CHINESE POSTMAN

Other books by Brian Castro

BRIAN CASTRO

CHINESE POSTMAN

Published 2024
from the Writing and Society Research Centre
at Western Sydney University
by the Giramondo Publishing Company
PO Box 752
Artarmon NSW 1570 Australia
www.giramondopublishing.com

Designed by Jenny Grigg
Typeset by Andrew Davies
in Tiempos Regular 9/15pt

Cover image: 'Old Chinese Postman in Traditional Attire'
courtesy of Chronicle / Alamy Stock Photo

Printed and bound by Pegasus Media & Logistics
Distributed in Australia by NewSouth Books

A catalogue record for this book is available from the National Library of Australia.

ISBN 978-1-923106-13-0

9 8 7 6 5 4 3 2 1

The Giramondo Publishing Company acknowledges the support of Western Sydney
University in the implementation of its book publishing program.

This project has been assisted by the Commonwealth Government through Creative
Australia, its arts funding and advisory body.

For Jaffa, Méabh and Niamh

I'll begin with an old Ukrainian proverb:
A woman's beauty cannot heat a whole winter's night, but a good, warmed vodka creates a blooming carnation in your belly.

John Hawkes once said in an interview:
Everything I have written comes out of nightmare, out of the nightmare of war.

And finally, Natasha, a postwoman in Vasylivka, advised others upon the Russian invasion on 24 February 2022:
The less you know the better you sleep!

How time-honoured custom reverts to ruin!

On summer evenings, during the vesper hours, after dinner, people used to take their walks in the parks, the gardens, and on the road leading up to the magic mountain. To see, to be seen, to make conversation, to connect with neighbours, shopkeepers and colleagues. There was always a low buzz of quiet exchanges. There was always soft laughter and sidewalk wine in front of the local art gallery.

No longer. Because the walk has become too muddy and slippery after the rains. And because of that solitary figure, that old man there, their *passeggiata* had all but been ruined. That's me there. I have a bad back, few teeth and I've lost my smile. And these are the Adelaide Hills.

That lone walker, yes, that stooping figure over there, that bitter and twisted man who only straightens up to look at treetops and sees nothing but fragments – ruins are his best friends. He sees only broken columns lying horizontally in the grass, symbols of fallen ambition. He does not know many people now, or only by sight. Most of those his age have passed away. *The killing zone*, he calls it. It occurs within a few short years. He is too old to connect with young energy; with their rapid rattle of rap; their pointers of no universal significance. Too tired to talk. Most of those he knew well are now in their graves. A heavy burden. Walking slowly is the most he can manage. Count the steps towards oblivion. And because he is loath to talk, others also stay silent as they pass. They sense something funereal that they should not engage with, something that may infect them. Like his cigar smoke, which they treat like asbestos dust. Environment; environment. They should all wear masks, he thinks. But they are all destined to die. Gradually, those who pass do not resume much conversation within themselves afterwards, since the hand of solitude and pessimism presses down upon them more firmly. They sense it, but it's not for articulating. It's a disturbance of wellbeing; a virus or a miasma: on the main street, over the town, the parks, the esplanade. Children stop screaming. Dogs stop barking. Choirs stop singing. The caravans have long gone.

He talks mainly to himself. Clears his throat often. This guarantees others will stay away from him: *To speak truth to power is a case of putting the cart before the horse. One must speak powerfully to 'truth', that is, rhetorical power to expose the deafening truth; the truth which is usually bare and dull. Bring on the catastrophe with the illusion. Oral art before going hoarse. The thing is, how not to lose effective words, both in terms of brain cells and through rigorous rote and painstaking transcription? Every process is lethal since words can fall through seams of syntax and can turn out to be their opposite when the process is completed. But that is all youth and myth. In time there will be detachment, and then disgust and then silence. Words fail faster than music. I dislike the political feebleness of poetry and hawk with contempt for those who try. But I honour those who have been tortured or imprisoned.*

I snort a lot. I spit. It saves on handkerchiefs. Better for the sinuses anyway.

He hates these italics inside the mind. People, especially writers, cannot read them, or they nod off. Less literary readers of ebooks confuse these declamations and emphases with popular highlights. Nobody takes note of anything. But writers are the worst in exhibiting their narcissism. There are too many writers with too much preciosity, who even after their deaths do not leave an impression of having been very memorable. They may have written fairly well, but since they were totally self-involved, they had no textual camaraderie, they leave behind a residue of grey skies rather than warm light, the former redeemed by distant lightning and faux self-humbling. No humour. No revolution. I forgive them for dying, but not for the afterburners smelling of ozone that gave them stardom. They should speak to you still, like Shakespeare, with diabolic emancipation, piercing reason, paranoid fantasy or drunken spit. One should still hear their laughter in the dark. But perhaps it is better for the observer to be acerbic and smile at how literary memory grows out of waste, of *schadenfreude* and shit. Shit is the highest form of subjectivity, more meaningful in defining the individual than the sublime. It is both dialogue and meditation. Medieval monks have now been found to have had massive intestinal worms. Wrigglies coming out of their backsides in their sleep. All because they fertilised their veges with human waste. Meditation was recycling, like night soil. Why 'night'? The stink was constant, twenty-four hours a day. Flies. Floating words like clouds forming and reforming: different each time and unpredictably so in terms of the winds of honesty. It is important to collect honesties upon dying, important to know its odours. Know thy worms. Consume thy worms. Worms make rich soil. Monks slept very little. They produced illuminated books; books of hours; which turned into short stories; legends; tales of chivalry. Worming their way into popular culture.

Writing makes matter out of metaphysics. To do it the other way round is an insult to life. Abe Quin...for that is my name. I am a scrivener. Not Abe Quill, though that would sound better. Abe Quin makes kirigami flowers out of newspaper. He loves to see them blossom when cast into the waters of the lake. Children are delighted by it. Capillary action is the scientific explanation; but what he makes is not above physics. It is not a metaphysics. Aphorisms should have the same effect of blooming, he thinks, without metaphysics or explanations.

They simply expand through leaping frogs of metaphors, which are physical, morphing in the liminal. For delight, just add water. Water finds its own level, as any plumber will tell you. It discovers and corrects and steadies the world. But these flowers have no smell. It is important that writing smells because life smells. Dogs are alive because they smell.

Metaphysics is nothing but infinite anxiety.
Fernando Pessoa

You give your life to your craft in order to provide some insight and life for others. But you die doing it, and not many care, having lost the communal nose for ordure. In other words, no one gives a shit unless there is sanitised order: chronological or narratorial. Shit is of the highest subjectivity, though they would gladly sublimate it. They would prefer my ashes on offer. The incineration of momentary memory is more presentable and purified at the end of the day of life than my wasted words and their struggle; the end of the privatisation of the self and the beginning of my mainmorte, a mingling of all the elements in nature, taken back by the earth itself, the lord of my slavery. This is what it means to be popular posthumously: to be received amongst the fish and cormorants. So let there be no separation of graves and bodies after I go. Let us scatter me into the infinite depths of the lake that lies in the valley below the gravestones. I have taken my language with me to the clay beneath the water, far from the gurgling and muttering above.

He still spoke a tonal language: ten tones in all; like *see* (high tone: *to stick*); *see* (middle tone; *to try*); *see* (low rising tone: *shit*). You had to be careful about tones. And thus he was musical, linguistically, without knowing it.

They said, those people on their evening procession, that old man Quin was once a professor. Of what, they didn't know. Certainly not of economics or artificial intelligence. They were sceptical of anything creative, that was not about scientific or technological progress. They also said he set fire to his library, which was in the west wing of a large house beside the Mount Lofty Botanic Garden. Since he had burnt out his former life he now spends his days examining with meticulous care the habits of small animals; their brevity; their fates; their tremors and fears. How at one point they will give up on survival because they are so small and almost invisible. But you learn how to get around things by being small. You had to improvise; be cleverer about existence; learn patience and the freezing arts of pure meditation and motionlessness. Kafka wanted to be really small. A beetle, perhaps. Or a Chinese, he wrote. I can hide if I'm really tiny. The Viet Cong proved how effective that was.

Quin didn't quite begin as a scholar. He came late to his bookcraft. As a non-citizen student, he was not entitled to any scholarship. They made that very clear to him; that he had taken the word 'Commonwealth' too literally. Those were the years of his hypothermia. He felt he did not belong anywhere.

In this new country I began as a walking postman...you know the type...pushing a three-wheeled cart in front loaded with parcels and letters...pushing along the sealed flat streets through the township in all weathers...pushing mail through slots in the doors of the shops, waving hello, good day, great weather, catching so-and-so at the back of the shop with his face between her moistened thighs. I carry the knowledge of a priest, pushing back to the post office and collecting the next bundle of gossip through a slot, rumour, all blur and deeply secretive, names well-known and names withheld. It's idiocy, this social hypocrisy replicated from town to town, suburb to suburb where all is known, and I arrive punctually every morning, consoling as a doctor on his rounds to listen, sound but not to enter into cupid tremors, knee-trembles or requited sighs. Sometimes my delivery is deliberately detained by a cruel delay, wilfully manufactured, for all of this bored me, and brought me what little mischief I could get up to. It was the walking that I liked; the thinking; my existence at the extremity of the epistolary ward reaching its demented destination and extinction. I asked for divine dispensation from daylight hours. No postman does night shift, they told me. There are not many of us left. We would work for nothing, though senior management are skimming off huge salaries and rewarding each other with expensive gifts.

They reassigned me, the kingdom of the post office. No reason was given save the reward of a bicycle for use in a hillier region. It was a kind of punishment, though for me it meant less thinking and more exercise. Which circumvented my thinking being and allowed my instinctive being to be astounded by the natural order of things. I liked being astounded: by the slithering of a snake; lovers at lookouts; suicides. I once found the body of a man who had shot himself inside his car, which was parked on a lonely cutting off a dirt track. What I was doing there was of course the first question the police asked me. I said that because I missed walking, being now a bicycle postman, I walked at night to retrieve the sensation of being astounded. This wouldn't have sounded very convincing to them. But then, if I had said more truthfully, that I take refuge from sadness by walking at night, it would have augmented their suspicion to the point of an immediate arrest. Affect and truth are a diabolical mixture. Language, however, was made to be masked, composed of the virus of cliché and misunderstanding. The logical thing the police should have asked me was whether I was expecting to be astounded. But they didn't.

Perhaps astonishment was too complicated in their book of motives. They asked me if I knew the deceased. I said I did not and did not look into the car because it was dark. The man may have been asleep. But you had heard the gunshot. Did you touch the car door? No. Then you would need to provide fingerprints down at the station.

They visited me three afternoons later. A policeman and a policewoman. I invited them into my small house, a one-bedroom weatherboard cottage prone to bushfire. You walked in the front and came out the back without any turning. They looked at my shelves of books and walked straight out the back to where I had a small upturned sailboat. A mountain was a strange place to have a sailboat. But they didn't ask that question either. It's Australia and people should always have a boat in the backyard. One week later, they came and told me it was a suicide. They were grinning, as though I was off the hook. All suspicion was over. I may have to show up at the coroner's inquest. That was the real reason why they were grinning. Big joke. It's never over.

I am the Chinese postman, out in all weathers. As you know, the Chinese Postman Problem was an algorithm proposed by mathematician Kwan Mei-Ko. In 1962, during the Great Leap Forward, when thirty million people in China had died of starvation, Kwan Mei-Ko used Eulerian graph theory to minimise the distance walked by a starving postman in delivering mail, preferably passing each street only once while returning to the origin. So I understood how to eliminate mileage by studying the vertices, never traversing the same street twice, thus eliminating the perils of repetition-compulsion and of useless passion. People, mainly, are inertia itself. They tread the same paths.

Sometimes he didn't complete his job until dawn. He liked working at night. His dog kept the other dogs quiet. They knew by his dog's smell that the party was friendly. The Union said Quin couldn't work except in daylight hours. But he'd received confirmation that he could, owing to a medical condition. He was allergic to sunlight, like an albino.

There is nothing much you can do to ameliorate or euphemise the word 'gunshot'. You could do a lot with a word like 'shotgun', used figuratively in phrases like 'shotgun wedding', 'shotgun shack', 'he rode shotgun', etc. But 'gunshot' only emits peril and portent. Its report is totally enveloped in time and that is what you told the police. Back to front now, it wears a jacket of time, cloaked by the night, its crack no longer immediate in recall and as I do not have a watch, I had no idea of what aspect of the night had ushered me into that menace of a gunshot; whether it was the freezing cold, the incipient flurry of light snow, the anticipation of joy.

But apart from all this drama which has only accrued of late, Quin was normally obsessed by tidiness, by spelling, by rubbing off stains on the carpet. How quickly it arrived, middle age. He remembered his father's shuffling gait; not quite balanced. The life remaining was not one that Quin had imagined: the disruptions to one's rhythms; the noise and untidiness magnified; people get louder and louder and do not understand Mendelssohn, and it is too hard to explain because there is no explanation in music; the earth also shuffled; not quite balanced, wild with contingency.

It was as though, now that he was released into the countryside doing night shift without a watch, it was as though he was licensed to use verb tenses interchangeably. But like his mother's conjugations, there was no future tense. He was free to deliver mail in any order or on any specified route, as long as all was done within twenty-four hours. On daylight schedules he didn't hurry or try to get home early. There would be long days when the sun had already gone down and he would be trudging up the hills with his bicycle, completing his duties as cooking wafted out the windows of the cottages, and sometimes a woman would wave to him but not too often because she was often too busy with cooking or children to notice him fiddling with her letter-box in the half light. He preferred not being noticed since he received a private satisfaction from depositing a missive into a private box like a sneak-thief taking his pleasure from a sleeping girl by leaving her a ring or a necklace stolen from someone else.

I only ever waved back to one of them. It was by coincidence that I had not only seen her up in the hills but had met her in the city and then there she was now, looking very pretty, a month before what I will call the Lookout Incident. I remember that day well. In the art gallery in town I had seen myself in the glass doors like an installation, my father looking back at me, his eyes squinting against the glare just before he died into the light. I remember him saying that death was the only deadline for a journalist. As a journalist he trained himself to notice things with the instincts of a policeman, mainly about people. But he did not seem to care about what was on the periphery...a particular tree, the light in the late afternoon, peculiarities of feeling. He did not know that the key to understanding anxiety was to realise one was missing something loved and longed-for like home, because as a journalist he subedited emotions and was often disappointed that the homeless realities he pursued did not fit. He moved on, like I did that day, wandering into the labyrinthine alleys of cafés and cannabis. I noticed the librarian's wife working in one of them, and when I waved she beckoned me to enter, asking if I had a day off, to which I replied that it was a postman's holiday. I should have said it in French if she had been French (though I found out later that she was Ukrainian), that I was *un facteur en balade* and with that waltzing ballad upon my lips ordered a Pernod, as though I were in a small bistro in the snowy Alps greeting the entire tavern with a sense of intimacy: *messieurs dames*. Surprisingly, she began to speak with an accent and a slight lisp and I immediately felt I was no longer a blind spot in this footlight of the foreign, which is something only foreigners thought you believed, understanding that struggle was necessary in order to understand. I read somewhere that when someone is attracted to another, their pupils dilate. I put on my dark glasses. Indeed, the light was blinding in the café, where skylights had recently been installed.

The shyness of hypothermia: it arrives with the numbing of the body while the mind continues to think, warmed by the inaction of the body, which is now fungible, drawing off its energies for glacial communication, already decomposing but composing letters of love, constructing bridges across crevasses of feeling, paradoxically avoiding any breakage in this ice cocoon in case it melted and translated into public sociality, declarations of love, heated arguments, the horrors to come.

How do you translate solitude? How do you translate the wind, the town rearing up in its shouts from illuminated football stadiums and the silent deserts of isolated lives in the cross-streets of weed and concrete, litter and bitumen? You can't. That's why, I was saying to her, to this foreign woman, that hypothermia, like reading, is so important in shutting out the world, like hibernation, sleeping in the frozen happiness of books. She confided to me that her husband practised something opposite. As the town librarian, she said (I heard it as *libertarian*, but that was a matter of hearing, a choice for the foreigner, tuning in and out of differing registers), as town librarian, she was saying, he busied himself with getting rid of books. Digitising and disposal were his job descriptions. He did not read. I suggested to her that he put all the library books in a shed in the hills, and let bushfires do the rest. With this remark we had become thick as thieves, smoke getting into our eyes, alcohol into our blood. I remember telling her there was no such thing as an 'open marriage', which her husband foisted upon her – a man's idea of having his cake and eating it – it was most likely he was having an affair – which seemed to give her liberty from him but instead meant it was unlikely that happiness or pleasure for her would eventuate in a simply brutal encounter with somebody else. The balance was always unequal. An open marriage, I said to her, was like an open parenthesis, a diversion in which I could see the reason for his not reading and for the holocaustic disposal of books. It was his reason for experiencing external realities rather than involving the imagination in them, and by isolating himself and declaring an open marriage he was sacrificing himself to voluntary blindness and the immolation of ideas. Did she suspect there was another woman? No, she didn't think so. The children seemed happy enough, those canaries in the mine-shaft. But they didn't look like her; maybe they weren't hers. Then, I said, I shall send you some notices from *Neighbourhood Watch* – and some entries from my diary (which I neglected to add).

So, I addressed all these thoughts *To the Householder*. Of course, she had invited them. After all, I am the postman. But they would remain unread since I write in a microscopic hand on the inside of envelopes which I manufacture myself, having done a course in origami – no cutting or pasting, just folding – a dove, a crane, a flower – and then the testing of unfolding without tearing, when she would toy with discovery and misreading. But this never occurred. I would find these folded micro-dove-letters thrown intact into the bin, without deconstruction or de-origami, without the butterfly-dust of love disseminated over her eyes, my miniature script remaining heavily useless and sticky with affect.

A week after his last visit from the police, her house was for sale. The shutters were closed; there were no children in the yard; no dogs barked at his approach. The letterbox was filled with real-estate leaflets and junk mail. He imagined there was something left for him but there was nothing. He did not find out for quite a while that after losing his job, the librarian drove to the lookout that final time, passing his own house on the way, traversing a route he knew well. Perhaps he threw my paper flowers into the pond to expand them, but I do not think so. An open marriage, like an open book, always harboured betrayal. People simply do not trust books anymore and look at the misery of those writers who stir up grief like I do, delivering disorder on my linear rounds.

He told himself it was a gunshot/shotgun; a backfire from which he was lucky enough to escape.

That was many years ago; in another time and place, but eidetic phrases kept recurring in phases of time. When Quin started writing his diaries and stories rather than unsent love letters, his script enlarged. He was no longer hiding, folding his work from the world, and he was beginning to collect things instead...coins, stamps, minor experiences...no longer being pushed out of his own life.

A bowerbird hides its treasures in the strangest places. For many years, the poet Robert Adamson kept a pet bowerbird called Spinoza, who brought troves of words.

AD – *Anno Domini*. After death, we used to say as children. Who died?

HD – She was a poet. Hilda Doolittle. I do very little, so I'm a kin. I would have loved to have been a poet, but I think you have to die young for that. I could not have done an impersonation of a Dylan Thomas because it's too hard to drink that much, although he made amends in the mornings by swilling tankards of orange juice. Apparently he felt foreign everywhere except in the beginning hours of inebriety.

ADHD or a nonlinear memory? It was a fact that Quin thought only in bowers of vignettes; in images of vinelands with soured harvests; garlands of misery; vintages of memory and desire. But that sensory material stuck even when unstuck, and he scrabbled to make sense by being toneless and dry.

Clarice Lispector, the celebrated Brazilian writer, suffered third-degree burns to her arm from smoking in bed. It may have tarnished her great beauty.

Ingeborg Bachmann died of complications suffered while falling asleep with a lit cigarette, setting alight her nightgown. It was just three years after the suicide of her former lover Paul Celan. Her erstwhile lover Max Frisch had previously written a play entitled *The Arsonists*. From her photos Ingeborg appears to be very beautiful.

Why do beautiful women set fire to themselves?

But then Quin thought of unprepossessing men like himself; and like Elias Canetti's Peter Kien. We all do it through unhappy affairs and disordered lives. We smoke; and then we burn diaries; and then we burn books; because our perfectly smooth and reclusive existences have had their voices stoppered by semi-colonic hiccups of neurotic memories; we have been turned upside down; destined to stutter for the rest of our lives.

Clarice Lispector – *My parents* (who spoke Yiddish), *stopped in a village that's not even on the map, called Chechelnik,* (in Ukraine), *for me to be born, and came to Brazil…so calling me a foreigner is nonsense. I'm more Brazilian than Russian, obviously.*

What constitutes a foreigner? Is it not a person who cannot dwell mentally in one place? Is not a foreigner a stutterer? The stutterer's voice is the voice of homelessness: it jumps here and there and keeps trying to return to somewhere else with the energy of a wren. But a wren is small and fragile and has a life span of about five to six years. On average, foreigners move house every one to two years. Mostly, internal migration occurs in about a year. The worst thing you can do is to move a war-torn migrant into a nursing home. They know that death was never going to be home. The question is: do you deepen yourself or do you spread out for others?

Memory is all I have left, but this kind of memory may be a form of dementia. I wonder whether I'm outmoded or antiquated or whether I'm in the vanguard of affect; the affect of failure. Failure is the affect that is most important in the future world. I possess this and cherish it above all. Again and again; here and there. No one should be rescued from pessimism and failure. We should be in love with tragedy; the tragedy of the planet and of ourselves. I only wish I could hide memory effectively from all those do-good rescuers. There is too much *faux* in the world of the so-called real, so that you have to hoard those real things in case they are transformed overnight. After all, in this sanitised world, dying is a failure and shitting is not transcendent, even though Chinese emperors had their excrement read like fortune cookies.

Little by little he's losing his life: losing his possessions and gaining depression, obsessions and repressions. Quin of course, was a *saudosista*, a member of a little-known society of melancholics. It's normal for him to have an editing consciousness, but what is it for? He is forgetting the vernals, the springs – when lilacs last in schoolyards were plucked for young lovers – fuckers – his life of weeds now an auger for further disaster. It intrigues him. The Country Fire Service came and put out the fire before it caught to the rest of his house. They are good men, the firefighters, volunteers, and they shared his whiskey as a mark of his gratitude. Ashen-faced. From that point on he always said that he had to go home, whenever he found himself in a social situation. But what is home? It was simply something to say when he felt tired, or that his heart was giving out, a tachycardia making him uneasy. Had he remembered to turn down the stove?

Then again, home in the hills meant bushfires, falling trees, blocked drains, network outages, blackouts and leaking roofs. He was going to get too old to manage repairing things, will perhaps have to put up a beach umbrella over his bed. The isolation suited him though, and when that was disturbed he grew difficult, disturbed, depressed and then started to build structures: sheds, boardwalks, bridges over the various creeks. He managed the heavy timbers with a number of trolleys, dollies, barrows and ropes. He felt he was homeward bound in this way. It was a lot better than building ideas. Ideas, he felt, weren't useful in war. In war, you thought about dying; if you didn't die you thought about wounds; and if you weren't wounded you thought about defecation. Would you break cover out of personal decency? Attract a killer drone? It was not something hummed at luncheon parties. He would have to travel to Ukraine to see for himself.

Homeward bound after schooldays in Hong Kong, his mother used to wait at her window, making sure he'd got off the bus at the right stop;

and he, just six years old, would wait while his mother opened the door of their tiny flat with the three locks; she was barricaded against intruders. He and his mother lived in a world of fear and suspicion and a bowl of mandarins was their only reward for a hard day's separation from night, his father's dissipation and anger. His father's long gone now. His mother sighed with relief at the funeral. Now I'm freed of him, she said again and again. She was genuinely happy. Her happiness turned out to be the result of dementia. He and his mother had some years of complete silence and peace sharing their prewar flat with a series of dogs, their silent farting and incessant licking and careless grooming punctuating the nights. If there were a fire, it would be hard to undo all three locks on the front door.

I sit nervously in my sanctuary-room reading, anxiously disquieted by quietude, doubt, thought as feeling, kneading thought with feeling, but mostly worrying the beads of voices I hear in the distance growing a little louder as they approached and then fading after they passed, with great relief, imbibing all the intoxicants of alcohol and tobacco, to and fro, ebbing and flowing with meditation and then with the impending threat of the social. I do not understand why it has to be so, unable to shake off this other dialogue with myself and the louder dialogue that would disrupt my inner pit within a pit, this joust pitting itself against others, waiting for the inbox to be emptied until I can leave this heavy work of normal existence.

The fire is smoking the room and I am no fire-philosopher thinking 'I am' because I think, but instead, inhaling fumes that send me into a dizzying trance and I imagine how trances are induced in mystics, not by an involuntary communion with spirits but by a willing surrender to the burning of substances like the smell of burnt souls at Christmas barbecues. Christmases were always the worst: divorces happened then; arguments; family breakdowns; irreconcilable differences; and thank God, perpetual silence until the obituaries. Too hot; too hot; there must be snow in one's thoughts in order to understand oblivion. I need to build a hut to defend my solitude against marauders, rampant acquaintances, life brought too close.

He never quite believed in Cartesian dualism, of the separation between mind and body. He was fond of saying that 'the body was the mind' or 'the mind makes up its body', or 'think with the body and feel with the mind'. He was looking for meagre rewards in life: cycling (endorphins); sex (self-pleasuring and watching thinly built women of a certain age crossing the road with alluring swagger), drinks (that brought a peaceful silence). Nothing much else in these dimly lit dusk-days, but it all warded off early dementia; perhaps not the drink; but perhaps the willed forgetting of a past distemper.

Quin wanted to spend the rest of his days in Amsterdam. His thoughts were all about canals and narrow buildings. You think where you are. Repressed writers loved narrow buildings. He was never more at home than in the Frank Lloyd Wright-designed hotel, the Banks Mansion, Herengracht 519-525, 1017 BV Amsterdam. The happy hour there featured free whiskey. Nobody socialised, and if they spoke, they discoursed in low whispers as though in church, happy in their mortal meditation.

Spinoza became his model of stoicism, religious ostracism, non-conformism. In winter, Quin wore a dark cloak, something which saved Spinoza from a knife attack – one can employ it artfully, like a matador.

I have had the library rebuilt. The tradesmen took forever because it was an insurance claim. Tradesmen are the lords and barons in Australia. They know a PhD can't help you build a house by yourself or repair a ruin. In the meantime I watch battles between spiders...when you transfer one to another's web. Nature is a constant battle for territory. Euthanasia, on the other hand, is decolonisation; an eschatological study of end things and their disburdenment and disposal.

When you depart this earth there'll only be a handful who'll remember you, if you're lucky. But whose luck? You'll be dead and out of contention for memory. A few will read and think back and maybe, just maybe, like an old opera score, a crackling diva will cast about and sing your images, loves, and words of loss. Times change and younger critics will score for a piece not nearly so memorable as a vague subject invented for themselves. Strange how I see it all before I go, passing so quickly when the dusk is dimmed through dust or whispers of rain. It's not a sad moment; just a lucky one amongst those that occurred more briefly and more painfully. Point counterpoint. The phantasmagorical grim reapers cast by magic lanterns are discarded for the liberating presence of out-of-doors nature where *thinking is presence*. I am where I think. An outdoor toilet is the best for this purpose. Indoor toilets with their tiles and mirrors presage death like operating theatres without hygiene.

Nature is a purgatory no doubt, Quin was reflecting, but the promise of a *Paradiso* is too ideal and weak, failing in the presence of what we *do* know. Dante knew the impossibility of paradise. After nine circles of hierarchical moralising, the pilgrim is absorbed by a tepid love in the empyrean. Exile saved Dante from this fate. And so I cycle and cycle, all those kilometres purifying me of the literary, a cyclic exilic. I'm not interested in the successes, the famous, the bestsellers. I ride for the infamous, the dead, the ignored. By riding I'm exhuming them, bringing them into existence through the traverses of space and time, reliving their time, breathing their space. In this way I free myself, but not them.

Quin would have chosen exile in Amsterdam. Now he's considering Kyiv. He wants to be there, where he could think. It is, and was, a beautiful city. But there were his dogs to consider. His dogs do not know the difference between the outside and the inside. There are no borders. They come into the fire and warmth, then they go outside to experience the brutality and cold. It's all the same to them. Change and thrill. There is no exile for them, which is a peculiarly human affliction.

He did not set fire to his books deliberately. It wasn't an *auto-da-fé*. It was in the days when he smoked Havanas, just after his retirement, thinking he wouldn't have many years left, lighting up his pension. He fell asleep listening to César Franck's *Quartet in D Major*. He dreamt he was in Kraków. He could smell the Nazi occupation: sweat and pine flavours. In the forests, they were shooting people falling forward into ditches. There were dark, snow-lined fir trees. His whole lifetime of reading was about disasters and wars always in a setting of natural beauty. In the cold, the dark fog, the misted streetcars. His stub fell onto the Persian carpet.

The world has become more punitive than ever. We want to punish every misdemeanour because of individual self-righteousness since it can be instantly publicised; 'self-empowering' it's called. If you mention the word 'libertarian' it is inside a glass bowl; ready to be observed with a sarcastic smile – 'self-empowering' – but the irony is rarely let out – that the new libertarian is the new dictator.

So many years have passed. Almost thirty years ago now since I took this dusty volume of Robert Frost from the shelf, and for thirty years it has been uncared for, and I find my first wife's signature and mourn her handwriting. Those dog-eared pages of famous verses with her naive annotations now objectified into sad memories, her scribblings in the margins. Mostly the lecturer's words, no doubt, which are obvious and analytical, but bearing her own thoughts as well. Now I am the remarker of these comments, remaker of them, and am saddened by these reforming hands of mine correcting her naivety, her scripts of time, remorse and all the deaths from roads taken and not taken; by my not turning back for fear of time's curse and life's remorseless advance. I am always in a correctional and a confessional at the same time. Wilful forgetting was what you did when young. When old, feelings revive like Lazarus in times when frost on the cleared ground allows one to skate on what has been and what could have been and it all comes down to an era of optimism and adventure that became too hard; the brief joys too brief; flakes of sadness scattered by forever shooting forward and not backward-bending for reflection, which sent memories into the sky. All led to holes in the ice and hypothermia. Such things are brought to us because we lived and lived through them without pausing on account of pain. Pain is there for a purpose: it slows you up so you have to sit quietly and think.

I snip my Frost between interruptions; in and out of moods, some never to be retrieved. I can't bend to the long dark night of extinction. The heart keeps ticking with aphorisms: Time's arrow carries knowledge in its fletching: What bird's feather primed it? What quill and colour? What brief life which occurred when? Which has as its grim purpose, the aim to kill. It was all about the killing fields. You died seeking revenge.

I am fortunate to have this small dam outside my writing window, which can swell to deep greens in winter from a tiny muddy pool of turtles and yabbies. From the water's reflections, I observe the weather and sky, not the other way around, as I am always concerned with the lower levels of earth and life, small patches of communities of plants and insects and pond life. I believe this determines the existence of tiny canvases, from whose concentrations and grids one can measure pulsing life itself.

In the summer, some trees turn white, their branches shedding bark in the dry heat. They're like snow trees then, in a paradox reserved for nature, and it is then I feel great sadness for not having the sensation of sadness in the same paradox of cold depth and heated listlessness, unexceptional now, both my feelings and the season; trivial, my thinking turning into dreaming. Am I losing feeling? It could be a relief, but then, fearful of timelessness, I still want to keep in touch.

A terrible start to the year of the dead and dying. I felt the weight in my chest, lugging something heavy with every breath. It has gone on for a month, along with aches and pains. It's probably time to write.

But no writing comes to him because he is not made of writing anymore, having lost faith in that form of manufacture, the fabrication, the story without bones which has to be remade in someone else's shape and not lived through. Grave-robbing; scene-stealing; masking; causing grief; mischief-making. He's through with all that novel-writing; it's summer reading for bourgeois ladies. Who said that?

Then again, concentration on such matters demands silence. It isn't ideal in a war. The Ideal isn't a place where you are in a paradisal room filling up notebooks. The real place for writing is in a noisy place with hammerings and sighings, traumas and drunkenness, madness in the corners. That's when everything happens para-dyslexically, out of your control, and *you have to put things in order.*

He has always distrusted *moods.* Not grammatical moods like the subjunctive, tentative in time, wishful, but he distrusted sentimental moods, nostalgic moods, moods of loss, moods of no loss, moods of detachment, no moods. He now looks for them in vain as one who lives only in detached memory, constantly seeking a future emotion in diminishing time, not finding a single worthwhile mood in which to feel anything. This memory can deliver neither sadness nor hope and the barrenness of feeling is for once strange to him, its emptiness like old perfume or a tasteless, dusty meal made out of fragments of the self, the remains of the whole.

I'm only ever feeling good in the early afternoon after a few lunchtime drinks, and soon enough I'm ready to write in a language melting into scorchers and have an enjoyable time too, without fretting over masked balls and hydration and certainly not publication. On the other hand, language of course, is the root of suffering. You don't get joy without nightmare. I wish I could be acquitted of the unconscious. And so we die and we die unconscious. Death isn't a memorable event for long, and the language of the aggrieved lasts until the next season when the rabbits have regrouped.

Then I read poetry, still learning the rhythms; the grimy humility of Larkin; the wounds of Glück (pronounced 'Glick' like the sound my dislocated shoulder made fifty years ago...the clavicle was also a clavier without wires)...she had so much to repair...she grieved so... the collage of Ashbery and most of all, the wreckage of Lowell; mad

Cal. We all should have picked up the revolver, and not put it down too early. While empty, it makes a sound like 'glick'. While loaded, it's anyone's guess.

The weather's been temperamental and so have I, as I do not have the means of outdoor exercise. I'm losing the spelling bee and the colours of butterflies and the sounds of dragonfly wings. I only want to go out when I've had too much to drink; dreaming of reality, I die in the justice of the interstice. By the way...

My little dog has already lived more than half her life, yet her loyalty surpasses mine. I chided her for stealing the Roquefort and for barking. She's only doing her job scaring away intruders. Here she is asleep at my feet oblivious to all but to be together, now, listening still for each other's dreams.

I always used to hurry things, making books, wanting them to be finished and whole. Then I learned patience and now as with poetry, taking time to think through a particular reciprocation in feeling as only a good poem can do. But still, it hurries me, this life, and while the breaths are deeper and more spaced, I still hear the language fading in and out, trapping life with a net fine as silk, looking for what has weight and fill, which is less and less. At least the main house is fully restored now; too big for one inhabitant; great for boisterous guests.

Professor Quin (now retired) was, and still is, a collector of bric-à-brac, *tchotchkes*, or (in Polish rather than Yiddish) *czaczkos*, trinkets, and pretty girl students, with whom he had no serious relationships except through letters and emails, even before #MeToo warned off professors just before they leapt from the ivory tower. He puts it down to being

Chinese and not being 'out there' and not 'getting out more'. Besides, he preferred a good lunch to a good conversation, was unabashedly shy and possessed a residual disgust gifted to him by his father of the uncouth behaviour (of the *goyim*); his father, who at five foot two (*his* father's first name was Bonaparte), exuded eternal charm made more enticing to women through superhuman retention of desire. Somehow Abraham Quin didn't inherit this conquistadorial line. Hello. This is me we're speaking about. But I know enough to also know intention never eluded instinct.

I married three times and now, sometimes in a provincial place, I meet a woman who's scared she'd be number four or five and tells me as much, that buying her a drink may be a sign of a divinity not welcomed or perhaps too wild and dangerous. I didn't see a compliment or feel the power, but it must be strange not to be able to even *play* at being seduced. I must be in Adelaide rather than in Paris. Too many lawsuits, and no flirtation. No imaginary assaults either, because sex is beyond me unless coerced. Better to lead a smug life and not go anywhere. Do not touch. That constitutes assault. Don't even look. That constitutes harassment. Thank goodness a pandemic saved me. There could have been so many other lives from which I could have taken flight on account of my precipitation. I'm fond of speedy Hermes. He's the protector of thieves, travellers and orators. A woman once said to me that I was very gregarious. I think she meant it as a compliment. But *gregarious* is also an anagram of *egregious*. I never wanted to stand out as egregious. The flock was my mob. I was always a good soldier, one platoon commander said of me. I never aspired to the officers' mess. One mess of envy and spite. But I knew I was a good shot, even though I was a little unsighted. In my mind I never missed.

Since writing letters is the only thing I can do now, I am always misread and am told I message with too many gaps. I write to women to express things no man would ever dream of doing, because men like to not express themselves, not because they have to be 'men' since it is not about strength or power, but because words are simply too inadequate for the practical world with which they have to deal without succumbing to elaboration or 'bedighting'. Epistolary adventuring is a dead art.

His solitude is enough, but the days are long and are growing longer. There was no more time for time itself: the concept of it vanished. He simply had too much to do to get to the end of his life.

No more raptures. That was the trouble with age; there are no more raptures. Except for the time he was happy because he was going to ferry over a Persian woman named Hasti (whose name was full of irony), with whom he would share his life. But nothing occurred. Once the vigour of life was over, opportunities became rare or non-existent. *I think about you often*, he wrote to a woman friend from another state. *You too are in my thoughts*, she responded. It was nice of her if she had not typed the following sentence as though on second thoughts: *These days I'm too tired to have adventures.*

Ironies abound in life, the latter without linearity or internal development like a Shakespearean tragedy, the former falling thick and fast, warm rain heavy as lead upon the theatre backdrops. Mortality is close by these days; the smell of the earth receives those who are only surviving for the moment. I go from door to door like a doctor, practising for another's death in my *passeggiata*. Through closed doors and curtained windows, I can hear women in the stillness, murmuring to themselves, on the telephone perhaps, birds twittering in the night for fallen chicks and windblown nests, for drugged and wayward children. Ironies abound in circularity, things come around to their beginnings, one is a child again but there is no renewal. One's mouth is a mouth of a small stream, emptying into the vast ocean.

An ocean of recurring dreams, like the dream about a train taking him to the Gulag: the hymn *Panis Angelicus* being sung in the background by Andrea Bocelli; huge expanses of Siberian permafrost and taiga and snowdrifts and a few pine trees out in the middle of three days of nowhere and the train stops at a water tower and the experienced amongst them – men and women – jump off as the locomotive is still screeching to a halt, a few people going off to defecate behind a stand of spindly trees trying not to look at the others and suddenly the train starts up and chugs slowly off and everyone is scrambling to get on and only he is left behind because his trousers are around his ankles and he trips ripping his pants and the others are yelling for him to hold out a hand but the train speeds up and there he is a lonely figure in the landscape of snow a dot diminishing into clouds of steam and snowy mist and he is maybe the first to die in the next small hours surviving fear and then hypothermia and then fear again as his body kicks and his mind ticks and slows. I don't want to dream of this anymore, he says to himself. But he thinks only of warmth and bread. Of writing the word 'bread'. Trolley-loads of baguettes he'd once seen delivered to a vast Parisian café from the train station, baked from the original recipe, *les traditions*, stuffed into tin garbage bins lined with newspaper, still steaming from the bakery. And he thinks of that time when a girl was looking cold in thin stockings, her coffee steaming, waiting for someone, a man perhaps, walking from the train station to see her again after some months, a cigarette between his fingers, older now and more experienced, may have walked past without her noticing, not wanting to go in because he does not love her anymore and after pausing to study her back walks on. So, I walk on along the railway tracks and the snow is now a fog of cotton wool, angel's hair we used to put on Christmas trees, fleecy fibreglass, curly commas, the latest invention which scratched your forearms and left a nasty itch. And of course, reminding you of how you thought this was the true way, following the railway sleepers, the only math visible of progress and survival to return to the water tower where perhaps another locomotive will stop to convene another sleeping car of languorous prisoners in my recurring dream and I will climb the ladder with great intensity, never failing to observe through the snowstorm a different smoke in the distance, the darker, heavier, optimism of suppressing the death-wish and not concealing it, me and then not me, rabbinical rocking as though of an inconsolable infant, survival-oscillation from nursing trauma, the memory of horror lightened only by the recall of a girl in thin stockings with her back to the window, denying and not denying what was passing by – a train of fire and steam, buffet cars of baguettes, an ex-lover, listening to the roaring and the chugging beneath of un-commemorated history.

But mainly I dream about being lost in a foreign city, usually an Asian one, though when I try to recall it, the scene turns Kafkaesque, with one major addition: I am looking for a toilet where I can urinate with dignity – six-star hotels are best – well-appointed and well-frequented to avoid the embarrassing wet patch in the front of my trousers – because of my prostate, though I have never wet my bed, but now I'm traversing the castle-emporium in dire straits – and in my dreams I can never find a clean toilet as they are always ghastly toilet bowls so it is better not to stand too near and hit or miss to the peril of my shoes. It's an old man's obsession of course, to be dignified, to still carry the eau-de-cologne of attractiveness though there is nothing left but chagrin and pity for such incontinence; colitis, bloating and diarrhoea still to come. But public inconveniences are almost indescribably public, these shitty cubicles, sometimes with no partitions or doors, so shoppers roaming these department-store castles can see very clearly what you are doing, these jurors in your trial, and these no-privacy dreams are the worst, establishing your guilt, since no real urinating could ever take place with eyes behind you and faecal matter before. Shall I wear a nappy rolled? Part my shirt-tail behind? Sometimes the toilet from hell occurs in a nice country house, where doors are never lockable, and even though the bathroom is spacious, it is never clean and someone has stuffed clothing: bits of underpants, socks, etc. down the bowl and all that would be impossible to flush away, so I'm thwarted from urination and worse, I may now be blamed for this crisis. Then I'm condemned to wandering again to find a clean, well-lighted place, but there is never a drizzle of taxis in front of the arcades and the people do not understand me because I'm asking for a *bathroom* instead of a toilet, and I take elevators which go sideways instead of up or down, so no public convenience is available to me. I always wake disoriented, not relieved but with a profound sense of loneliness strongly intimating this may have been purgatory rather than hell since there is only a salvational chance of now going to the toilet on a familiar and habitual trajectory of prayer.

The late poet Dorothy Porter once suggested we write a book of toilets-from-hell together, which certainly would have sold well, though that project never got off the ground, probably because poetics and shit didn't mix. It was the year that Helen Demidenko won the Miles Franklin award for literature. The year I left for Paris. Before leaving Australia, I made an inventory of all the odd toilets I'd found and experienced, because one had to *experience* a toilet to know about it. Pure mechanical theory was not good enough. So I listed outback pit toilets, which were incredibly deep and which smelled like rotten cabbage and you had to agitate a broom before entering to ensure a snake was not behind the door. I found on the south coast of New South Wales a toilet in a rental house perched on a sea-cliff, which had a large spin-wheel beneath the bowl and a crank like a railway signal lever, sending the waste centrifugally into the ocean. Then of course there was the dunny can and the now extinct dunny man who collected your waste painfully on his shoulder draped with an old, stained towel, for whom I always left a bottle of Tooth's beer at Christmas.

That 'I' is in the sentence again. He was racked by arthritis and it was poor form to speak in the first person about pain without poverty since sympathy was never forthcoming from anyone who was not a flirtatious lover. Speaking of which, he liked to write letters when he was a boy, mainly to girls, since he was never really obtuse or casual or pushy enough to take to conversation or presence or boastfulness. Intimate letters, and now emails, were for the pathologically shy. He was protected from blunders and forearmed for rejection. As an adolescent, he sent an extract by Catullus to a girl whom he referred to as Lesbia, but he didn't put inverted commas around the quotation, thinking anyone would have recognised it. Thus an early reputation as a plagiarist. Still, it was in Latin; meant for a five-finger exercise in mutual translation. Now, as an old, somewhat embittered letter-writer, he referred to himself as an epistolarian, which gave him a clerical status, but very few women cared or even tried to play the game once known as intellectual flirtation and now referred to as grooming, or worse, as scamming.

I received an email: *Dear Professor, I am reading one of your books on the doorstep of war. You once wrote about war eloquently, so the critics said. I do not believe anyone can write eloquently about war. If you could find the time, could you please answer that question?*

I do not reply of course. The correspondent sounds female. *Iryna.* Russian female. Means 'peace'. Good night Irene. These are all scams. I get a lot of them. They want a pen-pal, then secrets and then money, in that order. Money pays off the secrets. They are usually men with some education. But then I get many without grammar: *Dear Sir, I want degree research your work; please send me all research to help how enrol me your university.* The 'block all' button doesn't quite filter them out.

He returns to reading E.M. Cioran: *On The Heights of Despair*, and *A Short History of Decay*. Schopenhauer on *The World as Will and Representation*. Hard thinking concretises a quiet life. It is a respite from the chaos of solicitors' letters with their direct and indirect routes to liquidating his former properties and endowing his ex-wives. Being rather old-fashioned, he answers all correspondence of this kind, though such duty guarantees the impossibility of fruitful meditation and by erasing the first 't' in that word, encrusts it with blackmail. His lawyer, who was about to retire, seemed to absorb money through endless mediation.

According to Schopenhauer, the Will isn't such a great thing. Though it is born of need and is our vital existence, it is also our death. Imagine willing your day and failing at every turn. Death, on the other hand, makes life possible because it is serendipitous. Just hanging around the corner. The Will, or will-power, is ultimately the will to death. That's why we make wills, Quin was saying aloud to himself on his walk through the Botanic Garden. Having no offspring and no legal will, other than a bequest to the wildlife sanctuary at the apex of the steep hill he crests on his e-bike, he thought of 'Iryna' again, and of his own 'eloquence' in writing about war. It was an accusation for sure, a scammer's Pawn to King 3 rather than the usual opening move. He was being studied. He pedalled harder. The chain came off. It made a sound like 'glick' and then there was silence and powerlessness and frustration.

In his youth, in his student days, salad days, before the internet and emails, he cleaned the toilets in Fisher Library at Sydney University. He was adrift, reading French and English, inflamed by Baudelaire and bored with Milton. Toilet cleaning was not his choice but it was out of necessity through not being an Australian citizen, since he was not entitled to a scholarship. So he traded shit for library privileges. The men's toilets, of course, were always the worst. From there he learned how to research via graffiti. There were the usual chestnuts: *To Be or Not to Be: Shakespeare. Being and Nothingness: Sartre. Do-be-do-be-do: Frank Sinatra.* But then there were more unknown and sophisticated names: Barthes; Foucault; Derrida; De Man. *Written shit does not smell.* He borrowed their books from the Stack because he was an employee of the Library at Night. The LAN, before it became known as the Local Area Network, gave him an auxiliary status as a night watchman, an ex-officio security guard. His mother, working as a local seamstress, embroidered the letters 'Fisher Security' on his overalls. He was a fisher of thieves and ideas, armed with buckets and mops. And he was a hider of books, putting them behind shelves of medical books or Old German, or histories of the Alemanni.

Ethics is a fucking white detergent, he wrote back in texta on a cubicle wall under a racist slogan. He was thinking of his lecturer. He wrote the word 'fuck' in English and then in Chinese traditional script, making a point multilingually, since 'fuck' only had force in a monolingual world. He wished there would be a lecture on ethics and toilets, but Professor Burnheim SJ, who taught Ethics and Metaphysics, would probably never use these toilets, not in a cubicle anyway. Maybe he was in his second relationship, burning his home and leaving the church – no one knew what Jesuits could do with split hairs.

Ten years later he revisited his labours and was relieved to find that the wits had not changed: *Watership Down: you've read the book; you've seen the movie; now try the stew.*

Instead of completing Law – he was bored with Torts (people were always doing wrong to each other, so why not just walk away, rent somewhere else?) – he wrote a manuscript, entitled *Cleaner Dreams*, sent it to a small publisher called Wildfire and heard nothing until the *Sydney Morning Herald* reported in a back column that the firm had burned down under a suspect insurance claim. There were no photocopiers in those days and carbon paper was expensive. Besides, he had written it in longhand, in a microscript to save on paper, something nobody would bother to read. Life was about to get harder.

These days he had great difficulty in the mornings. He would get up and go straight to the bathroom, groaning and moaning. He reminded himself that most people in peacetime did not die heroically. They died on the toilet seat or collapsed trying to make it there on their knees, *driving the porcelain bus* as they colourfully say about vomiting. His dogs were alert to his howling. Afterwards, he would light the fire. Fires everywhere. He thought of Iryna in an imagined Poland. In its violent history, in its concentration camps, she wrote, God had never appeared. Not once. Not even to argue with Moses. Any disputation was a fizzing bullet, a tank shell that burst the eardrums if it didn't annihilate you. The Nazis had flamethrowers, invented by a German of course; every bush was burnt; every book afire. War. He wrote to 'Iryna', who was probably a bearded scammer, sitting there in the Kyivan summer wearing only rimless glasses: *What about the dogs in the Donbas?* This non-sequitur intended to shove aside the irritating accusation of eloquence. Surely no one could speak eloquently about death; about prostate cancer; about the hospital ward and its cocktail of smells? Dogs can be trained to smell cancer.

And indeed he had been a member of every animal society, donating small amounts of money to each, until he read about mismanagements and scandals and then eliminated them one by one. He rescued pound dogs instead. Usually, German shepherds, which no family wanted once there were kids. Paid extravagantly for a high fence around his three-acre farm. He liked neither fences nor fencers. It was where he parted from Robert Frost. Fences were only good for self-promotion. My land, your land, makes us one, but individually, fences make profit. Suburban boosterism. Frost had country cunning: real-estate hikes were good for property development: sewerage, electricity, surveyors' pegs, and once all the paddocks were subdivided, you were set up for life. But Quin was convinced that really good neighbours would not complain of wandering dogs. They'd feed them and send them home. No boundaries were necessary. And there weren't miles to go in the valley before we all slept.

Two men turned up and tensioned wire by pulling the strands with their truck. They didn't speak to him the whole time, except to tell him they preferred cash to an invoice since he didn't have to pay the GST and they, of course, didn't pay tax. He drove to the ATM several times that day, anxious about having so much in his pocket. Was it enough? He had to keep the dogs in the house all day.

The answer from Iryna about the dogs in Donbas was rapid. Not enough was being done for all the abandoned dogs. Dogs were great survivors, s/he wrote. They became feral once they were left by their owners. They scavenged amongst dead bodies and chewed off what they could. In Donetsk s/he had seen one dragging around the bottom portion of a leg, the boot still on the foot. Professor Quin, s/he wrote, could you donate something to the UAAA, the Ukrainian Association of Animal Advocates? This would enable some dogs to be reunited with their owners.

So here it was: the scam. He deleted Iryna from his contact list. He removed all correspondence from his 'sent' list. He didn't as yet know how to block a sender. There was a follow-up email: 'Alternatively, you could come to Kyiv to do a reading in aid of our animal charity. Perhaps in Poland, if I can get there.' This was now getting catchy, like a Jerry Lee Lewis tune. *Great Balls of Fire.* He decided not to reply, given that he had no wish to visit Kyiv while the Russians were building up a large depot of tanks on the other side of the border. In his comfortable armchair in his newly rebuilt studio library (stocked with books he bought from Oxfam), he read Victor Klemperer and dreamt of disaster. Then he started thinking about Poland again. He had been to Warsaw before. They were incredibly literary there. They lived their history, though there were hardly any old buildings left after the war.

But something stuck in his mind. A public reading. They were usually disasters. Foreign audiences didn't get the puns or alliterations or the irony. He had once read in Warsaw and Prague with the writers Janette Turner Hospital and Frank Moorhouse. The latter was not only a very good novelist but an even better raconteur. He was frank and believable. Quin had fun, but his readings didn't get much attention.

His introductory puns on 'more house, less home', and 'a turn in the hospice', denoting how writers were always *unheimlich*, fell flat except for a light Freudian chuckle tinkling in the treble clef, coming from D.M. Thomas. Afterwards, in a palatial restaurant near the Charles Bridge staffed with white-suited waiters, the hefty bill came at the end of the night. The raconteur immediately produced a card. It was generous. Unfortunately, it was a hotel-membership card and not a credit card, upon which all of them fumbled and then pooled their interdenominational cash. Quin, who was always forward-thinking, had USDs which settled the evening into a stroll over the bridge lit with riotous parties and fireworks. A memorable event, even though the exchange rate was against him. But yes, Beckett would have been pleased that someone else was shelling out more than words.

He couldn't tell stories. Fragments were what fired him and he should not have tried to join them together for stories. Fragments got him fired from the reading circuit. In Australia, nobody came up for his signings. Nobody bought his books. Still, he got to see Warsaw, bombed out of existence in the war and now sprouting Stalinesque buildings of the nineteen-fifties, looking as though a slight earthquake would demolish them into modernity. Kyiv, though, was purported to be very beautiful. It had a river, parks and boulevards. Iryna was a nice name if pronounced properly. It rhymes with 'scrivener'. In boarding school, during the holidays, he stayed with a Polish friend whose mother was called Iryna. Wójek told me Australians pronounced it as eye-ryna, sounding like urina. It was a much prettier name than that.

This memory took him back sixty years.

Wójek Strzelecki was a gigantic Polish boy who hated rugby and loved rowing. He was non-aggressive and stayed away from trouble. He had what was called a large wingspan, meaning his pull on the oar sent the boat slicing through the water faster than the coach's motorboat. In his house I learned a few Polish words: *dziękuję ci*; thank you; *dzień dobry*; good morning; *do widzenia*; goodbye; *przepraszam*; pardon. I liked the sound of 'pardon' best. It had so many 'z's' that it softened the request into a bequest, sounding like something between 'present' and 'depressant'. Yes, his mother said, if you forgive me Abe (she pronounced it *Abbé*), I will perhaps buy you a present. *Proszę*? Please? (Also 'sorry', or 'pardon'.)

Iryna liked to lie in on summer Saturday mornings. Nude. While I sometimes brought her tea. As a fourteen-year-old, this was very exciting. In the evenings we had blueberry soup, cold. Wójek was a lucky boy. I said *przepraszam* and *proszę* a lot to his blonde mother who bought me lots of presents like colourful Ukrainian sweaters when she went on trips abroad. But mainly she liked to see me in my Speedos. Her most unusual gift was a box of condoms. *It's for the girls in your life*, she said.

After trying one out on himself, young Quin had no other employment for them than to investigate the word *condom*, of unknown or dubious origins; one being that in the nineteenth century a British Colonel Condom issued them to his troops to guard against the proliferation of French sexual diseases. The phrase *French letter* sounded better, *lettre d'amour*, which as a spermatozoan epistolarian, Quin much preferred in his romantic naivety to the *English cape*, whose cloak and dagger intimated pillage and rape.

Now this younger Iryna was starting to sound genuine. He was imagining a reading in Krakow, in deep mist and wet air, the city growing dark at three-thirty in the afternoon and he, in a warm bookshop, where the audience understood English and laughed in the right places, which never happened in Australia, being applauded by a local.

I am losing my sensitivity. Which is useless and a burden to carry all of life. Perpetual longing; nostalgia; these are hypochondrias; aggressive illnesses; wounds which are enjoyed, their pain just on the other side of eros. So it is best to lose all these sicknesses and to recover the present, the phenomenology of astonishment without a backstory. But the burden of it, the longing for a time that was unchanging – that was what he was denying himself. Survival meant not going to those places in the past; quicksand, the lot of it; treacherous for the solitary if bearing a burden. But what mattered was the trivial pursuit between partners: the loss of a favourite book or manuscript; the misplacement of a love letter that was latently discovered without exciting jealousy; the abandonment of vengeful or attritional memory; the wilful lack of understanding as to what truth was and what was fabulism, taking form in the extremes of the imagination and which only come to fruition without the weakness of sensitivity. Which is unempathetic but ethical. Isn't that the real definition of *Mensch*?

Faith has never provided a supplement for the failure of his senses. Indeed, he is with George Steiner, who said that dignity is carrying your own suffering (after a passionate assault of course). Don't whine. Get on with it. Pessimism has its uses and abuses. It soothes you and protects you, but you should use your brains instead. Differentiate feeling and thinking. That's what books told him. Steiner too, had Alsatian dogs. He once said he would die for them rather than for his family, if he had no choice. Strange thing for a Jew to say. But since George's wife had died, it was probably both paranoia and companionship that drove him, living alone in his Cambridge bungalow. Not strange bedfellows for someone who was Jewish.

When he reads a writer who is little known but harnesses the most exacting of the senses – music and heartbreak – he cannot resist sharing and yet does not want to share it with others. A grievous novel provokes a resistance that is embodied by its loss. Once read it is predated upon, used up, made one's own in its edification, squandered, but then, after a few years, not even one memorable line is left, save a feeling of the memory itself, but not a memory of its feeling; rather of empty rectitude. Quin wished he could feel passionately again. Literature's reach should be like the tentacles of an octopus, which, according to Sy Montgomery, a woman Quin would like to meet and know, contain three-fifths of an octopus's neurons. Thinking is not done in the brain but in the arms. An octopus can change so fast, from colour to colour, from texture to texture, from shape to shape, that it can experience a kind of rampant synaesthesia. Its dance can operate as a nervous impulse and its movements are never quite equivalent to our representation because most of it is done in secret; under ledges, in clouds of ink, covered in sand. An octopus is a novel at work. Einstein may have been something of an octopus: he said that for him colours are feelings and numbers are tones. Einstein played the violin. He said he wanted to have at least eight hands.

But Quin was not Einstein even though he once slept in a bed at the Bissell House in South Pasadena, a bed Einstein occupied while visiting Caltech in 1930. Anna Bissell, whose father Melville, a vacuum cleaner tycoon, had built the 'Shingle' house on Orange Grove Avenue, now known as Millionaires' Row. The boutique B&B was free for visiting writers in exchange for a reading at the library.

He felt strange sleeping in Einstein's bed. It was very soft and very high. Next door, the bathroom boasted three showerheads and a tiled bench where he could sit and be hosed with warm water from all directions. He had a public reading at the library on Oxley Street the next afternoon, something which kept him from sleeping well in that soft, high bed. Besides, the crickets out in the garden were very loud. He closed the window. They seemed to be in the room. He thought of putting each cricket in a matchbox. When he was in primary school his classmates sold fighting crickets in matchboxes. They also tied thread onto dragonfly tails so that when they flew, they could be reeled in like a kite. Nothing escaped in childhood.

His father regularly went fishing in the South China Sea. He was not sure if these fishing trips were real or fictitious. His mother said they were fishy and no doubt knew there was a woman at the heart of the matter. It was difficult not to suspect where his father's money went when he was supposed to be on the South China Sea. He always came home broke, but when questioned, told wondrous tales of encountering Communist Chinese gunboats and flying fish. Sailfish, he said, could jump out of the sea and stab you in the neck. He'd seen it happen. Nothing escaped him. After one fishing trip, he said he'd caught a small octopus and put it into a jar with a screw-on top and punched a hole in the lid with a nail, to provide oxygen, though he knew little about undersea life. He said it was a present for his son. This would prove to his wife that his absence wasn't a fish story. He described the flat and oily sea in the way Joseph Conrad would have done, the red and green lanterns on either side of the night-fishing junks, the warning gongs and stiff bunks, a distant typhoon whipping up the water on the horizon. My father also told me of plague boats drifting aimlessly about with no crew. He placed the jar next to his bunk. In the morning, the octopus had escaped.

Sy Montgomery, the octopus lady, describes how octopuses can undo the lids of latched boxes to capture the crab inside. They can also shapeshift, and slide into two-inch openings by flattening themselves, and then changing colour before hosing down any intruder with ink. He was thinking about all this in Einstein's bed and the crickets were driving him mad. He sought out the source of the noise and found that it was a recording from a small machine inside the cupboard. You could change the channels, choosing between sea sounds, foghorns, birdsong and frogs. As it turned out, what he heard were not crickets but frogs. He unplugged it, but he still couldn't sleep. He needed to have faith in himself. His reading will be fine, he told himself. He will make his way to the library early, check out the ambience, meet the staff and test the acoustics. The head librarian will make the introductions, acknowledging the Bissell House, the beautiful blonde heiress who now owned it, and the rather awkward and distant writer from Australia.

But it did not go smoothly. He read the octopus story at the library. There was a man at the back, an Afro-American, who wanted to join in with the reading. He rapped loudly with every line that pleased him, and swam his fingers and arms through the air, enjoying the beat of the reading. The small crowd was agitated. The rapper wore dark glasses and rocked his head like Stevie Wonder. *Octo puss!* he repeated. *Ya gotta stay loose! Forsaken Kraken, awaken now!* The head librarian was on his cell phone. *From the bell jar flee back to the ominous sea!* The reader found himself enjoying the rapport. *Octo puss, ya gotta stay loose!* He gave the rapper the upraised fist. He thought of the three-way shower, the crickets. Escape! he emphasised. Set yourself free! *You have no bones for Davy Jones!* His reading was now totally directed at the rapper. He snaked his arms in the air. *Ya gotta get smarter and a whole lot sharper; ex-cape from yer fuckin father! Use black ink!*

Ain't time to think! He was now reading in unison with the rapper, both of them miming an octopus. It was too late. Two policemen arrived and handcuffed the rapper from behind. The crowd murmured and some applauded. His reading was compromised, though in retrospect, not in the way he would have thought. He was not with the crowd and anyway there were no old rappers so he was now accepting their apologies, signing books for the beautiful heiress, shaking hands with suits and ties, wishing he could change his shape, slide under the door and glide out into the night in the opposite direction from Millionaires' Row.

He looked up the UAAA, the Ukrainian Association of Animal Advocates. Printed out a Cyrillic alphabet compendium and searched the lists of patrons. There were quite a few Irynas. Maybe he will arrange to meet her in Krakow or Lublin.

Krakow would be different to US cities. It would have a long history of wars and repressions. He would wander through the main market, the medieval Rynek Główny. He would queue to see the Royal Castle and the site of Schindler's enamel factory, which now houses two museums. He would if he could. He thought of all the airports he'd been in; repositories of rudeness: people running over your toes with their trolleys; on the plane, a large person sitting in your seat; in the next seat was megaphonic all-night talking, laughter with someone across the aisles; farts and snorting. The flight attendants were all in the rear galley; impossible to get their attention.

He couldn't summon up the will or the energy to do all that flying and suddenly, to his relief, there was a pandemic. Russian forces were now building on the Belarussian border. Then on 24 February, they attacked. Could he go now, and get involved? DFAT, the Department of Foreign Affairs and Trade, has issued severe warnings to travellers. The skies are closed above Ukraine.

He wanted to show his care. He wrote to Iryna, discarding all suspicions of her fakery, promising any help she may require, within his means, feeling quite excited by this new *aventure épistolaire*. She did not reply.

So therefore the alleged scammer has also had to flee, Professor Quin concluded. Suspicion returned. Funny how Iryna addressed him by his title. He was Chin to his pupils. *Qin*, he would inform them, was the old name for China, pronounced 'Chin'. Uttered twice for good health. 'Old China', old mate, China plate, his high-school nickname. He felt brittle. Iryna's silence returned him to his solitude, his memories of slights, his losses and lovelessness. After a week he wrote: *The Ukraine is much in the news of course. I follow every bulletin. I watched the movie* Donbass. *I studied the maps and plotted the Russian attacks. Learned the names of the main streets in Kyiv. I do fear for your safety.* But he postponed sending the email.

He *is* involved in this war. It is the first war with a positive intention to defend, identify, and show one's colours. All the other wars in his lifetime were wars of deliberation, reticence, fear, in the end, proximity, corruption and compromised withdrawal. All these earlier wars were somewhat literary and diaristic; they reeled out like memoirs of pain and failure, not worth fighting, paradoxes of wars, liberation or deliberation. Defeats brought poetry; victories brought ideologies.

I think back on the past, that unpromising life wrung out of cold-water tenements, when something happened. Literature like a Russian doll in the drawers of time was hatching. Bitter depression, already viewed through a telescope, emerged at age nine, not inflamed by Enid Blyton or W.H.G. Kingston, but brought into focus through a Virginia Woolf exchanged for ten comics at the hawker's stall. It was the first time a book *disturbed*, took the 'I' out of him. So 'I' became 'he'. He stayed awake slapping at mosquitoes, desperately trying to decipher it. The flat reeked of stinky tofu. Something had to give, a melancholic surrender of life, he wrote to his friend Ginnie much later, having lived most of his life backwards, without discovering happiness. Ginnie would always answer in single lines: *Anhedonia is not without pleasure.*

Ginnie was not my girlfriend, just a good friend. It was rare in Australia to have good girlfriends who were not sexual objects, who were not traditionally gender-oriented and whom one did not exploit because of that very fact. Ginnie however, was also Polish and Indigenous, a strange combination found mostly underground excavating for white opals in Coober Pedy. Therefore she knew what it was like in Australia to not only be non-Anglo but to be assumed as a migrant and a lesbian. The eight ball was always in front. Her early education was in missions and Catholic schools. Perhaps being more than triply displaced in one's own land was what bound us together. Ginnie was like a sister, but she could have been a lover.

Perhaps he was unsuitable for the normal world. The damage that literature does is to make you unsuitable for the real world, but not for imagined other-worlds. It opens the prison doors but lets escape an eternally unfulfilled desire. He wondered whether it was better to live without desire and to accomplish simple things every day. Why he can't relate to ordinary people is still a problem. There always seems to be a subtext in what they were saying, their words like spiders in a letterbox, but it was really he who could not speak without feeling fraudulent, like an actor on stage who could not believe in his role. They must think the same of him, stepping back, spinning on their heels in supermarket aisles, suspecting he was carrying a virus, a biblical plot soon to be released unto them. But he wasn't carrying handwash or the last packet of toilet paper. And he hadn't travelled for many years. And he felt guilty about having travelled at all. Ginnie agreed with him. *The pissoirs in Paris are privations*, she wrote pithily. Would you go all the way to learn that bit of information? How did *she* know? Had she always been heading for the wrong toilet? Travel was finding out that you never belonged. Only *imagined* travel worked.

Vespasian was Emperor of Rome between 69 and 79 AD. He placed a tax on public urination ('money doesn't smell') and on the excrement of sinners, which he called 'the gold of expiation'. His name is more famous for the urinals in Paris named after him, the *Colonnes Vespasiennes*, than for his deeds as an emperor. In the nineteenth century in Paris, these pissoir columns were often topped with advertisements such as: *Entrepôt général de la Parfumerie Hygiénique, rue de Rivoli, 79*; as if sanitation was equivalent to the masking of odours. Perhaps the sign itself disinfected the latrine. These columns were like telegraph poles for dogs. Though passers-by only saw the backs of those who were urinating, they would have observed the different finales of shaking, bending, straightening and patting. Sometimes you paid

the cleaning woman standing outside. In any case you had to spend a penny or a sou for the discomfort of public toilets, a tax on dreams in the eternal return of sleepless nights.

Ginnie had a treatise on orality and anality; something she researched by interviewing colonoscopists and dentists. 'They are sceptical of each other regarding germs,' she said. 'In the end, shit does less harm than mouths.'

I adored the pithy as I adored Ginnie. We spoke in monosyllables when we went on that trip to Coffin Bay together and you could have counted the words spoken on a thousand-kilometre drive on four hands. She was not the model of someone who spoke on the phone for hours, or who needed emotional support, or wanted to fill you with knowledge in that educative way; no, she left you with incomplete and multifarious alphabetical symbolisms like the Kabbalah and you had to mull over those at your leisure. And if you struck it lucky, you might just sleep with her in that ungraspable way...mysterious and lustrous and infinitely desirable because of her curiosity and pliable indifference...until she met a woman, several women, twice as brilliant as any man. But our trip to Coffin Bay was really about death, though I didn't know it at the time.

Raining heavily now, and he thinks disjointedly because of its drumming, unable to seek references in books, rainy books – *Henderson the Rain King, Rain and Other South Seas Stories, The Hawk in the Rain* – copies which he was beginning to lose in his vast library because they were uncatalogued, placed willy-nilly on disparate shelves, and now he was losing his eyesight, which came with panic attacks and claustrophobia and not even the paper bag he carried around with him in order to breathe into and count the breaths, had any use. Every Tuesday, in the tiled clinic at Mount Barker, he watched as in a Buñuel movie, the razor approaching his eyeball.

But if his father were still alive, he would have patented an electronic barcode system which would be stuck in every book bought or lent; borrowed or stolen; and all you needed to do was to scan the shelves, your handheld beeping when the code was detected and there it was on your screen: title; date acquired; author; contextual interest.

Of course, if there is no time, there is no death. So in a way it is better to be demented since there is no sense of time in a demented state, he thought, as he imagined being caught by the security guard for *not* having taken anything from the store without paying. The guard would be full of fury. Where do these Asians get off? Up their arses? There are guards everywhere. Alarum. He carries a paper bag with nothing in it. The guard wants to look in it anyway. Alarum. The trouble with being foreign is that the people around him were treating him as though he had the plague or was dim-witted; speaking slowly and cautiously to him, sometimes loudly, as if he were a baby. Goodwill hunting or is it entitlement speaking? Lately, this world began to spin as well. He couldn't stand on one foot for more than thirty seconds. That, he read, was a prediction of a life at its end. Not more than ten years awaited him, if he were lucky.

But he is neither foreign nor demented. It's just the wild air. Around him, all those different faces, none of which were recognisably interesting. Was this the stage of age when nothing more was attractive or astonishing? He remembered in the Paris Metro when that girl, a Picasso painting of parts, folded her hand over his on the crowded carriage rail; classically deeply transmitting something; Iberian grief perhaps. Now alas, his reclusion insured the being of one who only counted his pension. Counting is behovely. It focused the mind and drove out the demons of premature climacterics and senescence. Mathematics was retention, like romancing a stone. If he kept up this practice he would live to a hundred. He felt the edge of the wind most keenly when he was not counting. He was vulnerable. Indeed, in the interior, there was no outside. No thick skin. I circle the same story: October 1962, at night, in my dormitory.

They've tried to short-sheet me again but this time I've tumbled to it quickly, being paranoid as well as neurotic, perhaps with as many crossovers between the two, and have sprung their trap early. It's cold and the crows have long cawed their way to water and to roost and here I am listening to the priest intone his prayers up and down the aisles for JFK, and I, the arch-enemy of them all in my regulation two blankets, under suspicion – 'The Red Guard' they called me – was several thousand miles from home. That's one way to explain the rise and fall of dissociation.

At the .22 rifle range for cadets, he was a dead shot. Sharpshooter, which now they call a sniper. Then he graduated to a .303. Both eyes open; get the blur in the shooting eye; squeeze slowly, slightly below six o'clock; breathe out; bull's eye. He enjoyed the kick and lift. Grudgingly, they stopped calling him four-eyes. Vũng Tàu came to mind; Phước Tuy province. He would have gone as his father had instructed him by aerogramme, and may have toughened up if he had survived, a point-man rescued by nervousness and an eagle's eye as long as he had on his bottle glasses and didn't stop moving. But that was not it. He would have gone because of a death-risk. Not a death-wish, but an interest in a wager on God's existence. His classmate Lionel, a fat boy who sent a photo of himself in fatigues, didn't survive a mortar attack (they had to pick up the pieces the next day, but would have missed some, or got some wrong – there were all kinds of other body parts). He still would have gone to try to prove something about death to himself. Perhaps death *was* God? It may have saved him in giving away any belief in God. But he would have gone because there was nowhere to belong, except to the already lost; if he were alive in 1936 he would have gone with the International Brigade to Catalonia. His thesis was on Norman Mailer; who knew war; who was belligerent and knew how to box. Quin's father would have approved. Now, being a war journalist was different. You were there; you reported what you saw; you weren't a wimp making it up. Go!

He didn't know what to feel. He had spent a summer with Lionel's family in Moree and the two boys went out and shot rabbits, skinned and gutted them, dressed them for the table. Lionel's mother never wore a bra. She leant over the sink and Quin's desire rose. At night, fourteen-year-old Quin fantasised about farm life in Australia; a Wonder Woman cooking a rabbit for him without a bra. There was just one thing wrong: Lionel and Quin forgot they had to break the rectal bone of the carcass and empty it of any remaining spoor before handing it over for cooking. This was one of the finer points of dressing a kill.

None of that explains neurosis, which Freud defined as the opposite of psychosis. The latter with no reality, no door bolted to steel hinges like the former. We had to take off our shoes before ascending the marble stairs to Dorm 4 and fifty smelly boys rose silently under the threat of canings to make a silent peace with God, family and country matters. Psychic damage. It came with corporal punishment. Some of the boys evaded caning by letting themselves be preyed upon. You could defend yourself if only you had the words. Can the past be expressed without the turmoil of one ego being replaced by another? Damage. Are not words already an other? Damage. He was pubescent then and would not know anyone of the opposite sex for a decade and had only his library of voices which he'd gathered around himself until they started fading to make way for money calculations, unnatural disasters and the precariat of pestilence. If not for these practical traumas, daily doses of reality supplements, an aid to becoming someone other, then what else would have engendered reflection or even reflexive verbs which could have buffered the shambling fantasy of not seeing oneself at all? Sweet loves, dead or soon to be dead. Damage. Sometimes he glimpses them on the web, aged and bloated, still working as head teachers, for whom he once had a yearning but never made a move to touch their coloured frocks, seeing himself reflected in the loving headlights of oncoming horror like a wombat on a freeway. They all had flat Anglo-Celtic names, seldom more than two syllables, innocent of the advertisement of truth...that they attracted him...maybe even Lionel's young mother, for whom there was a fleeting heartbeat...who would have been thinking after her son's death that all the king's men...and then this diffusion of sexual longing fragging his narrative, the result of his hermetic observation that creation was all work without the reality... unravelling in the same way as nature's woven hardship of survival drove intermittent self-destruction...leaving holes for readers to fill. Something that worries me; irks my memory like lost objects; lost sayings; untidy lives. I was unhoused; all over the place. Put it down to damage. It's okay, you know. Everyone's damaged goods. The rare ones have happy families and ivy-league educations and then three or four marriages. They come through; they hate ill-health; life can be bought. But in Quin's case, what couldn't be bought was that sharing of thoughts and feelings, *us against the world*, the team who built a fortress, even though constructed by means of creaky scaffolds. But in his experience, partners were always busy, obsessed with themselves, plied with ambition and were always having to prove something through darkening moods and gender agenda, and the fortress wall caved in that way, and let in the world to plunder the painstakingly kept secrets stored over time, now open for all to see...ha-ha! We all knew it wouldn't last.

I sip my whiskey from my telescopic cyclist's cup made of silver, circa 1887, imbibing all the microbes of the ages. Then I have second thoughts – better late than never – dosing the cup with isopropyl alcohol. Embossed on the lid is a tandem bicycle, with the woman on the front. Age of the pre-suffragettes. She steers and gears, he supplies power as the engine room. This would equate to women's liberation later: he, hard-wired, a dinosaur; she, nimble and clever and good with instructing him. In the distance, the spires of the towns and the barns of the villages. Idyllic, save for the year 1887: the *annus mirabilis*: Queen Victoria celebrates her Golden Jubilee marking fifty years of her reign. Zululand becomes a British colony. The Theatre Royal in Exeter burns down and one hundred and eighty-six people die. The British Empire takes over Balochistan. Oscar Wilde is appointed editor of *The Woman's World*...etc. The cup leaks. Isopropyl alcohol is giving me a stomach-ache. A man is delivering carnations at the front door with black gloves on. My mother loved carnations. My mother is dead, I said. He nods in sympathy and turns quickly on his heel. My mother died a long time ago. Probably during the time of Boccaccio, though she was no storyteller. I could imagine her in a plague, rationing our food, counting out pumpkin seeds, boiling up five banana peels. Counting is important. Why am I receiving these flowers now? A mistake, surely; but maybe a prognosis, or maybe a prosopopoeia. There is no note with the bouquet.

At the height of the pandemic he wrote a series of apophthegms: saying he should begin writing in pencil, where everything can be erased and the handwriting improved with the body's shaping, so that lightness, craft and humble shavings should not last beyond the moment of creation, the smell of wood, some graphite, scenting the lone pine forests of perennial disappearance, the forever of lost time. He was inspired by his friend Ginnie, who said there was nothing of importance that was not brief.

Henry David Thoreau: 'I am a pencil.'

Janna Malamud Smith: 'My father is a book.'

Nadine Gordimer: 'A serious person should try to write posthumously.'

His father was a tension highball – all bourbon and temper – he had a genius for striving – never giving up – though in the end giving up was necessary, giving up on marriages, futures, see how old he was when he gave up! Crushed by appearance. But let the real seduce the real – those beautiful women of the imagination and their first deaths, when he got it all wrong emotionally, not hearing the silence of the icebergs and their subliminal creaking, finding out pretty quickly that there was no woman for all seasons – and that there was no lasting joy save in a nanosecond when measured by the universe's terms.

But hey, I understand cool. Phlegmatic, my humour. The epistolary my favourite method. Do you read me? Probably not, these shuddering wings of butterflies leaving only powder on the page which one blows as drying pounce over ink, but there is nothing afterwards, as though I am being dreamt. He wasn't like his father, for whom writing always had an addressee, any response a challenge for pursuing the case as in a law court and not in courtship or even courtly love. No, father was father, the patriarch, menacing, litigious, and no one writes to the patriarch.

I would like to slip into reading again like an old familiar slipper after all these years at the factory in Hobbesian boots, one leg in fear, the other in contract. But how long will it last? How long before the scribbling itch returns and speeds past, overtaking the slow train of thought only to come to grief at the level crossing?

Sitting up late Sunday night: each loaded chamber of his revolver a lessening option. Meditate on its weight, the heft of its cross-hatched handle, smell of fine oil. My father's Smith & Wesson is always larger than imagined. No one writes to someone who packs a gun inside the big lapels of his double-breasted suit. If there's a war on, you won't feel lonely, he said. In a recurring dream, I try on his jacket. I forget that I am on my own and then I wake and *am* on my own and what a reprieve! Ginnie writes in a moment of levity: *I have dreamt whole books, but they are all forgettable.*

A famous historian said we had to limit Asian immigration because if you walk down the main street of Cabramatta they are all spitting. On more than a dozen occasions, in outer-suburban railway stations, blond or shaven-headed young men hawk and spit very close to me until I am of no doubt they mean to spit at me. I presume someone spits for someone to watch the spitting. Perhaps it is a sign of solidarity. Epidemiology of semiology. But it is not a football field where everyone spits together out of physical effort. In Australia, being Asian is a physical effort. During natural disasters and pandemics, the illusion of being the same is no longer the same. I remember a huge bushfire darkening the skies at midday and reddening the skies at midnight.

Then came the pandemic hot on its heels. First, it was 'evacuate!' then 'stay at home!' I had nowhere to go anyway. There was a police car on the corner. My dogs keep up their barking until it drives off, sullenly, it seems.

I remember the guy two places behind me in the supermarket queue saying loudly as I bought toilet paper: 'Even the Chinese have to shit!' Was it a statement of equality or one of surprise that humans were similar?

I recall the man in a suit and tie making a zero with his thumb and index finger as I rode my bicycle past him. Did he mean 'all good', or 'don't come close' or something else entirely? Apparently, Quin was told by one of his students, it was a far-right call sign.

I found a note in my letterbox which said: 'Dear neighbour if you need any deliveries please don't hesitate to call me. I can get you groceries and leave them at your door. Elizabeth.' Somebody has reached out. I still don't know who Elizabeth is. I wish I did, so I could continue some correspondence, and by chance, experience as Baudelaire did, a *correspondance*, of the sordid, the corrupt, the damage one can do to relationships and oneself through a forest of symbols hidden in letter-writing. There was no return address. That was the catch.

I can't remember much else about earlier wars except deforestation, sardines on toast, hungry dogs and soap operas from Brazil. I guess trees don't ever travel, but I think they chat. I watch them closely. Dead trees or cut trees or burnt trees fill me with an empty grief I cannot express.

Apophlegm: Choked with the flegma and humour of his sins he shouted: 'God grant me apathy forthwith!' to relieve his aches of recurrence: one good thing; one bad thing; hope or regret; looking out the high windows of his mind onto low eternity...the line of graves he can see from his house. He was cursed with an expiation complex. Perhaps something lingering in the gene pool about penance. In a more quotidian manner, he paid his parking fines immediately. He even suggested to the Adelaide Hills Council that they have an expiation reserve set up for each ratepayer, so that it could be paid into by repeating offenders, accumulating before a fine was issued, thus becoming an efficient revenue income for the local government, plus removing unnecessary paperwork or paid overtime.

I was given a Japanese calligraphy chest, circa mid-nineteenth century probably carried on and off American ships led by Commodore Perry in 1853. Someone had carved an anchor on its side. Such barbed weights must have been intriguing, quite like briefcases of the time. It is a dark wooden chest no larger than a US Army ordnance grenade box. But what smells it harbours! Old lives, multiple secrets, aged coffin wood. In the top section, there is a secret compartment in which you can lift out a tray from the whole. Beneath is not another chamber but a very shallow section, only deep enough for secreting a special letter from an envoy or a lover. A fragrant missive perhaps, hidden from prying eyes, which can only be identified by scent. Or maybe poison, if you lick the paper. There are always these chambers of the heart made shallow by time, undiscoverable for their deep meaning. No longer secret, unsophisticated in the technological age, they become memory through the reinvestment of story, without smell, without experience. But how frivolous are books without the engagement of the writer in total desperation? One needs to put oneself on the line; go out and confront danger; lose one's lover and all one's money. Then tell me you're trying to write. Dostoyevsky had it right. I went to Baden-Baden. Lost at the casino, skied down a slope at night, misspelled everything in my diary after they rescued me in the blinding searchlight of a snowmobile. I may have had a slight stroke and may have begun speaking in tongues. These lapses are becoming more common.

She who thinks like a cryptic crossword is the lover of my dreams. Clue: *Lawrence, a Freudian dyslexic, wrote* **** One has to go figure. *Tunc*; (Latin) *at that time.* I would probably have removed the asterisks, though Ginnie wouldn't have done so, reprimanding me for reading too much Durrell. Missing letters reminded me of gunshots. At that time, many of us owned guns and had short liaisons and abortions. I do not need guns now, nor dream of making love in starry-eyed cane-breaks, or reconstituting elaborate time schemes for future marriages in a precarious age. All is in the past. *Just as well*, Ginnie wrote, *dementia has its uses.* These days I thresh the corn and wheat of my language and think of my connectedness to nature and try to think thoughts to their end by writing them in the sand. But the beach does not please me. Sitting there makes me uncomfortable, I am swallowed up by the least literary of gestures. Too much nakedness. Snow, however, allows me to think to the end. All because I am still an *alpiniste*. I want to climb the cold alone. However, neurosis is now reaching every height and depth. I once tried to come to terms with Mount Kosciuzko and equipped myself with ropes and crampons, but there was an easy environmental walkway to the top. No magic mountain; no cigar. My friend Ginnie possessed an ear for a tongue; the nose of the wolf; a slip of the Freud. Aphorist *ne plus ultra*, she was melancholic and angry at the same time, each an antidote for the other.

Life. At first, you count the bad moments. Then the moments of joy – and our joy increases with this counting.

Counting was a kind of discipline and panic, like a Pascalian wager or Faustian pact. There is a purity about counting and chanting, I said to myself, one act contained inside another, moments within computing, in the same way as one human relationship necessarily remained rhythmically imbricated in another, and that in this lock-step, in this keychain of events, the crowning achievement was to arrive at one's death by design; a counting-down; T-minus x to lift-off into nothingness. The expiation complex manifested in boarding school in the form of countless decades of the rosary. You worried the beads, counted off the prayers, paid for sins. The result of all this was to make you a second-tier bureaucrat, a functionary abiding by all the laws, and like Pontius Pilate you cleansed your own hands after cultivating your own garden. I was not like my father, who understood corruption and thereby exposed himself to the rottenness of the State. He didn't care about being cleansed or baptised into its power.

In 1525, Swabian peasants revolted against the aristocracy and clergy in Salzburg. The bishops barricaded themselves in the Hohensalzburg fortress. They defecated out a second-storey window onto the peasants. The rebellion failed.

I was never good at philosophy. At university, I skipped a whole passage of Plato in my tutorial because I found it tedious and somewhat constipated. Plato doesn't say anything to me, Quin commented to the sniggering of the other students. Plato was no poet. He strains at metaphor. Quin's tutor, who had bad teeth, repeated his gaffe to the other classes. It came back to him like Chinese whispers and though he was not identified directly, clearly saw himself in the third person. From then on he moved easily between the two.

I've left most things behind. I do not want to blame myself for uselessness. No one should have to live with the blame of uselessness all their lives. Dinner with sparkling people would have been good, but that has proven to be just as useless and although he never forgets one moment of it, others always do: wiping him off the map. Years later, no one is recognisable anymore. Ginnie writes that she is living alone by the sea, pocketing and counting stones and taking them home to protect them from the weather. *People are dead but stones are alive*, she writes. Ginnie is making love with several women, but only by letter. She has one heartbreak after another. Letter-writing is dangerous, I tell her. The virus can live on paper for a brief time. *That is all the time love needs* – Ginnie's last words.

Visions now of the Indian Ocean lapping grey upon a nether shore. A red-brown desert awaits. A red-brown job. They warned him, the fortune-telling women, about thinking clearly over what job he should attempt, advice he didn't take in this case and was down to his last five hundred dollars, imagining the emptiness of the landscape; the silence of the suburban afternoon; the terrible grieving at sunset. He would need to get a day job.

His despair forms on cloudy afternoons on most days. Something is irritating his memory and he swears he cannot die without finding the source of it. He would need another body in which to die and they will file past remarking on how well he looked in death when he was, in fact, nothing but a dried cricket in a matchbox whence no noise emerged on summer nights to tangle their dreams of self-congratulations for being alive. In this subterfuge of death, he would be free to investigate out-of-body experiences. This would not be easy.

St Teresa of Àvila was a discalced Carmelite; i.e. she walked everywhere barefoot, particularly enjoying rough ground, barnacles on rocks and pebbles on the beach. As a child, she stuck gravel in her shoes and called this a present from God. She was born a noblewoman in 1515. This may have explained her desire to have adventures, fight wars and explore South America. But she joined the convent instead. In her fourth meditation, the Devotion of Ecstasy, she writes about how to achieve the moment when the consciousness of being in the body disappears. Michel Foucault, who also wrote about this, proposed that the ancient Chinese perfected the prolongation of the sexual act in which time, 'which aged the body and brought death', was exorcised. Teresa calls her ecstasy a 'happy pain' followed by a moment of strangulation in which her body levitates in a fiery glow. Thus one is in union with God and wakes in tears. *Bonjour tristesse*. Orgasm is brief. It can be achieved in pain or in relief from it. Ginnie, pocketing heavy pebbles, was gathering beating hearts in the sand, weighing her down against any levity. Friendship, unlike love, is not light, she said. Her punctuation was always superb: commas, colons and especially apostrophes, which she loved most because they took the place of something missing, like that which was irritating my memory: aphorisms; apothegms; epigraphs.

Somewhere along Coffin Bay in South Australia, gulls alight to wait for the oyster boats. Sometimes they get lucky. They pick up an oyster, drop it on the rocks from a great height and eat the innards. Once he and Ginnie visited those oyster farms. Ginnie rhymed with skinny and her stick legs wading in the blue bay water made him think of an ibis or heron and she was very happy in the water, indigenous to it. She was also a genie which often came out of a bottle, after long periods of silence. He was just out of university and they had come on this long car trip knowing this was not a sexual trip but some kind of knowledge-gathering about friendship. They told each other about their first sexual encounters and in the telling they were sexualised, but not for each other, though there were moments, brief moments of happy pain. There was a girl, Pamela, he said, who was tall, willowy, had long black hair to her waist and wore satin bell-bottoms – it was the early seventies – and she asked him to accompany her to a movie – *Summer of '42* – and after the movie, in the cold glare of the nightlights, she kissed him and suggested they go to bed at her place and he didn't know what to say because he hadn't done it before and he was never going to be able to do it like Hemingway and he thought he would start by reading a bit to her from *For Whom The Bell Tolls* – ('But did thee feel the earth move?') – and maybe kiss for a long time, until she asked him why he liked to kiss so much. He thought then what a weight it was to have sex, what a waste of good love, which wasn't present. Nor was there ever a good war for a good love. *You see*, Ginnie said immediately, *the unbearable lightness of it*!

At Coffin Bay, Ginnie and I ate oysters and watched the gulls and the seals. You know, you really are neurotic, she said without a sign of irony, having reviewed my novel on Freud's Wolfman, which can be distilled down to letters, wars, cataclysms and intercourse. She was staring straight at me without pity but with great curiosity. When she was ironic, she always looked away and spoke to the wings as though she were in an Elizabethan drama, discoursing with the dead. It's like an oyster making a pearl, she continued, not referring to my novel. The struggle of making. You make or you self-destruct. Nacre lines the inside of the shell and then a foreign substance, some grit or sand, gets in between it and the shell; irritating isn't it? Imagine a pebble in your shoe or a thorn in your bum. Pure suffering without being able to remove the source. The oyster's reaction is to cover over it. Keep working at masking it. Baroque, don't you think? Like the Catholic church. The Catholic enigma is that you self-destruct. The Judaic shibboleth is that you *make*. And *macht* became destruction, not freedom. Do you dare to eat an oyster?

Ginnie was always smarter than I was, or more ornate. She ran an antique store. I immediately thought of my shopping list when the pestilential lockdown came. Berocca for my hangovers. Water and wine and bread. Shopping lists never end or evolve. They just repeat themselves. Ginnie asked me, while I sipped a sweet wine, if the world was ever my oyster. I said no, it was always the aim of my doppelgänger. He was always much freer in the world. Ginnie nodded and kept silent. It's what I always liked about her. Sometimes I think I would have proposed to her if I hadn't known she played on both teams and I would be ignored but not jealous because girls together had a certain vicarious attraction for me. Equanimity fluctuates, like most things on the spectrum. I think back now and see that her silences were punctuations. Her world was cast with perfect sentences, syntaxes and precise breathing. Syntax was philosophy. The grammar of all thought. I think she was writing me but I can't be sure. I would be immensely flattered. All I know is that she knew every provenance in her antique shop, dating objects better than radiocarbon. *Dry salvages from the shipwreck of history*. When she was ironic her apostrophes to the wings addressed what was dead inside me; things that needed to be disinterred from their italics. I told her about the time I was in boarding school when I was about twelve or thirteen and my voice had broken so I was useless for the choir and had to do technical drawing, sitting there with other broken boys, drawing a cube in oblique and isometric views, but instead, I was sketching Leonardo da Vinci's helicopter with a nude woman lying beside it, when the priest caught me doodling and placed his large hand on the nape of my neck, a hand so large it had previously belonged to a wrestler – he could bend horseshoes, it was rumoured – and the hand squeezed and pressed down hard on my neck, lifted me almost out of my chair and dropped me back, patting the back of my head, all without a word being said. Maybe that was the irritation in my memory, a spell of strangulation, a levitation fit for a priest in his devotion to ecstasy. Tears came to my eyes but I had not experienced a union with God.

The last time I saw Ginnie was at my mountain home where my new wife Yuliya and I had invited her for dinner. I picked her up in an agitated state from the station, both her wrists bandaged. We inquired of course if she was all right. She brushed it off by saying she fell onto the barbecue, but I was thinking that if you fell onto the barbecue your hands would be burned, not your wrists. I put her into a taxi late that night as we were all quite drunk and I slipped the driver a handful of notes for the fare. I thought of the way my wife and I had always taken taxis, especially to the airport, because we were without children and my wife had a good job, but that was long before our divorce.

The last time I travelled was to Paris, where I was writing a pearl of a novel and when I returned it took some months before I found out Ginnie had killed herself; three empty gin bottles under her bed, a mess of pills on the Louis XV side table. It is only now that I've detected the real splinter in my memory because I had not realised she had waited until I was well out of the country to feel fully freed or fully abandoned, thus reminding me of that rhetorical device, that address to the dead, for it is only now that *he* knows he should have stepped out of the body of his work, levitated, and looked outside of himself to look out for the other.

I sent the email I previously wrote, and had archived, to Iryna. She wrote back almost immediately. *I am now in Lviv. I am safe. And, by the way, my name is Iryna Zarębina. You can donate to the dog rescue through this link.*

I was not immediately interested in a donation, but I was intrigued that her surname was of Polish origins and that it ended in *ina* rather than *anka*, which meant she was married. In Polish, *Zarębina* is pronounced with a nasalised *ę*; like the name of the Polish-Jewish writer Natalia Zarembina, who in 1942 was the first person to write about Auschwitz-Birkenau.

I donated to the animal advocates after looking at their website. I wasn't sure it went through on the card link since this would automatically send a notification to my phone. There was a delay of course because there was a war on. I wrote again to Iryna hoping she was safe. Lviv was bombed a couple of times. *If you can you should get out of the Ukraine. I understand you can go to Poland without friction at the border. My warmest regards, Professor Quin.*

I am more like my mother every day. She saves and saves and is more than thrifty. She is of course dead. But then I am growing into her. Saving and saving every day. You can't take it with you but you can leave a legacy. Living in depression and melancholia, only she doesn't drink and has an occasional cigarette which she enjoys without inhaling, her legacy to me was lethal. She employed tenses interchangeably. Poised, she was thus always present in the past. All the things she has been through. The Japanese occupation of Hong Kong; the drunk husband; the abusive neighbours; alienated children; two miscarriages; the death of her two-year-old; poverty; starvation; emigration; dementia. It is happening *now*.

There used to be two small fish on our plates on Fridays. Caught by our piano-tuner. He used to say, 'eat rice', 'eat rice'. It was the Chinese way of saying 'bon appétit'. The fish was full of bones. My sister and I picked at them like kittens. A sparrow was making a small nest on the upper ledge of our balcony. We watched it while we ate. The piano-tuner was an old man who owed my father a lifelong favour. He tuned for nothing: one hour on the last Friday of the month at noon, with his tuning fork and lever, leaning over the piano like a mourner over a coffin. I would hear him playing octaves: B♭ – B♭; B♮ – B♮. I honed my pitch and could have told him I could have tuned it myself with a shifting spanner. But I didn't. Later in life in Australia, I would distil Mozart from magpies, storm scales from koels, and plainchants from crows. Much later, the insistent, industrial F♯ of tinnitus.

Mr Wu came on time every month. One day, when I was old enough, my mother told me that he was saved from a Japanese beheading because my father intervened and claimed they had the wrong man, whom they accused of stealing firewood. My father, who survived the end of the war by playing the clarinet in a band, said Mr Wu was tuning the piano in the officers' mess at the time. But it was my father who took wood from the back of a lorry. That night the Japanese beat up the innocent Sikh guard on sentry duty.

Two small fish. We picked over the bones. 'Eat rice', 'eat rice'. In our rice, we found some blackened, tiny worms. They were bitter if you didn't pick carefully enough. Since then I have become very good at forgetting. A master-forgetter of taste. As an anti-Proustian, I only remembered the sparrow. And I drifted off into being someone else whom I could see very clearly in hindsight but was unable to determine his motives at any moment in the past. My grammatical tenses change all the time and I am reconfigured.

Dusk. Sometimes I hide things so well that I can never find them again. Like memories that can be semi-translucent; or a fountain pen, a present from a past relationship that may resurface when used in writing. You know they're there but do not want to even look to find them for their use. Too many memories. The dogs follow me around, knowing where everything is, but they don't nose into my writings.

I am curiously restless, imagining an ideal love affair being offered me, curiously venturing forth through its open doors and finding there no hitches to romance, no small idiosyncrasy that provides rebuff or embarrassment, no stain which will have to be removed time and again. Solitude is my friend and nothing real of this sort can ever come to me, I had figured a long time back when I came to this country and realised pretty quickly how the girls who were very white and blonde seemed to regard me as an ink spot needing white-out, or a blind spot into which they collided, their pity misread by me as interest, their clammy clumsiness as appropriation.

Suddenly you are tired and you stop caring about how you look and grow whiskers instead. You delude yourself when a young pretty girl smiles at you, but she is thinking you are an old man and she needs to make way for you, you who are lumbering by with shopping bags and a stoop. I have dispensed with everything except my bicycle and of course the daily emails which promised everything but delivered nothing. Of my bicycle, I stare at it a lot and meditate on its quadrilateral and its triangles. It is a triumph of design and what it makes available in freedom of being and exploration stems from geometry and physics. Thinking and motion; thinking in motion; outside of time.

I thought more and more of Iryna. I wonder what she looks like? Would I meet with her in Krakow? Would she begin speaking with an accent and a slight lisp and would I immediately feel I was no longer a blind spot in this footlight of foreignness? Since I had little Polish, would I give her cash to buy us drinks on the terrace of the Copernicus Hotel? There would be other signs: holding your hand in both of hers to give you change in case the coins fell, and you cupping her hands saying the change was not necessary, as though you were convincing yourself you were buying intimacy; care with conversation; allowing brief silences between drinks and when things were not too busy, sitting with you and holding your eyes when you allowed it.

The shyness of hypothermia and the dream of love sent you into a trance.

It was like when he first sat on a surfboard at Soldiers' Beach. He didn't know you had to get ahead of the swell and catch the crest of the wave. He was always missing it. But then he was just happy to miss it, watch the others speed away towards shore. It was calmer where he was, a bit behind, not waiting for anything. Then he realised he was being swept out further and further. He was another foreigner having to be rescued. He gave up swimming. The sea was not his element.

I think back on childhood, the unpromising life of father-failure and mother-melancholia. Out of lower middle-class proportions in a prewar tenement with just cold water – we showered from an urn, luke-warmed – a moment of respite when literature became a secret weapon. But before that, bitter discipline, sour vomit, ammoniacal feet in urine, maniacal beatings. Something had to give, of course, a side issue of life-threatening consequences. Hypothermia set in. So here we are, a fossil buried in us which told of a past life and here are we in all the different places called the past, all the frozen layers which have held us for a time, a relic which could still be exhumed but without life, like re-reading a once-favourite novel where our original time had moved on and we are now stateless, lost and disappointed, the exhumation propelling us into a futureless deep-freeze. No surprise that the word 'literature' contracts into itself, mistaken for literacy or literalness. Perhaps it has had its time.

I ride my bicycle through the hills. It gets harder by the day. Recent bushfires have seared my routes and I have to avoid the blackened paths, once riding past a battery-hen farm still glowing with embers, a waft of roast in deadly sizzle.

The smell of chickens and their manure came back to me as a childhood memory of coffin wood. From the age of five, I lived above a courtyard owned by Chinese launderers. Chickens raced between trestles and steam, ironing boards and starched sheets. Quite a few people down below and on the floors above died during a short period. Perhaps they moved there to die. Perhaps it was a kind of extended family, a community. Perhaps there was a plague. Cholera! My mother would shout, covering my nose with an eau-de-Cologned handkerchief. Heavily carved coffins often appeared outside. Then they came lumbering in, seemingly by themselves, followed by Buddhist monks, with incense and chanting. And there was always the smell of chickens and their waste. I dream of that smell often, an odour that I call coffin wood, a shade of sandalwood and odour of the wet markets that I cannot remove from my nose on winter mornings. But now, sixty-five years later, I cannot recall it. I can only recall *him*, in that chrysalis, growing alongside me.

He told his old friend from another city that whilst having an affair he felt it was always necessary to tell of it to a friend for all kinds of psychological reasons, to presage divorce...to salve his guilt, to make it public, to warn of his future unpredictable direction, to legitimise his love, to exacerbate what was already a distinguished desperation, to refuse further help. His friend Ginnie would have gone to bed with him in a state of complete intoxication to assuage whatever they were thinking together, of whomever, or with some sexual allure or fantasy, perhaps even with cool indifference, inadvertently courting pandemonium. Counting minutes, his friend Ginnie brushed her coffee cup onto his lap after his confession; a Freudian supralapsarianism. If we fall, we burn. A scold. Ten Hail Marys, she said. Ginnie had dallied with joining the Carmelites. He was not scalded by the hot coffee and they parted on friendly terms, a kiss on the lips, a lingering hug, and then he caught the last train home, knowing there was no one at the station to greet him, and in the depths of the moonless country night, made the long journey along a forest path while dogs barked in the distance. He smelled coffee on the train, coffee in the forest, and finally coffee in his lonely bed, which he had from then on always associated, the smell of coffee, with divorce, and mostly with cows in the night who came up to greet him along a barbed wire fence, their mustiness replacing the smell of chickens. Translation. How do you translate solitude? How do you translate the wind, the sea beating against rocks and the town rearing up in its shouts from illuminated football stadiums and the silent deserts of isolated lives in the cross-streets of weed and concrete, litter and bitumen? You can't. Unless you're in turmoil. Then, translation comes easily through estrangement and disengagement, though it is hardly ever revealed through words and books. Not many can give a book full attention while in a state of turmoil.

Iryna was now a bit more regular in her emails. Her husband, she said, could not leave Ukraine. By the way, she wrote, it is no longer referred to as 'The' Ukraine. That was offensive. The definite article harks back to Russian occupations and is a residue of imperial control and subjugation. 'The Ukraine' insults us with derogation: 'the frontier lands', or some such thing. We are a sovereign nation. Not a frontier. Even though *Ukraina* means 'borderlands', we are a sovereign nation.

Iryna was feisty and meticulous. He rather enjoyed this aspect of her, treating him as an ignoramus.

He was happy for a while. He went out on his bicycle more often. Thought about how Australians still call the desert plain from Ceduna in South Australia to Norseman in Western Australia *The Nullarbor*. The no-tree land. Rather naive to just look on the surface. Indigenous people call it *Oondiri*, meaning 'waterless', which is more accurate. Not 'the waterless'. Look beneath the surface. Why should white people expect trees when there is no water, when in the past there has always been water? Same with *Aborigine. Ab origine.* From the origin. Why the Latin? Look beneath the surface. Some time or other, the origin will be all of us. *Koori, Kuarna, Murri*, etc. All these colonial white classifiers who masqueraded as ancient Greek or Roman explorers and discoverers missed the point when fifty thousand years ran beneath the inhabited land. Learn the language.

He stood corrected about 'The Ukraine'. It was a huge parcel of land, expertly cultivated, fertile and grain-abundant, centred around Kyiv. It was not a border region or a frontierland. Look beneath the surface at the nomenclature. Where culture is, there is always agriculture. Yes, the name means fertile. And deep; and lush; and most of all, linguistically unified; the bread-basket of Europe and the world. *Ukraine*; pronounced *Ukra-ina*.

I'd always thought 'home' was where you stayed a long time. Then you left it and made another home and then another. Until chronic anxiety developed and 'homelessness' became the norm. Nothing is stable until you find an ideal, and that is always in the head, a mobile suitcase of words and debates.

Forty years ago, in the Blue Mountains west of Sydney, I jogged along a track on a sharp ridge regularly, but now upon visiting my old haunts I walk it slowly expecting danger around every corner. People come here to commit suicide. Lookouts abound with signs warning of unstable rocks and clifftops. It is good that I push my rented bike ahead for it acts as an advance guard. When you arrive at the main lookout and gaze across the valley of aromatic and hallucinogenic sassafras you see a sheer cliff face where a group of Marist Brothers once painted a giant crucifix in white. I don't know how they did it – perhaps they abseiled down, boy scouts of God, for that was what they were good at – pouring buckets of paint horizontally then vertically in commemoration of a fallen brother who had been caught midway down because there was a knot in his rigging. You can't climb a rope hand over hand, he was thinking, especially if your hands were starting to freeze. You just wait to die. It was a winter's afternoon and the rains came heavily and the novice's climbing partner was too slight to pull him up again, backtracking in alarum, calling for rescuers with a winch, but by that time his companion had perished from hypothermia. I wrote to Iryna. I said it was the same with me. I'm too old and frail to haul up a choking dog, whack it hard on the chest, upside down, even in the wheelbarrow position. I failed my dog. I failed her when she needed me and she trusted me to help her.

Ropes were what one learnt in the novitiate. You trained without experience for the greater glory of God to climb the human coil. There was a rope around your waist and a crucifix at the end of it.

All that chanting and self-immolation. In the same way, they played Aussie Rules football with a live possum in a gunnysack. Cruelty is an initiation to toughness. Men of God. I had no truck with novitiates, though the famous writer Thomas Keneally was a trainee priest across this same valley in a seminary from which he had departed early before abseiling and possum-kicking were installed. Iryna wrote back. *You must not blame yourself. You must let things go in time.* Every time she writes, I am chastened. My shallow bourgeois life is put through the wringer.

Back home in the Adelaide Hills, I spent some time on my weekends sifting through the skips behind the library, collecting books that had been discarded. I did not look for classics or best sellers (or what appeared to be best sellers, judging by their lurid covers), but for writing which seemed to be about isolation. Sometimes, though rarely, I would come across a Ludwig Hohl or an Arno Schmidt or Wolfgang Hilbig – I don't know why it was always German-language writers, particularly those who isolated themselves in provocation and self-pity, who interested me, and whose books were marked for disposal. I presume there was a grimness to their prose, an exacting greyness, frozen in place on sooty walls which did not appeal to sunny Australian readers, nor perhaps to many women. I cannot recall the grey feeling itself now when I read them. I can only imagine the *grisaille* of my youth: the first flush and flutter of grimness, of being besieged, or as the French say of a crumbling stone wall, *lépreuse*. The night-time wistfulness fantasies are more real than the real. The only true way was to isolate yourself, to cultivate your own garden as a leper; away from urbanisation, modernisation and the minority manipulation of nationalism. The carriage of spring, joy for jumping, was nothing compared to the excitement of the pessimist who had no home and was always eternally unhoused – but was periodically, nomadically, loved and received. That was true freedom. Living in romantic hope that a lover would take me in. Checking the backs of envelopes to look for names of love, sometimes two or three times a day, or placing them on the desk simultaneously, that strange emotion rising and falling, now almost alien, gave me great solace in futures and failures. Sealed with a kiss. Girls used to print that on the backs of envelopes: *SWAK*. It must have been rare, like monitoring the heartbeat of an exotic bird flushed out of the wilderness; I do not even know its colour or its song. Once upon a time, I must have been joyful for half a day, knowing there was no next time, surprised there was, walking on air because of the afternoon post. Sprouting, budding, those springs and groves now hurt me, unrecognising age, passing as a stranger passes in a busy street kicking at falling leaves. There is no returning this way. Write something each day: this preachment is the death of writing itself. I'm obsessed with death or the dying process, how to process your way to death with all its weariness, and tiredness of living because you have seen it all. Nothing more to say, so why say it? It's a better option than a mobile phone chat.

He had always loved the cold. For years, cold was something he could control, light a fire, put on warm clothing, make love, drink a bottle of whiskey, catch the beauty of a woman in a beret when she turns her head slightly in the wind. Hold hands. Warm toddies. Then it all changed. He could see himself aging. His core temperature dropped. An inside cold, much greater than outside cold because it was frozen anxiety that enveloped him; a time-capsule sickness; childhood memories of his heart beating in his throat and lungs; his mother's refusal to light a fire, switch on the radiator because all that took money and there was no money in times of war, she said. For her, the war had never been over. There were no moments outside catastrophe. During those childhood years, melancholia was seeping in like oil under the door. Something spilt over inside. But now you do the habitual cleaning up. You stop the indulgence of the banal and wring out the failure of the quotidian, of these inverted decades that were once tortuous, now melted down to unguents of sighs over old wounds. Velleities, but no actions.

A somersaulting palindrome of dates asks the revolving questions to come. Why were you familiar and suddenly not familiar with me? How could you know me like my double and then withdraw into silence as if embarrassed by my closeness?

The past is the past. What if ex-wives died? You would mourn them of course, but what exactly in the distance of years would make you sob?

For over half a century I was stalled. Back and forth. Can there be a new start? Crank up the life engine? Perhaps I should retire from communication. But then I have been retiring from that since I was born. Items: order a book; buy a shaving mirror and rice. Luxuries for passing the Beatles' landmark *When I'm sixty-four*! Only sixty-four! 'Confounded fool!' Montaigne used to say to his morning mirror. I guess death is a little like this: blurry vision, voice rattles and rampant nose hairs, a sense of panic and claustrophobia at the world drawing in its horizons; back to the numbness of the cradle. My strength ebbs and flows and there is a longing to leave, so as not to breathe. In the sun the world is slightly different; but then the chainsaws fill the air and one feels like dying all over again. Bushfires are a constant threat. Reading doesn't help; to know death like a writer is hardly the case of really knowing extinction. To know death like a writer is knowing the lonely banality of heartbeats, the shuffle to make tea; not having the capability for social involvement. To know death like a writer is falling asleep in an armchair. At sixty-four Patrick Leigh Fermor swam the Hellespont – 'because Byron did it' – and at sixty-four, the watershed for me, hardly walking or seeing, the sky strange and calling for twilight, when the sun has moved too slowly like a migraine, I filled my life with damage in the hope for more verdant fields. What does it all mean? Perhaps confusion. At the differentiation between disorientation and the purpose of memory, which is the letter writer's cabinet of wonders, one hardens oneself once more, even when the soul is porous with failure and sends a deliberate chill to sadness: move aside, make way for hypothermia! One more cry. A new partner. A love interest. Perhaps it will be Iryna.

When he was three or four...it's the age when memory is first retrieved... his half-sister was dating an American sailor. One day, the sailor, who was also a good dancer, took his sister and him to visit a friend in Kowloon Hospital. He can't remember much now, but there were men in bandages and some were struggling to walk along a short passage bordered with parallel bars. They scared him, these men swathed in white bandages, peeking out at him from the deep recesses of their facial wounds. There was also a young child with bandaged stick arms, who lay unmoving, attended by a nurse. There was a war going on in Korea. His sister's boyfriend gave him a 'Dixie Cup', a sailor's white cap that was too big for him. He also received two campaign bars, with blue stripes and a small black metal star. At three or four years of age, this was all quite exciting as well as traumatic. They then went to the sailor's destroyer and he was carried aboard on a steel ladder off a launch. He was taught how to raise and lower a six-inch gun by turning a wheel. You didn't need a lot of strength for the muzzle to rise and fall. In the end, he burst into tears, terrified at the rapidity of the large barrel descending on top of him. This was how war first came into his life.

Then there was the shelling of Quemoy in the Taiwan Straits. The British army in Hong Kong trotting out columns of tanks as a show of strength. Then the riots of '56 when his father loaded his revolver and put on his police volunteer's steel helmet and his mother strung up paper Taiwanese flags on the balcony to deter would-be looters of the flats of Communist sympathisers. And then Australia...and Vietnam.

He knew something of what Iryna may have been feeling, but he also knew how survival in a real war meant so many other feelings were on hold or were quashed altogether. For a long time, he didn't dare write to her for fear of speaking banalities, of false beliefs, of succouring hope for the wrong reasons. In his silence, she wrote: *If you are any kind of a writer or historian, and I don't know if you are, then your greatest enemy is forgetfulness. For us Ukrainians, we will never forget, but for the West, an easy solution to end conflict is a diplomatic one. Unfortunately, I cannot see this anaesthesia as working simply to put the suffering patient to sleep, only to wake up another generation bewildered by fear and loathing. My husband is in the military now and we are not in touch for obvious reasons of intelligence leaks, spies, saboteurs, loose lips and sinking funds disappearing into nothing. My daughter and I are instead listening to a free cello concert under the arches of the Art Nouveau Lviv-Holovnyi railway station, and there is a young couple in front of us walking to and fro like zombies, as though the music were a temporary balm for grief, but their constant movement does not show evidence of solace, rather of catatonia. My very kind regards, Iryna Zarębina.*

Oh, how the world was so full of sorrow! Quin was now thinking not of sorrow but of those women that he had known who gave off the scent of sorrow, great pheromaniac that he was, more astute than a dog, working his way around their tragedies, being the grand uncle, offering nepotisms to his female students, noting that lesbians took him up seriously, he didn't know why, perhaps because they weren't worried about abuse, knowing expertly how to overpower him, in a prone position, two of them giving massage and solace and finally, rewarded by their publication as a poetic duo of sapphic requital. Oh, sorrow! His sapphics knew all about the carpentry of sorrow and in many ways, he gave advice, offered readings, and was their Chinese confessor. But they didn't know or were not interested in the professor's patrilineal devotion to teaching and yes, praying. Good heavens! Professor Quin had a Jewish father! Who might have witnessed the burning bush consumed to ashes in the crackling voice of Mao, whom so many feared and revered in the sixties. Quin's father saw the end from his office chair in Shanghai; his lace company confiscated; the factory windows smashed; he was leaving for Mexico to start a small publishing business for God's sake, from lace to publishing. Not for his wife's sake. She would come later, or always second or third. No, little Chin Chin and his mother would be sent for when he made it to the other side of the world. But in the meantime, Quin's mother got a job as secretary of Chinese Women's Affairs and dallied with a Communist cadre and burned all the paper Taiwanese flags in her small brick kitchen stove. She made enough money to send him to a convent school run by American nuns: the Maryknoll Sisters of St Dominic from Westchester County, New York. Chin Quin was the darling of the Fourth Grade. He won prizes, came first in the year, and gave speeches that had his classmates rolling in the aisles by mixing bawdy Cantonese puns with sober English. It was a great cocktail. And he was always going to be in the company of women.

Now Ukraine had a Jewish president. He wanted to know what Iryna thought about this. *Putin*, he wrote, *has succeeded in uniting Ukraine against Russia. He has done it by ignoring its history: the Holodomor*

famine; the Bandera-Nazi collaboration; the fact that Russia wants
to be European. He has given Crimea back to the Tartars. But he is
overlooking the most important thing: the one thing Hitler was afraid
of was the laughter of the Jews. Without humour himself, they always
had it over him.

Even though he was hoping for a reply, he didn't get one. His self-
styled role as an epistolarian may have been over. So he read *Le Livre*
du Voir-Dit, written in the fourteenth century, which means 'the book
in which truth is spoken'. So even then, they would spruik a tale as
a 'true story'. Why did Quin want to read this medieval book armed
with his dictionary of ancient French? Because it was the story of a
noble girl who sent a poem to an old poet and by doing so began a
love correspondence. This went on for a while and grew deeper and
deeper. Nowadays he would have requested a selfie. But her poem was
her profile and the old poet began writing an epic in which he inserted
her letters and his poems, and if there was wrongdoing, 'they would
conceal it from God'. Quin loved this licentiousness. Love was the
truth after all, even if it involved the self-deceit of an old man or the
deceit of a young girl hungering for fame. (We should remember Quin
abandoned studying law and would have succeeded as a criminal
defence barrister had he pursued self-deceit.) In 1362 Guillaume de
Machaut was sixty and the noble, beautiful girl Peronnelle was sixteen.
Professor Quin dwelt for a long time on this literary grooming. If only
he would write the book of truth made from real correspondences! He
made another donation to the animal advocates.

But Iryna had a daughter. If her daughter were eight, what age would
that make the mother? Thirty? Forty? Then the gap between Quin
and Iryna would not be that far apart. Respectable, even, since he
had always looked young for his age. He could name his book *Forty-*

Seventy. For some days he took his *passeggiata* in the botanical gardens with a smile on his face. The other walkers wondered what had happened but were too afraid to ask.

Iryna's emails became more cryptic, written almost in code, with long dashes. She may have sent them from her mobile phone. There were no formalities: *Today more confiscations – for the good of the country – we've run out of everything except grief – which is in never-ending supply.*

He thought he might give her some breathing room. It couldn't have been comfortable being an internal refugee, moving from place to place with a daughter and a husband fighting on the eastern front. Quin settled in to read all of Vasily Grossman's books. Grossman deserved diligent readers. He was a chemist after all and was careful with writing and observations as with formulae and pills. He reminded Quin of his father in this respect, a diligent father who travelled a great deal doing his imports and exports of all kinds of commodities. He sent his son many stamps, torn from envelopes teaching him to steam them from the envelopes. Then he sent six-year-old Quin a blank stamp album with blotting paper, stamp hinges in a small tin, first edition envelopes and a starter kit of stamps from all over the world. Quin began and then stopped; started and then grew bored; wrote his name painstakingly on the cover followed by block letters: *PHI-LATELY*. Stopping and starting like Morse code, he stuttered his way, filling the album and then the next and the next. His father, he now realised, was an epistolarian *par excellence*. He must have written to countless foreign women, who sent him first-edition envelopes sealed with a kiss – *¡SWAK!* – philogyny, like philately, paid dividends. But Quin had put them all aside in his library and forgot about his dead father, the stamps and all the worlds of love and charm they brought him until the fire. After the fire, which burned most of the books in his library, he found that the stamp albums were only singed on the spines and that the stamps were all intact inside. 'When books are packed tightly together,' the guide at the Hôtel de Soubise which houses the national archives in Paris said, 'they tend to survive fires.' She pointed out the singed spines, the finger and thumb indentations at the top and bottom of centuries-old books as countless scholars pulled them off the shelves. Yes, books are a burden for the old. No one wants them now; much easier to carry a laptop or an iPad with whole libraries in them. He had hurt his lower back many times lifting the stacks. Archiving the books by subject. Stopping and starting a new collection. Then he came back to his boyhood stamp albums. He looked up some of the old Chinese stamps online. The Communist revolution-era stamps were worth quite a lot of money. Presumably, nobody wrote much during that time for fear of imprisonment. The first Ukrainian *zemstvo* stamps (issued by Russia in 1918) were also quite valuable, and he had at least two albums of those. Perhaps he should send them to be valued by a reputable philatelist society. And then, surprising himself, a series of King George VI worth $16,000 each. But his were not in mint condition.

Friday at 4:15 p.m., Molly my dog died after choking on a piece of chicken breast. It was an agonising death but it took only thirty seconds or so. She will never again be trumpeting her way to my studio or heralding me home in the afternoon. She will never again be sleeping on my deck or under the house. She will never again be hunting rabbits in the bushes or snoring on the rug before the fire. Such a good dog. Such a dog crazed by food. And food killed her in the end. I do not know where to turn. I cannot have closed doors for fear of choking. It was a lonely death and the second dog I'd had to wheel out to the car in a wheelbarrow wrapped in a blanket. My favourite cotton blue blanket was bought many years ago during my lonely stint at a new job in a new city in Adelaide. I have not eaten for two days. My heart is beating strangely in my throat. I know this is nothing compared to what is occurring in Ukraine. But it is grief all the same. And it is a loneliness one does not ever want. It is not the same as solitude. I now have to hose down the wheelbarrow and collect her food bowl and leash and put everything in the garbage bin. She lives in memory alone. And I don't want to read anymore. At least, not for a long time.

Then again, grief might be a kind of wallowing.

He didn't know how to perform the Heimlich manoeuvre. He had no idea of what to do. He was in a panic. But it only took about twenty seconds for her to die. And that was because of his inability to act fast in any capacity.

Acting fast is beyond an old man, and now he realises he is uselessly meditative, unable to think fast, unable to do anything without thinking slowly through it. He was an old man. He needed to acknowledge this. It was an existential threat and a warning. He was split into time scales. Like Mr Wu the piano-tuner. Back and forth, trying to find the right octave vibrations dictated by a tuning fork.

Anyway, he was always *unheimlich*. Never at home. Unhoused. Not knowing the *secret*. Back and forth. He sent another donation to Animal Advocacy. But he didn't know if they received it or if it was all funnelled to the war effort. It didn't matter. He had failed his animal. He was therefore going to try and rescue others.

But he didn't send anything by email or text or Twitter. He didn't know why he would want to be networked or publicised. He wanted a single recipient. Someone who would understand what he was feeling or doing. That was it. But there was no one. He learned this when he was ten years old. There was no one out there. When he was sent away to boarding school in Australia. There was no one there. And the fact was, why would they even care? When his parents didn't care. Or at least his father's strategy was to get his son educated and successful. Not his mother's, who only knew grief. The strategy was how you won battles and wars. In boarding school, it was the Lords of the Flies. There were racists. There were kind boys. Some boys delighted in killing animals. Now in his old age, he grew soft. He only knew cigars and fires and the burning of books. Those were not strategies. He drank too much and he didn't eat enough. When grief turns from mourning to melancholia, that is the measure of wallowing. Beethoven's piano sonatas ranged between *dur* and *mol*, the hard and soft; major and minor; sharp and flat. You had to fluctuate between moods; the frenzied and the calm; war and peace; struggle and grief. I poured Molly's ashes into the botanical lake at dusk when the *passeggiata* was over and no one was around, not even the ducks. Then I set a flotilla of kirigami flowers over her to bloom in her wake and I heard her trumpeting in the dark wind and bade her a last farewell, she who died doing what she loved best even though such excruciating agony gripped her in the last minute. But now it was a cleansing and salving moment to hear the soft churring of a solitary nightjar accompanying that dear dead dog.

Then Iryna wrote to him out of the blue. He must have sent a few lines about the death of his dog. *Is there anything I can do to help? I know how much you love your dogs. But please do not punish yourself by not eating. Nothing will bring it back. It is winter and the weather is so cold (it must be even colder in the Hills) you should keep your body strong to avoid numerous viruses which are around. Is there anything I can help you with to alleviate your grief?*

I think grief for death is the hardest. But, unfortunately, every life cycle should complete itself. So, try to look at it from this perspective. Please let me know if I can do anything for you.

He was chastened by this message. Her husband was fighting in the Donbas. Her daughter was sheltering with her in Lviv. He was just a grieving bastard because his dog was dead. And she was assisting him! In any war, he belonged to the side of the animals. It is pathos, but it is the pathos of a satirist, who sees through suffering as if the silver backing of the mirror was missing. So he carries a hole in his heart through which he can peer and by doing one tiny hard thing a day, just one, not multi-tasking hardness or difficulty, he can hear the stupidity of the gun shot while he is listening for a single bird call more beautiful than any soprano in an opera. Others do not have this luxury.

Pessimism is the only quality that survives shock. If you hear incoming artillery rounds, a friend conscripted to fight in Vietnam told me, you know it is meant for you, and if you're still conscious after becoming temporarily deaf, pessimism stands you in good stead. You can worm into it like a good foxhole. There you will find an atavistic silence. You will listen for the bird call and if you find it, you will know it is pain you have escaped, and you are then back in the world of unreality.

This hand; this life; this emotional ubiety. Wittgenstein was right: the world cannot be explained except outside of it when it records a cry of pain. And who is to do that? And what is pain? And how does it sound? We are not what we are unless a million light years from now we are observed by a technology of which we have no knowledge or imagination. Logic and linguistics just will not have any connection. And, as the cliché goes, who will hear you scream in deep space? And what would it mean? A whale song perhaps? With no idea of whales? Intelligence does not mean life as we know it. Emotion is not necessarily true feeling.

But he didn't hear whale songs; instead, the sirens of war; he saw the pink glow of bombed buildings, sandbagged monuments, the struggling ambulances which were not hurrying because of the holes in the road. *In Irpin*, Iryna wrote, *that is a town outside of Kyiv, the Russians shot a young girl and then ran over her body time and again in their tanks. Nobody dared come out to bury her. I found out she was the same age as my daughter, who has stopped talking. I told her that it was okay to stay silent because it makes you harder, and as you harden, you will stop speaking the nonsense of emotions and simply describe, almost uselessly, the way buildings collapse and fall, sometimes silently, in the night. These observations are the price of former loves and beauties. Hatred too is something that will keep you alive.*

I used to run away from grief; as fast as I could, to escape memories. I went to a Greek island – a holiday to restore myself when my wife died. I was covered in dust, counting tourist buses heading up the hills, donkeys standing sideways, honking in valleys silvery with olive trees and steeped in vineyards. I did what the local old men did: across the hilltops they hurled their sighs, early in the morning and at dusk, good for the chest and lungs, standing there in their off-white singlets howling for their dead. But one doesn't escape in the end: you have to deal with ashes and burials and ultimately the silence even though the world is filled with noise: the sea, the wind, the elaborations of existence. Everything pivots upon pain. It is the price of being born. Solitude is a hard but faithful lesson that one learns over and over again. Death is what it is; over and over again. Every time I cough I could see my dog choking to death, wagging her tail the last time, hoping I could save her.

But of course, he failed. He listens for her trumpeting and hooting but there is only a silence willed by other noises. He says to himself that grief is personal and cannot be shared, probably because it is a form of repetition-compulsion, a Freudian description of visitations until time depersonalises it. Shell-shocked soldiers relived their trauma time and again. And so he relived Iryna's sentences and unpacked their trauma.

I look after children in the evenings whose parents have perished. We are all carers and migrants now, living and working in a building in Lviv. There is a kind of plague upon us that is felt but unseen, a miasma slowly filtering through the building as I feed the children, wash them, and put them to bed until such time that a distant relative could come to carry them home on their backs. I keep them safe in the meantime, I, the woman in exile, always looking back in anger, tired of paying for the tragedies of culture and politics, cursing her parents for bringing her into this world, tired of this farce called life but not courageous enough to commit suicide, dragging sadness like a tail, never finding the kind of love she thought would have nurtured her, giving in to loneliness and dejection, who must run and keep on running before they tag us with tracking devices much more effective than the Star of David. I am so sorry to complain, but a strange thing is occurring in my heart. My husband is a commander of his military unit now. He will die for his brothers-in-arms, but not immediately for us and this is his survival method too and not his love. But however brief or elongated, death is perhaps easier for those who die and hardest for those who survive. This is my grief and my anger, both of which play games in my head at night. I had one text message from him a week and a half ago. He did not speak about love. He may be dead now or wounded, but the distance inside me is preventing any immediate grief. I am Jewish and he is Eastern Orthodox. He's an aberration because Poland is Western Christian, thanks to the Czechs. Perhaps we are made of different matter, torn asunder since the Middle Ages between victims and inquisitors... we were both, of course.

He wanted to reply but he didn't. All responses should wait. Sometimes they are too late but too late for what? To be an epistolarian is not to find solace in written words. It is actually to explore himself and to turn thought around to remove what Elias Canetti called 'the kitsch of sensitivity'. So it was not for 'communication' or soul exchanges that these emails flowed back and forth between them, but like the tide they simply pressed the sand tight underfoot and then released it to dry, the powder preventing any more running, when there was no marathon with real news afoot. Until the next time, when the hard-packed sand allowed new sprinting.

He was thinking before bed; before sleep, if he is given sleep, that when an enemy is bayonetted he may defecate in fear and pain. And that is also the smell of death, much stronger than the smell of blood, although the latter is present in a subtler way like the smell of fear, fishier, saltier, rubbery, something he smelt once in an abattoir. Death is never simple or defined.

What age does is make you want to unload all your ambitions, especially of immortality. It makes you want to cast off all the learning, the so-called wisdom, and confidence in your skills and craft. What you do take on into the emptied space is irony; the irony of memory loss, which like a brain fog, clears for a moment so you can look back, but then fogs up again, creating little openings through which the sniper of thought might fire, hitting the sentimentality which once was full of peaceful reminiscences and now becomes a stark pain in the chest. Like the way the glass doors in his new studio library, through which he once gazed at the lake and ducks, watching with interest through the double-glazing at the rabbits his dogs hunted unsuccessfully, are now fogged with sighs and pain.

Witold, my husband, had always been severely depressed. It was something I surmised came from his mother, who amongst many Poles, knew of the camps but chose to ignore them. At times there was the smell. At others, the religion. Religion put up a barrier against empathy. His mother always emitted the smell of guilt. It was indescribable, but it smelt musty, like old clothes kept in a damp dresser, or incense during High Mass. Witold, from what I can gather, is now having the time of his life, liberated from his mother, who is still in Kyiv, unwilling to leave. Perhaps he is fighting for her right to her home. There is nothing like the dance of death, as you so eloquently described in one of your novels, which enables you to survive.

There are more ironies of course, in his own life, which he shall come to in time. Time passes quickly in disguise as old time, reiterations of retinal imprints, scenes, pains. The irony of his dog, obsessed with food and choking to death. The irony of his not eating, told he would be malnourished if he didn't, choking on forced food. The irony of not being at home, each time his neighbours encroach on fences and borders and his own inability to be outraged, which he knows will lead to selling up. The irony of not ever having a home, which like a caravan, he tows and carries with him. The Jewish wanderer; the Mongolian caravanserai; the evader of ownership and merchant of contemporary hand-to-mouth; the tailor and tinker of all commodities and needs. Perhaps nomadism was the core of a hollow man.

When you're young you do not grieve as hard. Is being forty still young? He supposed so. The young stay younger these days, since it's the old who do the grieving for them, for all the others. He thought these things but did not write them to her. How will he even move forward without knowing what she is like, what she perhaps looks like, and thus, as a blind man, without the power to invent, to delude himself, he can only speak the truth as a blinkered being living alone in a farmhouse with two dogs now. Should he get another one from the pound? Should he do his rounds on his bicycle? Visit the forests? Listen for the familiar barking of all the dogs he knows and who know him?

He did not hear from Iryna for more than a month. In a way he was glad to be freed. He didn't have the energy to intensify an epistolary relationship. It demanded deep empathy with empty words; sometimes rich words with an attempted evasion of feeling which confined him to subterfuge.

I was trying to love matter.
I taped a sign over the mirror:
You cannot hate matter and love form.
Louise Glück, 'Archaic Fragment'

Reflective glass is a dangerous thing. People, like birds, fly into it and are concussed.

Old Chinese postmen – let's say in the Qing dynasty (photographed by Nadar or Fauchery) – carried a covered cage on their heads strapped to their chins. This was how they walked their birds on their rounds, killing two chores with one duty. When the cloth was removed, their canaries sang cheerfully, gave warnings of dangers from other birds, went silent at midday in the heat of depression. Ancient postmen ('in the before days' as the caption reads) also sported a long pipe to help them survive the tedium. This soon became a symbol of authority, the mark of a civil servant – it was long and thin like a cane (churchwarden-style in English climes), except that it afforded a touch of opium to add somnolence to serenity.

I deal with trivia and fret over trivia. Speak with the bureaucrats; think with the wise. But the wise are, sadly, missing in action.

I am much dispirited. It is a desperation that much of technology defeats me. I am learning to type again on soft keys that do not clack or rebound. I am without much manual control after a slight stroke. A temporary disruption of the flow of blood to the brain. A Transient Ischemic Attack. That's when the dogs bark and the caravan moves on and I, left behind, ponder my lack of adventure, lack of faith, lack of intimate friendships. One thing I do know well is that age and its related incidents occur very rapidly. Death does not approach from a distance but attacks from round the corner, faithful to suddenness, fateful only in hindsight.

My dog comes in through his trapdoor. He brings in the smells of the outside: dampness, mud, vegetation. He is happy inside, by the fire, but he is much happier outside where there is excitement, danger, warnings, the *qui vive* of life where he can join in barking with the other dogs. I am unusual because I, who am normally outdoors, come inside to the fire for words. Outside, there is no use for words, because they are unnatural within all the other readings; of smells, of movement; of the shape of the hunt.

For a while I was losing my eyesight. I couldn't see myself anymore and wondered why I made such errands for my emotions, driven inwards without a vision of how I am seen or read, as someone not to be engaged with, a little unpredictable and certainly not normal. Normality works between like and like in the same way a labrador recognises another labrador, some ancient memory that calms and consoles. But in what is unlike, there is a brief curiosity and then a quick evasion of an uncanny which could only presage trouble. So the dogs bark...etc. But my sensibility has been blunted by age, by time, by drink. There is nothing anymore at the end of this rainbow. Borgesian blindness has not opened up libraries of hope and fabulous tales. I read Cioran and sometimes curse my birth. Though birth is not an option. I've tried dying many times. But then, you can die into someone else's life. You can read their biographies and autobiographies. By entering them, you forget yourself briefly.

I look in my shaving mirror. *Mon semblable* was like me but he threatened me with his similarity. I was alone, but *he* was unpredictable.

I was imagining what it was like to be Ezra Pound. But I couldn't. Nor could I imagine what it was like to be William Butler Yeats. Neither of them could have imagined being a Chinese-Jewish professor. Orientalism has two sides to it: one is a curiosity limited so much by otherness that it is impossible to *be* Chinese in order to imagine being one; the other is the cultural depths and layers into which one must submerge, which would not have been available without air travel, immersion, extended networks and above all, a fluency in language and dialects. In the same way I can only see myself destined for Ward No. 6, as in Chekov's short story, where an incurable paranoiac who hides in cellars and avoids people in general, an *agoraphobic*, above all, awaits the rumour that a *doctor* is going to call. Just like a neighbour, a spy, an investigator, an executor, will undoubtedly call on me sooner or later.

I recently spent almost a thousand dollars on a plumber who spent less than thirty minutes on a blocked sink. I tried many things but the blockage, like a sore tooth, aggravated me. I could have solved it with some muscle and a plunger in under an hour and saved myself nine hundred dollars spent on electronic cameras and hydro jets. But I did not have the requisite knowledge, which was cheap but unobtainable amongst dissolute professors. You learn not to live in hope and not to live in haste. One dissipates the other. But you have to pay for it in both cases.

I look in my shaving mirror, which is not often these mornings, and I think about the dead. The dead have nothing more to offer the living. The living, soon to be dead, will also have nothing to offer in the future. Nor can their writing, which if they are lucky enough to leave behind, even luckier if it is read, resurrect itself without overlays of contemporary reconstruction, which is in terribly short supply (as everything is cinematic and all too unambiguous), without trying to regather a real time long past, a life lived poorly, a culture abstracted from commonplaces...all of which cannot be archived in the head, in the heart, without recuperating from the dead their singular and peculiar desolation if it is reachable. That is the most accessible legacy left from the journey between the shaving mirror and the smoke of the crematorium. Smoke and mirrors.

It is simply a matter of surviving the days. The days come and go without promise. In the limelight of youth, failure is but a game to be revisited, often romantically. Then in middle age, there may be some success, but there is mostly bitterness. Of course it's the bitterness you remember as you grow into success. But in old age you want to remember nothing. Erasure is more common than remembrance and rightly so, for in rubbing out one also erases the hurts and the embarrassments and the idiocies. At my age, one is the grand seigneur of nothingness. Tabula rasa. One walks around the truth. It is a great comfort to feel most mistakes are past and could no longer be made again unless one has dementia. One learns, unless one is a complete fool. One's mind, nevertheless, is a geography of anxiety, a nervous, sinuous network of mini-crises, of impending doomsdays, a mapping of all the angst it took to reach this point, still living, still struggling. Joy seems naive with the hindsight of how fleeting it used to be. There are now fantasies and brief enthusiasms instead and possible women like Iryna remain longer in the mind than their stay in reality, attempting not to drink in order to banish them in mind, or drinking to drive them away in reality. Soon all these states seesaw, the world going up and down, until one's legs no longer provide the spring for the upside after the downside. But a vast horizon is what I am seeking and probably will enjoy most if achievable, that boat heading without a compass to adventure, or towards the end, in itself supposedly an experience of the greatest magnitude: finally all done. But I know more than anything, that nothing much will have been achieved, that there is a horizon of books which I will not have read, lives untold to me, favours offered and turned down for want of time, and I will be the poorer, not richer, when I am done, cast up on shore if lucky, a happy hour if only from the rigours of the journey.

The above are all wood shavings, chips, leftover sticks. I have built a hut, a gîte, a clochàn, call it what you will. I have bought a small plot of ground beside the cemetery, which no one wants, for a very cheap price, on higher ground behind my house so the bones wouldn't leech onto my land even though I dug out a metre-deep cellar into the earth, which would keep me warm. This monk's hole is where I pay my debts for having a comfortable house, a library and a few acres of trees. The postmaster went guarantor, which was nice of him, but it took the Council three months to decide. I claimed it was uninhabitable, thus avoiding the planning delays. I said I needed a shed for my tools when I worked at maintaining my farming equipment. In return, I would tend the grave plots; throw out dead flowers, replace upturned stone.

I think I'm healing. First day without real sorrow. Did yard work; cut wood; snapped twigs for kindling. Swept steps. Started the tractor-barrow. Washed clothes. Fed remaining dogs. Yes, it's good to do outside work. Now inside with a fire, which isn't really very warm. But good enough. These duties I impose upon myself. I like the discipline, the muscle work. Now the sun comes out for a little while. It lights up the water and the trees. Crafting life is like crafting writing. Body and mind work together.

The ash tree beside my studio drops winter buds, pretty bunches of dark burgundy beads.

The year just goes on and on without any lifting of spirits. It's as though one hurdle and one grief isn't enough to pile up. The gods need a bonfire of catastrophe. I see myself with too much indulgence and not enough gumption to grapple with the difficult things of ordinary life... why grey skies are perpetual, stoicism, the disappearance of childish joys. They all need to be faced.

Indeed, he had a nice spinney of fruit trees which needed to be pruned, netted, harvested, fed. In winter he bottled the fruit: pears, plums, apricots, apples; put them in the steamer, sipped to test the fermented juices. He needed a cellar. They all have cellars in Ukraine, he noted. The Russkis waged war like they did in 1941, flattening everything. You could survive in a good cellar except for a direct hit. But then you had to get out of it for food and water. He thought of a cellar with a thick glass floor, then read that some cellars were cool, but others were warm, and too balmy for wine. It depended, like graves, on the state of the humus. The posthumous were all around, breathing out their sulphuric warnings: accidents, indulgences, obesity, gluttony, and of course, grief. They have washed their hands of it all now and the responsibility has fallen to the living. According to the apostles of Christ, or to the apocrypha of gossip, Pontius Pilate washed his hands a lot, which Shakespeare probably pinched for *Macbeth*. According to Anatole France (with a name like that, how could he not be believed?), the aging Pilate was exiled to Sicily for the violent suppression of a riot, where he lived contentedly as a farmer, suffering from obesity and gout, and was cared for by his daughter in the baths of Baiae regretting the loss of his governorship in great detail but dementedly forgetting who Jesus was. (He was always a conscious pilot of contemporary politics.) The daughter was a solace...did she wipe his feet with her long hair? Did she massage his back until a vague desire emerged of his days with young Nero in the massage-room tingling with anticipation, like Jeffrey Epstein's frequent in-house phone calls sending Ghislaine out for more girls for his three-a-day orgasms? Not really. The old Pilate was supposedly fonder of his dog than of girls. That may have been a good cover for his obituary. The afterlife was always a nest of lies. It was said that he died from drinking poisoned wine sent to him by Emperor Caligula. It was framed as an ultimatum. 'Die like Socrates!' the message read, delivered by a tall Praetorian Guard. Maybe I'm making all this up.

I now suffer regularly from gout. The pain at night is excruciating, so intense that a brush from the finest silk stocking can generate red-hot needles of torture. Yuliya, before I married her, used to send me her silk stockings in the post; worn only once, she wrote. She said it was a reminder that the post was erotic. Now silk only gives me pain, spiritually and physically. Gout and love, I concluded, were both self-inflicted. Was there a lesson in this, or was it simply the result of indulgence, or the domestication of indulgence?

I now suffer the loss of my books and the loss of all the books I've gleaned from the municipal cast-offs. All twenty-four cartons of them, which I cannot fit into my new studio and cellar. Since my bluestone hut is constructed round like a yurt, there is no room for bookshelves. I wish I had Montaigne's large mill house. The stone cast-offs were donated to me by a decommissioned quarry. I went out there on a foggy night with my neighbour in his truck and helped myself. I lined my cellar with sandstone and then used hardwood beams for ribs and cedar slabs for walls. Chocked the whole thing with newspaper and lime-mortar, laid the stone from the centre and worked outwards in a circle using a masonry saw and then finished it off with a round tin roof from a fancy chicken-house someone didn't want. My body grew stronger, then weaker, as I settled down to my daily task of reading. You see, reading weakens the body.

But the loss of my library and the recoveries in my memory which are a combination of damp lines and feint dreams leave me in a black hole during the long nights with no future sun rising, except a black one emitting crematory smoke and reflective voyeurisms preying on widows in black, sometimes granddaughters in colours, as I dream of silk stockings and of holding them up to my nose and lips. Robert Walser could well have asked: *Aren't lost thoughts always the most beautiful?* And of course they are for a collagist, a gatherer and paster of daily extinctions found often in newspapers and the minor arts; whole newspapers which often turn up at one's feet when you've already torn out the literary pages in the café. But lost thoughts are only ruins for me. I live hard and I try to live strong but all I see are ruins and fragments because that is what aging is all about: losing sight not for the sake of the recovery of beauty but for the observation of ruinous revivals; pasty pages windblown and finally anchored in mud, textual collages of moods, excisions, razored precision. Have a look at Elizabeth Hardwick's *Sleepless Nights* and you will see what I mean.

I go slow on most things for fear of tripping up and then the irreversible emendation which is what the hurry of youth taught me... hastening along slowly has been the norm but there is this anxiety in the gut, a prelude to something dire perhaps, which is the inevitable result of productivity in the capital way: the harvest beforehand; the pre-thought profit; the prolongation of the moment; the wastage. I anchor myself in things: wood, iron nails, coloured glass. The beauty of everyday things. In Ukraine, all of these things of matter and memory have been blown to smithereens by the uncouth youth of the advancing Russians.

He used to play golf. He thought it a silly game but its frustrations, i.e. putting a small ball in a small hole, guaranteed discipline, muscle memory, anality and delicacy. The only thing he hated were the other golfers and the club mentality. They were almost all white. One day an Indian player came along. He beat all the odds, coming in at two under par. The club didn't invite him to join. They said a woman, an *associate*, had marked his card, and that wasn't valid. So he disappeared. Quin was the only maverick non-white. They accepted him as an honorary Korean, since Koreans were now on the PGA circuit. Then along came

Jack. Jack had a cockney accent. He said his brother was at Dunkirk and the Jerries stitched him up the back with three machine gun bullets while he was wading out to one of the rescue fishing boats.

Jack was a real gentleman. Jack didn't see the point of eating vegetables because he said his wife Marge only made vegetables and though he was convinced that veges were more healthy, he could not feel any appetite eating them, raw or cooked, and at times read Claude Lévi-Strauss to try to make sense of this whole cooking and eating thing, but thought it better if he drank a lot of wine beforehand and could then say nice things about Marge's cooking, but mostly he snuck down to the mall and had hamburgers and when he felt particularly Jewish, as he was, ordered pastrami and pickles New York-style and came home saying he was not really hungry, but he always helped her cook vegetables, calling her his beloved Margarine and suggested they start a garden of greens because he liked cos lettuce and would eat that and horseradish like a horse, going yum yum, just to please her. Now Quin said to Jack in the golf club, the room was full of people, that he had floaters in his eyes, not pie floaters but all kinds of three-dimensional shapes shifting like holograms and these geometries were populating his sight, not wishing to complain of his numerous and various eye operations, but saying he could live with the imagination of them, that he could understand exactly what Maurits Cornelis Escher was driving at with mathematical inspiration, revolving 3D figures right there in the cornea, which was Escher's middle name, at the same time Jack was saying that with all the veges Marge ate it didn't do her any good since she had had bowel cancer and had died in his arms, as he said, *exploding* there in his arms, and he had her contact lens cases, all pristine, for anyone who wore contacts and needed them. *Gratis.* He gave Quin the plastic containers in a plastic bag. Quin, whose eyesight was so bad he would try anything, thought he might use the soft lenses, test them out, see what Marge may have had imprinted on her retina just before dying. At home, he went straight to his magnified shaving mirror. All they did was to make the world blurrier.

Then one day Jack didn't turn up for their prearranged game. Jack had died of a heart attack in the shower. Quin didn't find this out until much later. He explained it to himself that Jack died of heartbreak. There was such a thing medically: grief caused inflammation. An attempt to fight an attacking pain like grief releases a whole lot of chemicals into the immune system to block the invader masquerading as a virus.

Lives and memories break through into my heart and I suffer from breathlessness. Of course this is just a reaction to panic attacks, but also paradoxically I am smoking cigarettes, which may explain the breathlessness but also calms the sadness and the crises. So there is not a lot of hope for me. No news from Witold on the eastern front. My daughter Marika is terribly disturbed. She is Daddy's girl. In the so-called 'orphanage' (internat – both boarding school and place for dumped or displaced children), where I volunteer, she helps me to track down names and records. It's amazing how war erases writing, burns papers, bombs archives. But there is always human memory left and together Marika and I tie these together in little bundles of felled family trees. You would be pleased to know we have a program with dogs, bringing strays into the orphanage to befriend the children who are suffering so terribly from loss and confusion. Your donations are making this possible, not only for the sake of the dogs, but for the children. You see, dogs are not as tough as people think. They grieve too, for their families to whom they have been so devoted, a hundred per cent of the time. They too have long memories, but now have to make new friendships and relationships. Some of them return to the streets to find their homes, which no longer exist.

Tomorrow is my birthday. I will be forty for god's sake! The only thing I know about all these years is that they have passed in stress, hardship, poverty and disappointment. I cannot really think of any moments I have been happy. That's why I am not interested in my birthdays! They just remind me that I am getting older for nothing!!! I have started a poem called 'From Kharkiv to Kyiv', but so many things get in between and I just can't focus on finishing it, another reason for my depression! Take care. My very kind regards, Iryna.

I thought of writing back quickly with sentimental salmagundis but desisted. There was a war on. An indecorous p(l)atter to be sure, under the circumstances. Besides, starting a poem, *una canzone di guerra* no doubt, was serious business. So I wrote that in a poem you've got to balance eloquence with immediacy, fresh water with chlorine, otherwise you get algae where you don't want it, which looks colourful but is deadly for the poet...forever.

He regretted saying that immediately after sending the email. He was being patronising, a paterfamilias. Forget poetry; he ought to write songs. There is some gold, some influence, to be found amongst the stubbled dross. Like Serge Gainsbourg. Or Leonard Cohen. In Ukraine, the poet, novelist, singer-songwriter Serhiy Zhadan would do a recital in Kharkiv and huge flocks of girls in very short skirts flooded the auditorium. Quin foolishly yearned. Quin foolishly dreamt. He needed adventures and explorations.

The lingerie catalogue is a close companion to my maps and flight manuals.
John Hawkes, *Adventures in the Alaskan Skin Trade*

But his late style had turned into cold collations of Eros and Thanatos.

He didn't really want to start a literary discussion or worse, an argument. Creative people are always over-sensitive and it was better to stay out of the arena if you weren't a gladiator, or worse, if you were an armchair philosopher. He'd had enough of these roles and in the end he was playing them for himself, not for others. Not for nothing therefore, he played them on the page, but his wives had more reality: the first understood artistic competition: they were both young then. He traded their house for an airfare. The second was advancing wave upon wave of feminism and was surfing hard to keep ahead of the swell. She would say to him: I'm off to Paris for the Third Feminist Conference. I will be some time. It was during her absence that he wrote his long epic poem *The Lingerie Catalogue*. He went dancing with a colleague whom he admired but respected. She would undoubtedly be documenting him. He was a good dancer. She wore tasty skirts. It was enjoyable and she reminded him of Ginnie, awkward and shy and fiercely intelligent. 'If you think too much about it, then you won't dance well,' she told him, perhaps as a reprimand for his instruction. The third, Miranda, fought the world, men, climate deniers, the upper class, private schools, abusive neighbours. She was physically too frail to do battle, but she was an artist in her own right, with several cartoons commissioned by *The New Yorker*. As a Canadian, she won the Guggenheim Fellowship in her year of living dangerously but did not live to take it up. They both had time to prepare for a long hospitalisation, but it was quicker than he thought. For his part, he was getting too old to keep up, either with ambition or grief. If he worked outside, on the farm, he was okay, fit and briefly enjoying life. But as soon as he went to his gîte, he was confronted with reflection, which opened holes inside himself, and all the memories and sadness came rushing in like termites. An old man should not spend time reflecting. Forget the shaving mirror. Stop shaving, stop washing, stop dressing up for a party. He should cut wood, build like any ant, commune with frogs and insects. Live in the present but don't be a hostage to future or past. Survival is not a magic key. Soldiers, particularly, know that. Darwin, actually, was crap. Quin disliked Darwin's prose, the brutality of the one-track-minded theory. Darwin was never a soldier or a sailor. The four years on the *Beagle* left him with heart palpitations, stomach problems and headaches. Quin noted that there were countless parallel universes, unfathomable light years in other spirit worlds, centres of intrigue forever unknown to one person's lifetime, which can all be found in the consciousnesses of small animals, driven by smells and chases, always joyous of the present.

There was also a kind of surrogate love. He was sorry he sent that quick email to Iryna. He regretted the loss of the penny postage, the pillbox mail, the afternoon postman on his bicycle. These were his deferral icons. Systems; and quite possibly, a kind of wisdom. On the flush button of his toilet he superglued an English penny. It reminded all that waste was taxed. So was mail. So was whatever was sent or discarded. The State was watching.

Speaking of which, during the Vietnam war era, he collected assault rifles. It was a hobby, nothing else. His favourite was the AK-47. It was, and is, a superb short-range rifle. It was light for someone as slight as he was, it worked extremely well, it seldom clogged up. He could disassemble it and assemble it blindfolded. The army's reasoning was that if you were caught up in a firefight and had no ammunition left, your American M-16 was useless. Your enemy was less than fifty yards away. So if you captured an enemy weapon, it would most likely be an AK-47. If it's in mud, then make sure the rifle is clear, press the button on the left with the recoil spring pin button and your dust cover; don't lose the bolt, which is the smallest part. Stick that in a top pocket. To reassemble, put the bolt back in and spin it until it lines up, put in the bolt carrier piston first, after cleaning the gas tube with a bottle brush, push down, reinsert the recoil spring, push forward and down, replace the dust cover, push the button. Pull the trigger. All good to go. He could do it in less than thirty seconds...both disassembly and reassembly. Blindfolded. It was like playing a good game of golf in your dreams. You just knew the ball was in the hole. I slept with my weapon and knew it would help me in any psychoanalysis because I could assemble myself and disassemble myself more than could any specialist in the field.

During 2017, in the second amnesty for firearm owners, he sold most of his weapons. It was as though he had lost an arm or a leg. Nobody understood. They applauded him but they didn't know why he was in mourning. His supreme skill was superfluous.

He had skills which he could have taken to Ukraine. He could train ordinary citizens. He could familiarise them with what the Russians were using; the latest models; the best personal defensive small arms. Ukraine was the next level up. He could probably get to Poland on a tourist visa. He could run a school there. The Chinese professor was neither redundant nor useless. It was the only 'just war' he knew.

But his knowledge and his muscle memory were both useless against tanks. Though if Iryna and her daughter were about to be raped, an AK would be useful for them. Just to know justice upon death.

That afternoon he reflected on his fatuousness. He put on his fluoro yellow rain jacket, his blue tights, his green helmet and he rode for Ukraine. Some cars blew their horns in support. He felt good, he felt sad, he felt he had done nothing except saying something. It was all confused.

Then the initial euphoria started to fall short. Wars were always long, tedious, numbing, their military strategies like tides ebbing and flowing. In chess, he learnt that defence was always better than attack. Wait for the moment. Of weariness, of boredom, of the loss of passion. Patience was a virtue which the Chinese knew in their bones. Time was nothing if you could destroy passion by waiting it out. Then counter it. Castle to castle.

He wrote to Iryna. *The only way to write is not to be too clever; just be drunk.* Cleverness was like a cleaver. It slaughtered the beautiful animals of creation...and self-destruction was its aim.

He was consciously and unconsciously being gauche, in order to put an end to developing intimacies. Nothing good came out of correspondence without presence, especially not continuity, just as nothing good ever came out of war, without prescience. But now that he's admitted his proclivities – stout and whiskey – he ought not to confess further. He needed to get through the day without a full load. There is no need to doubt that he began at about ten in the morning and finished about ten at night, getting through a mountain of Guinness and half a bottle of Jameson's and it is when he was slightly drunk that he did his best work, because he was fired up by fragments and fragments, according to Hermann Broch and others, brought new insights into form and ditched wholeness, which died with the traditional novel, suitable only *as summer entertainment for a bourgeois woman*...yes, such intermittent consciousness was as solid as matter, as real as ruins, as cold as a gravestone. Drinking will hasten my end but it foreshortens my pension, so the two may coincide at a happy moment when one is not in debt to the other. Women will thank me for dying; men will perhaps drink to me. Dogs will howl. Falstaff will piss. It is what it is; damned lucky to be thought over as scraps of rapidly fading memory.

Today I bought a good axe. A Fiskars, from Finland. It cuts so cleanly, so satisfyingly, that when you know how to place the log, you strike without doubt. That's what you need: total belief. Like you know when to put the golf ball in the hole. You just know. Nine times out of ten. But eight times out of ten you don't believe. But I dare not say this to Iryna. I still suspect she is a scammer, though it is easy to say I'm softening with age. Which is not a recommendation for trust. I need belief. I'm too old to be effective; knowledgeable enough, but not to be a bystander.

Tricks of light. I do believe I have some worthy stamps in those albums bequeathed to me by my father, but I have no idea of To Whom It May Concern in the sending off of them. Surely they, the experts, will steal some if I have not photographed each page tediously, better to do nothing, which is the Pilatus *modus operandi*, wash hands, drink wine, play with the dogs, not necessarily in that order. But there is a Helmut Schellenberger in town whom I approached by letter, wondering if he would object to my standing beside him as he scoured the albums. His reply took some time, no doubt on account of his wheezing through multiple requests from desperate divorced housewives and widows wanting to make good in a revenge play. Schellenberger gave me an address and a brief consent and a two-hour timeslot. So I prepared my briefcase for the time and place and revved up the Rover Defender and cleaned the doghair off the seats and wiped the dogsnot from the windows.

He resolved not to Guinness himself up that morning so as to be soberly smart and philatelically sharp-eyed. As it turned out, Schellenberger's place was at the extreme point of the compass from his own place in the hills, through a lot of winding roads and past many vineyards and orchards. Since Adelaide is virtually surrounded by hills except for an opening here and there into the city or to the sea, Quin needed his iPhone and GPS and took many hours trying to get the thing working, and when he realised it depended on actually moving, stuttered his way through the snaky roads. He was running late. He finally found the Schellenberger Schloss in a dark valley overhung by fir trees and drove into a large car park, like one of those reserved for sightseers and marked off for buses and tour-guides. There were no other vehicles. He rang the bell. No answer. He rang again and suddenly the door opened and a somewhat angry small man in a black beanie asked Quin in and told him to wait in the library, whose magnificence astounded the professor, but whose shelves were stocked almost entirely of paperback crime novels by G.K. Chesterton, Agatha Christie, Georges Simenon, etc. There was no fire or heating of any sort. From a corner of the room came the crackling of a radio, tuned to what Quin finally deciphered as codes, issued by an American electronic voice. It spoke only in numbers. Perhaps it was from an American naval vessel or aircraft. Quin sat there for some time. Then the man in the black beanie and large moustache reappeared and introduced himself as Herr Schellenberger. 'I'm glad,' he said, 'you were able to make it.' Quin apologised, saying the roads confused him, but Schellenberger waved his explanations away. 'Come. This way.'

They entered a large study surrounded by electronic equipment. There was a huge oak desk upon which sat a gigantic computer screen, several keyboards and a kind of kneeling chair upon which Schellenberger perched. 'It's for my back.' For a fleeting instant Quin thought he would also have to kneel, but where? Schellenberger pointed to the only other seat quite away from the desk, which looked like a dentist's or barber's chair. Quin sat softly down after handing over his briefcase. His legs were dangling up off the floor. The same sound of code crackling was playing like a mantra in the room, only turned down. *Seven, sixty-eight, forty-two.* Schellenberger wheezed and flipped through the albums with an eyepiece the size of a riflescope strapped to his head. He didn't seem interested in anything and tossed most of the albums aside quite quickly. Then he focused on the King George VI stamps, turned on an overhead light, turned the album upside down. He put a bookmark into that page and then got quite excited about an Australian stamp depicting a bearded, Indigenous warrior.

'This is misprinted.'

'I haven't tampered with it,' Quin said, offended.

'No. See here. It says *Aborigine* and under that, *Postage*, but the two shillings and sixpence price is only on the left side. There should be two 2/6, one on either side.'

'Oh. So it's worthless?'

Schellenberger didn't reply. He brought out a small camera from his desk drawer. Took several snaps. Then he retrieved the bookmark and photographed the King George series. He seemed to be wincing – Quin wasn't sure – with either pleasure or pain, or maybe envy and irony.

'Well, very interesting,' Schellenberger said, putting all the albums back into the leather briefcase, much more gently than when he pulled them out. 'I'll let you know by email whether you have treasures or trinkets.'

Quin went out through the mystery and thriller library. *Seven, Fifty, Eighty-eight.* Maybe it was a bingo game. But something strange was stealing into him, seeping from the criminology lab. He took the winding roads back home.

Dear Iryna, My mind is a swamp and to stay focused I tell myself that I have to talk to myself. So that there is another character, one amongst many. This way, even though I am entirely alone, I know that I am only one among many. That makes me happy for a time. Then when you send me your emails I realise how lucky I am that I'm not in a war. This is my bourgeois indulgence of fearing death for the sake of it, the soft edge of the ice cliff. I try to understand what you and Marika are going through. I feel helpless, though I'm enthused with the idea of flying to Europe, to Poland and Krakow, and thus perhaps we could meet if I buy your rail fares and hotel room? Is that possible? Would you like to bring your daughter as well?

He begins each day in his working hut with a moment of sadness. He takes off his glasses and watches the blurry form of his dog's grave. Somehow he might see movement: a rabbit, a bird, a spirit. He does not have to travel very far to tend the human graves behind his hut. Just across a dirt road and there they all are; not at all spirited; no movement. You erase the most important things in order to invent, because that is the way forward and the most felicitous because invention is bred from illusion and imagination, not facts. Ideas are far more life-giving; just to work through them is working ahead of feeling, which always drags and lags. For instance, in winter, when the windows of his hut are frescoed with moisture, when the light is milky in the mornings and the dark hastens earlier in the afternoon, he experiences what he calls his 'condition'. The Condition is about being connected to things... ordinary objects which are taken out of cupboards and then returned with the door closing onto them, which relegates their lonely existence to prolonged darkness. This alternating current between empathy and instrumentality becomes quite intense until the point at which he has to leave cupboards, fridges, windows, doors, drawers, all open for everything to be flooded with light and attention, otherwise they move him to the past, to the way things once belonged to living beings, who are now gone save that things remain, bearing signs of humanity: a chipped plate; a knitted sweater now full of holes; moving him past the past and to eternal breathlessness, a wound through which he breathes; misprinted stamps. *Colonialism still repays itself with its own mistakes*, he was thinking.

He is relieved by reading an author like John Keene, who wrote that 'loneliness is solitude unfulfilled by its own presence.' This lapidary statement urging solitude without anxiety stands opposed to the loneliness of depression, an absence-anxiety which is always needing to be filled by an other, more imaginary self. One can read this solitude wrought out of an idea in which a self *needs* an Other, which is what writing provides; an altogether weird empathy which is not transcendence or appropriation, but an openness to reception and invention...a *partnering* self.

On a more practical basis, he inquired into travelling to Krakow. The requirements were ambiguous. He could detect second-language shifting between officialese and tourism: they were trying not to sound like the Russians; make it more Western:

Poland schengen visa usually has short stay with a period of 90 days and visa expires in 90 days. Applicant is required to be present when applying for visa with total of 12 documents.

Ukrainian refugees continue to arrive in Polish cities. However, this is unlikely to affect travel and tourists are still very much welcome in Kraków! Aid is urgently required.

Auschwitz-Birkenau has fully reopened.

On the other hand, Australian consular advice was very specific. It inspired fear and angst in Quin. Should he even consider making the trip?

Do not cross into Ukraine from Poland. Follow the instructions of the local authorities at all times.

    A state of emergency has been declared in areas close to the Belarusian border. There are restrictions on movement and assembly in these areas. Carry ID with you if you're in these areas.

    Muggings, carjackings and theft from vehicles occur in large cities. Petty crime, such as pickpocketing, is common. Thieves often work in small groups. Take care in tourist areas and near hotels, markets, ATMs, currency exchange bureaus and public transport.

    Be careful of drink spiking. Avoid public displays of affection. If you think you are a victim, report it to local police and contact your bank.

Quin remembered a sign he once saw in a Shanghai hotel: *Prostitutes are not encouraged. No upping of strangers without accompany of house guest. If you think you are a prostitute please report to front desk.* At the same hotel a well-meaning attendant asked him if he wanted a wifey with no extra charge. Of course. Wi-fi. He would need wi-fi. He roamed the streets of the former French Concession and tried to map the past, the buildings, none of which were there any longer, but the cold, damp, cokey air was there, the screeching cyclists, the elbowing crowd. There was a row of small, cramped terrace houses that may have dated from before the Second World War.

Undoubtedly the worst hell of toilets would have been at Auschwitz. Not the visitors' toilets but the one used for former inmates during the Holocaust. Quin did not want to visit Auschwitz as he was fearful for his mental state afterwards. His insomnia and his nightmares would have driven him to suicide.

None of these scenes came back on their own. Quin was synaesthetic, blessed not with a photographic memory but cursed with a documentary admixture of sounds, smells, sights and tastes. If only he could spin unending skeins of these like Proust! But as a fragmentist and a brief, if not brusque, epistolarian, he only had momentary social connections between smells and colours, colours and sound, sound and music, music and numbers, numbers (particularly whilst counting) and every ingredient in the Chinese food he was tasting. The past brought him to old worlds, again and again, a huge weight in his chest. What seemed to be missing was the haptic: the touch of women's hands, the brush of their hair on his lips, the bra or no-bra barrier in their hugs. Those late afternoon lunches with his students, the waiters scowling at them as though his students were prostitutes, his embarrassment in seeing himself in the glass of the restaurants looking like his own father, those afternoons were now showing him how he had aged. But the haptic also disappeared, not with age, but with the correctional facility of the behaviour of grammar, university threats, malicious staff gossip and Covid. No touching; no intimacy, no wit or inspiration. Yes, the prison-house had now extended its revisionary theories to language, and the voice had been incarcerated. Fredric Jameson's critique of the 'absolute presuppositions' of Russian Formalism may well be applied today. There is no more voice; only how linguistics is played out under the rules that permit neither distance, irony nor redemption. Indeed, an ethical gesture towards suffering, something Adorno so prized, used to be the reward for wayward, though sensitive voices, even if poetically rendered, even after Auschwitz. Now the commissars know that readers do not know these things, since the human factor has been under attrition, or the human may be offensive to the ideal of sound-bite conclusions and rushes to theoretical judgement. The voice has been disembowelled, disembodied, deconstructed from the outside. Slick selling is so much a part of literature, thought

Quin. In daily life, because he was no salesman, he gave things away: lawnmowers and chainsaws (which he couldn't start) to an erstwhile gardener, books to countless students, an old motorcycle (because its velocity was unmanageable) to his mechanic. Besides, selling was an embarrassment. You had to believe in lying.

He did not lie about the smells of each dog he brought up and looked after. Swampy odours, taffy nuzzles in winter, wet fur sizzling before the fire. He no longer devoted himself to the human. Perhaps this was the source of his sorrow? Was he disembodied himself?

Iryna was saying in her last email – it was a new message, so the thread was broken in their correspondence – Iryna was saying that her friend Mariia, who is a veterinarian, stayed behind in Bucha when the Russians invaded her town outside of Kyiv. She stayed behind while sending her daughters away to Europe, because the sick animals in her surgery needed her care. Bucha was the site of many Russian atrocities. They shot people at random, pointed a rifle at her as she emptied her backpack of dog food and then on the next day, shot the young woman who was walking to get water at that very spot. The young woman was Mariia's friend and assistant. Mariia wanted to know why she herself wasn't shot. Perhaps the young conscript was reminded of his mother? She cannot answer her own question. When thirty days had passed under Russian occupation, townspeople began to get sick. There was little drinking water, no doctors and no medicines. So Mariia the vet began treating them with veterinary drugs. She said she had no right to die amidst all this carnage. She used saline drips for the very ill and dehydrated, animal antibiotics for those suffering from pneumonia. The Russians let out all the sick animals in the clinic when they departed. It was an ironic act of great indifferent cruelty, a liberation of dying and abandoned pets and other wildlife. Dogs and cats roamed the rubble-strewn streets, some on three legs, some dragging themselves on two front paws. Injured birds fell from their perches. A fox lay panting a few paces from her cage, her brush waving, as though she still expected help from humans.

Quin had no right to speak of himself. He once knew how to speak, but now his past seems to be composed only of vanity. The only response to the atrocities of war is silence, he said to himself. He was impressed that Mariia's story appeared in an ABC report a month later. More impressively, Iryna was entrusting to him her friends, her family, her fears.

PS: Mariia is finally leaving Bucha, at least for the short term. She is going to Australia, where her daughters have been living in Sydney with relatives. My very kind regards, Iryna.

He imagined Iryna with a crown braid or halo braid in the Ukrainian style. Blonde, perhaps. In *The Book of Truth-Telling*, Guillaume de Machaut recounts how in 1362, Peronnelle d'Armentières, of a noble family in Champagne, asked the old poet to participate in an *aventure épistolaire*, perhaps out of vanity, but more so out of an adolescent curiosity as to whether a famous letter-affair would blossom into a historical, literary romance that would carve her name in history. Machaut complies, but only on the condition their letters are concealed in a special wooden box with a secret compartment, an ordinary small, stagecoach mailbox in which wine merchants provided samples of their harvest in tiny bottles...to be sent to Peronelle's father...and during the night, the young girl would sneak into the library and with expert fingers and long fingernails, slide out the secret layer upon which the letter would be retrieved. And so it went, back and forth. If caught, her only misdemeanour would have been mischievously tasting the *cru de région*. Quin therefore, explained to Iryna that words had to have a secret compartment, *if you know what I mean*, he wrote, *since you are a poet*, and a poem should always be reciprocated with a book. He was awaiting her poem *From Kharkiv to Kyiv*. Quin thought of Eric Newby's *A Short Walk in the Hindu Kush*. Newby was a fashion designer turned mountaineer. Quin was a self-fashioned fireside epistolarian.

Every now and again I repeat myself. This habit of anaphora or repetition (even though they may not occur in sequence) is how my compositions are made: the eternal return nails down the box that is couriered to others. The letter is put together from earlier fragments, in the same way that existence is made out of bits and pieces distributed over time, disseminated over space, and not much goes to waste, not even melancholia which they say is a writerly indulgence. There is no real message and if there were one, it wouldn't be newsworthy. At each station we try to understand the journey, but it's better that we don't, so as not to frighten the muse.

He writes to stave off something: grief, pain.

Joan Didion: *grief turns out to be a place none of us know until we reach it.*

It's a place all right. It's always a place. If there were no sense of place then we would be tripping the light fantastic in fantasy land. There are some old men who, when their wives die, manage grief for a couple of days and then start ringing women, old friends, ex-lovers, taking cruise ships, living in high-class Asian hotels, getting massages, flying on, never staying still, until one day or night, grief catches up with them, when *nobody* is out there, when least of all, lovely decent women who have lost their partners, want nothing to do with more grief, either from an unproblematic self or from warring selves.

Travelling more and knowing less. His doctor said as much: long-haul flights are risky for you, she said. No masks, recycled air, imagine all those aerosols of sneezing and coughing. Eighteen hours of it, then heaving into your lungs the miasma of crowded airport lounges when waiting and hurrying then waiting again is the order of the day or night. No, Poland, she said with a sniff, is where my husband is from. He doesn't ever want to go back. Going back is like re-reading a history book from which you learn nothing. Eastern Europe, you understand, can bring you the Wild East, scammers, imaginary loves, bleak hotel rooms where the TV is only presenting long talk shows in languages full of Zs, Vs, Shs and Chs while your escort empties your wallet and steals the hotel towels.

Iryna said she could not leave Ukraine at this time. The rehabilitation centre for lost children needs her. These children have been completely traumatised, she wrote, some have seen their mothers raped, then shot, then buried by locals in their own gardens. The dogs give them a great deal of comfort. Animals take their minds off all the terrible things, at least for a few moments. Iryna said her husband Witold was still in Donbas. His last message to her was: 'We are getting cut off by Russian artillery.' He did not ask after her or Marika. Iryna guessed he had no time. But then she also knew he was cutting himself off from them in order to remain hard enough to survive. She brought his message to the Territorial Commander. He already knew the coordinates and the units that had been surrounded. If they surrender they will be sent to Russia as POWs. She knew that was the best outcome. The worst was not spoken.

The cold fogs up the glass in Quin's hut. He can see outside only vaguely: the dam, the ducks, the blurred water hyacinths. Space is suffocating him. If he thinks of war he can probably imagine having to last a bit longer in survival mode. But no war is without war crimes. No war is without genocide. His father had said to him when he was very little: It's better to be a soldier than a civilian. Death will be a little quicker as a soldier. His father let him hold his revolver. Officers don't carry rifles. Officers are often in close combat. They are trained not to be captured. How close? his son asked. Close enough to smell the enemy's breath and body odour. At another time he was heard saying to his friends that when the Japanese invaded, men threw away their weapons and uniforms. But at seven years of age he found his father's revolver in the bottom of the cupboard, a Smith & Wesson, which didn't have a safety catch, and he was strong enough to pull the trigger again and again. The bullets were elsewhere. But his father told him you always left one chamber unloaded, where the hammer and pin coincided, as a safety. Then you loaded five bullets. Four for whom you will kill or maim, one for your own mouth. The only thing was that the British required an officer to have a lanyard tied to the gun. It was a nuisance. With the cross-draw you could tangle it up with your thigh and in panic, shoot yourself in the balls.

Yesterday, Iryna wrote, a student string quartet came to the *internat* and played Beethoven's No. 16 Opus 135 in F Major. It was well received by all the children. It is amazing how music comes so naturally to children as enchanting and uplifting. Adults tend to sink into solemnity and sadness. The weight of the world is now trying to reach for the lightness of being. I have to relearn the lightness of being, she wrote. I was eleven when Ukraine became a political nation in 1991. I remember my mother switching from Russian to Ukrainian immediately. We all spoke Ukrainian at home; now we speak it freely at school. That sounds ideal, but overnight Eastern Europe had become the Wild East. Gangster cowboys came out of nowhere. Sex was openly on sale. All I wanted was some blue jeans. The state of Ukraine had become a blackmail state.

I recall, Iryna continued, the time Witold and I met at a demonstration in Maidan in 2013, during the protests against the government led by that thug Yanukovych, who is now in Russia. Yanukovych was a convicted felon who became president of Ukraine. He blocked free trade with the European Union. He wanted to make Russian the official language of Ukraine. We demonstrated night after night. We called it 'the revolution of dignity'. It was a Kantian moral imperative that we had value beyond money. Our parents joined us in protesting. Many of us were beaten with steel truncheons. The police didn't spare old people either. It became an offence to wear hard hats or motorcycle helmets. We were executing another renaissance, only this time the far right, who claimed to be victims as well as victors, were interspersed amongst us. The speeches which inspired us were by singers and actors. We sang the national anthem every few hours through the night, but we didn't know if the person standing next to us meant it whole-heartedly or half-heartedly. Whose nostalgia was it? The monks rang their bells in support from the monastery nearby. So religion entered through the back door. Holy incense, they were heady times. But music was what we needed most of all, from chants to chance. Witold and I danced and sang all night, to Slava of Okean Elzy; he is our Bono. Then the interior police began shooting live rounds from rooftops. This is when I learned how to set up food stations and medical stations. I learned how to be a nurse without training. I learned how to dress and stitch wounds. Suddenly you forgot all about the political complications. There was only blood. And time. Time was changing every minute; it was flowing into something new; it was no longer ours. It was a peculiar moment:

the deaths of the people around me meant also the death of the State as we knew it. What was beyond was still unknown.

After Maidan I did a three-year degree in general nursing. In February 2014 Yanukovych fled to Crimea and then to southern Russia. He is still Putin's friend, living his gangster life. His lawyer was the same Paul Manafort who worked for Donald Trump. Just imagine how the world would look with Trump and Putin in charge of Ukraine. *On that very pessimistic note, Marika and I send our very kind regards....*

Quin had a reputation for drinking. Though you wouldn't know if he were drunk. He held it pretty well for the most part. Colleagues told stories of his office fridge, which was stocked full of wine and expensive glasses from David Jones, different shapes for different drinks. He always made a point of supervising students in the mornings. Last one at one p.m. Then he did research, wrote, read and with some disgust, fulfilled his tasks in the tyranny of metrics. The university loved points, which converted to money at some stage. The reward was a drink or two, after which he became creative with the statistics. The only hazard was the drive home. He was careful. Drove slowly. Put on his wire-rimmed spectacles. Plugged in his hearing aid. He avoided major roads and their random-breath-test points. It would take him half an hour more to get home. He didn't mind. There was no one to greet him except his dogs. Who needed to be fed, walked, dried if wet. Lighting the fires in winter: that was a peaceful task. Then he would sit on the couch and think about Ukraine and imagine the bombs and missiles coming in at random. He remembered seeing the footage of the war in Bosnia; the neat country bungalows bombed to rubble, just some bits of lace curtain flapping in the night-time searchlights. Dogs being shot for target practice.

On his mantelpiece, a framed photo of his father and himself. He was about five.

Easter rising like hot cross buns; a birdman foreseeing the end of flight; all meaning lost in the gyre of age. My father always made us do the Stations of the Cross on Good Friday. He had converted to Catholicism. We went to St Teresa's Church on Boundary Road and did the hour-long meditation on the fourteen Stations before each image. Our way of sorrows. I wasn't thinking so much of Jesus. I was told that at three o'clock in the afternoon the clouds came in, the world grew dark and then my sisters and I would be free. Not to run around, play games or music, but to retire to our points of view. I went to our verandah and our balcony. My sisters went to the houses of their friends and my mother to her kitchen. My father always left after the Stations. He met silently with his cousins and disappeared onto a double-decker bus to the ferry terminal. The clouds came in. The world became dark. Christ died when Gong Boy appeared. We called him Gong Boy. It had a nice ring to it. But let me put Gong Boy in context.

Here I am in 1955, looking smug in my father's arms. I am about to go into kindergarten and am very proud of my uniform. My father looks like an old Albert Camus if Camus had not been killed at the age of forty-six in a car driven by his publisher Michel Gallimard. But you can see my father's predilections: the bamboo blinds, the Cochin China tiles, the Chinese balusters and the shadows of my mother's poinsettias. That was before our downfall. Behind us are some granite hills. To our left there would have been a deep scar in the rocks left by an American bomb which failed to find its target: the headquarters of the Japanese gendarmerie where my father played tea-dances at the end of the war.

But let's talk about Gong Boy. They were building a hospital which was cut into the granite hills. To do this they needed to blast out the rock and drive the pilings into the hill. They blasted day and night. No one cared about the noise. It was a spectacle, day and night. Gong Boy was the central player. During the day he appeared in the middle of the road wearing a red bandana and carrying a bronze gong with a flag, beating his rhythms and stopping the traffic. He was undaunted in his duty, walking into the middle of the road, remonstrating with drivers who tried to sneak through, yelling at stragglers to back up. At night he was still on duty, carrying a kerosene lantern and still beating his gong, yelling at the top of his voice at cars. Gong Boy was my hero. I watched him from my balcony. He could stop cars at will, was always on the job in bare feet and in all weathers. One day the blasting went awry. A huge boulder rolled from the hill, sped through the barriers and careened across the road. Gong Boy tried to stop it with his hands but it was useless, and the boulder crashed through onto the other side of the road and into a Vespa shop, injuring two customers and crushing three scooters. I thought Gong Boy was pretty brave to try to stop it with his hands. His gong was useless, which he knew. But he was going to challenge that idea. I wanted a gong like his, but I didn't know the word for it. My father was never home so I couldn't point it out to him. My mother thought I wanted a drum. No one understood that I really wanted a symbolic instrument to stop erratic behaviour and disorder; halt dysfunction. I'm uncertain of the things I saw but sure of the things I heard: the Gong Boy had no rhythm; he missed the fact that others could not hear and so when he banged out his warning at three o'clock on Good Friday, he was challenged by a fire engine racing to the other side of town, its siren at full blast. I watched him assert his authority. He stepped forward. But the firemen knew they had more priority and failed to slow. Machine against man. The Gong Boy stepped back a foot or two at the last minute but did not really give enough way and the engine raced, ploughing onto him. I closed my eyes, knowing as the observer from the balcony – my mother's fatal practice – that I could not look at fate with equivocation. There was a slew of blood, a latecomer's scream from my chest and Gong Boy was dead and the engine slowed finally to run over the pool of red leaving a measured tread which only faded yards further along. Two days later, as if to assuage my trauma, my mother bought me a small dragon drum they played during Chinese New Year. On the sides were carved a golden dragon encircling the whole rim. It seemed happier than the images of the Via Dolorosa. I tapped out some bossa nova beats on the pig-skin, but they had neither resonance nor importance; nothing as resolute as Gong Boy's gong, and I would have been better off had I not softened, not severed myself from the brotherhood of those with backbone, not been sensitive to nightmares, and had sung full-throated of the deaths my father had seen during the war without blinking; all those images so different to those I saw on Good Friday. It's what literature will fulfil when the time comes.

Dearest Iryna, I know and I see. In fact I see more than I know. Forgive my presumptuousness. Of course you must stay. Today it must be Good Friday in Lviv. Sing praise to Passover victims. Stay strong. It's what coaches tell boys after the game. Stay strong, stay hard, for next week's match. We all used to joke about staying hard. But honestly, writing pushes fear into the background. It is a connection of sorts which makes regret redundant because what is written is irretrievable. Quin.

Those who write too much are always resented, thought Quin as he busied himself with mending his bicycle. Those who write too many letters are also hated because too many letters become tedious and are always one-sided, preoccupied with the writer's obsessions, because letter-writing is now reduced to *communication*, which is often selfish, never really inquiring genuinely about the other, or worrying for the other. Now that eros is no longer possible in belles-lettres, it is imperative to address Thanatos as a warrior. Seduction no longer exists in wartime as it takes too long. I have to remember that, Quin was thinking as he mounted his bike and coasted down the road and narrowly avoided being hit by a car as he turned the corner. The driver blew his horn. Quin's mind was not alert enough, he was digesting this thought, that his mind was frozen in isolation, mild hypothermia causing a loss of judgement. But isn't that what happens when you love your symptom, when you enter the killing zone, when you know your birth was a terrible mistake and now you have to cheat to live, but never losing sight of the fact that ultimately death can never be cheated?

E.M. Cioran: 'A book is a postponed suicide.'

E.M. shared the same initials as Forster. *Only connect.*

Did yard work; cut wood; snapped twigs for kindling. Swept steps. Started the tractor-barrow. Washed clothes. Fed dogs.

Night-fire, which isn't warm. Inside me the nights are hard because the dogs don't speak. But then speech is something always in excess.

These duties I impose upon myself. I like the discipline, the muscle work. In the morning the sun comes out for a little while. It lights up the water and the trees. Crafting life is like crafting writing. Body and mind work together. The mornings are hard until I get into some rhythm. Then muscle memory gets into swing and the work feels good in its juices, the land brings forth growth in the harshest season. Everything is damp. The creeks flow, the dam is full to overflowing, the frogs let me know that healthy life has arrived. The ash tree beside my hut drops spring buds, bunches of blood-red beads.

He was happy retiring into such solitude. People who have never been solitary sometimes think of this as an ideal, but once they move to the countryside and their friends start to drop off, they can only contemplate moving back to the city, or they commit slow suicide.

Dear Abe, Russia is reducing everything in Ukraine to rubble. I don't know how to respond to such destruction. Regrowth will be beyond my lifetime. Iryna.

From Kharkiv to Kyiv
My town is behind me now.
It's not like a photograph,
Full of nostalgia, of turning leaves and parks.
It's not like wiping dust from a child's face,
Which is full of fear.
There are no photos
Either of the train or of my husband
In uniform, of his backpack and rifle.
He never said goodbye.
He was not there that day
My daughter and I embarked
After the Russians came
And raped me in my bedroom.
(I had just made the coffee.)
There are no photos
Except for those they took
Of my nakedness, hearing their cell phone shutters

Through my shuttered eyes and seeing the stillness after
Their armoured personnel carrier left.
There are no photos of the tiny train toilet,
Of the bottle of mifepristone
Blocking my progesterone
Nor of the bottle of misoprostol
Which brought on cramping,
The worst of periods, bleeding, terrible pain,
The carriage was red, swaying, and the knocking
On the door for someone else's usage.
Miscarriage of justice, of life, a shameful god
Was what I was thinking,
As I made my way back to my daughter
Through erasures: slats of light airbrushing
The yellowstone suburbs of Kyiv
Just coming into view.

Quin did not know how to respond. He was not a first responder; instead he would hesitate, paralysed, waiting for a sign. Her fury was no doubt filling up his world, but now he was sitting there, reining it in by procrastination, or diverting it at least, by reading. He read that in the siege of Sarajevo there were over ten thousand dogs without owners, at large on the streets. The Serbs used them as target practice.

In her book *EEG*, Daša Drndić has her narrator comment on the *Canis montanus*, a mountain sheepdog which prefers to lie in the snow. This dog, called a *Tornjak*, has been known to save the lives of homeless people by lying on top of them during a snowstorm.

Then Quin sends a message by saying that the humanitarian deadline in Australia has been extended and will soon expire. It means that with Iryna's qualifications she could work as a nurse or teacher. Would she fill in the online details and apply for a visa to Australia? Her friend Mariia, who is in Sydney, will know all the procedures. He suggested that she could even come to Adelaide, where he has a largely unoccupied house and a self-contained studio, into which he could move if necessary. Please contact:

Australian Embassy
13A Kostelna St
Kyiv 01901
Ukraine

The Embassy is co-located with the Canadian Embassy to Ukraine in Kyiv.

That Sunday Quin was frantic. He had misplaced his passport, which he remembers having rescued from the flames of his burning library. He always had a satchel ready with important documents, in case of bushfires or war. Now he could not find it. The last time this happened was when he was in Hong Kong, fleeing his first marriage and warming to a new liaison and unsuccessfully escaping a jealous ex who had head-butted him in the lobby of his hotel. As he lay on the carpet, his satchel was liberally flooded with a can of olive oil from Macau. He complained to the staff. How could they stand and watch? His passport had been snatched from his pocket in full sight. He had a flight to catch to Sydney. He went to the Australian Consulate-General:

23/F Harbour Centre
25 Harbour Road, Wan Chai
Hong Kong SAR

He explained what had happened. He was okay, though his nose was bleeding. Thank goodness he had never broken it, not even in rugby. The woman at the consulate was sympathetic, even a little respectful. He said he was burgled in his hotel room. No, it was not a woman. Yes, it was the jealous lover of an acquaintance. He never thought of himself as a raconteur. The hotel was not going to charge him for one night's stay. Quin felt no enmity, no animus. There was an absence of a rapport with himself and his life had a different order now, no longer measurable in terms of reflection and solitude and his right to be alone. Denied those and suddenly he was flying, a crowd inside his head was applauding, and this attractive consular official was in front of him and smiling not with pity but with interest, and yes, he had his plane ticket and could leave tomorrow, as though fleeing a war. He felt something of a hero.

The Americans, baby, was the catch-call in Hong Kong and he had met a number of them: filmmakers, flight attendants, advertising executives. He told them he was free and running away from a former life. Helen was from Long Island. Her father owned several art galleries and she was giving a talk at the University of Hong Kong. After her talk, she invited him back to her apartment on The Peak, and they had progressed, after much drinking and caressing, to long and noisy lovemaking while the residents below banged on the ceiling. Then they went out dancing. Hong Kong never slept and as he was flying out in the morning, they stayed out until the grey dawn, watching toy-like ferries bobbing their way across a dirty-green harbour. He didn't think he was in love. It was the first time it had happened in this way, but there was something intriguing him about Helen. She imported Australian Indigenous artefacts without much red-tape. Maybe they were fakes. She had a vague, faraway look which appeared dreamy or short-sighted, but she was alert to everything that was being said;

it was just that she was thinking about things; about the two of them, she said, *if you should ever come back this way...* She had perfect teeth and a dirty laugh. She wore nothing under her ultra-sheer pantyhose. The libido played to all the senses: sight, touch, smell and sound; taste entered as a third party called *style*. The sixth sense prevented premature disaster.

To this day I don't know why I took the morning flight. I guess I was looking for home.

Helmut Schellenberger emailed. If agreeable, he would like to meet Quin in his city office and the offer of a sum will be decided then. And could he please bring with him three forms of identification such as a passport; driver's licence; rates notice?

Quin took the bus into the city with his briefcase in which he had the stamp albums, his driver's licence, Medicare card and the latest Council rates notice. He still had not found the satchel with his passport. The only way to do that was to think hard while sitting in the bus with a mask on, breathing slowly, which was making him dizzy without panic and so he fell into a semi-doze, working backwards from everything he had done after the fire in the library. He would have put the black satchel in a safe place. There were many safe places. Somewhere not flammable. He finally located it in his head. Of course. The outdoor freezer, which he hardly ever used. Snapped into a plastic air-tight container. He was very happy with this discovery. A kind of satori in a Buddhist daze. Dementia was postponed temporarily. He did remember he didn't have any breakfast and was therefore light-headed, split into others, levitating, looking down upon his body. He mused in a kind of fever. As a child he was often ill, with all those so-called *oriental* illnesses. Germs were everywhere. The wide-open spaces of Australia would be good for his son, his father concluded; plus a country coloured pink on the atlas would always be somewhat neutral in the oncoming war between East and West. In the bus Quin reflected on the parts of his self. In those fragments would be the residue of the whole, he was convinced, like imploded stars, into which dark matter would open wormholes of different time. A sixth dimension of Proustian memory; encrustations of eternity. 'Until hell freezes over' was not an impossible time. It happened with his outside freezer, which survived and did not stop working during the great library fire at night below Mount Lofty, casting a warm glow for those who dwelt in the valley.

In the meantime, he had received an email from a Ricky Dupont, from the Department of Foreign Affairs and Trade. Ricky said that he was a first cousin, *just look at your Ancestry.com link.* Let me know if there is anything I can help you with. As you may know I am your father's cousin's son. There were three of us from that family in Hong Kong who emigrated when Daddy died. Your father used to ring mine when fixed-line telephones were the in thing. Your dad laid the handset on his piano and played old-time waltzes and my dad cried and cried. It went on for hours. I was the only one who was sporting and played hockey. Sonny was a fireman. Junior rode around on a Vespa and dated your half-sister...totally inappropriate. But now Junior, who is also known as Michael, is CEO of an NGO in New York. Let me know if you need help. Michael can also help. He's connected. I've read your books. Totally crap in terms of the factuals. But then, I don't buy into stories. Sincerely, Ricky.

Schellenberger's city office was on the fifth floor of a rather shabby building in Adelaide Central. 'Call me Helmut,' he said to Quin as he opened the door. He was dressed smartly, in a vest and bow tie. The room smelled of pipe smoke. Virtually every desk and floor space was filled with albums, books, newspapers. 'How do you spell *Presbyterian*?' he asked. Quin spelled it out. 'Not many people know how to spell it,' Schellenberger was impressed. He pushed a tin of pipe tobacco across the cluttered desk. *Presbyterian Mixture*. 'A very good blend. It has Latakia in it. Reminds me of travelling in Turkey. Have you ever been to Turkey?' Quin said he hadn't but he understood the Bosphorus was very beautiful. 'It's where East meets West,' Schellenberger said, 'where the Ottomans meet the Christians.' He produced a pipe with a very long thin stem. 'Do you mind?' Quin shook his head. He would love a cigar, but that meant a burning library. 'In this tin I have some of the rarest stamps in the world.' Schellenberger didn't open the tin. 'I'm not going to light them up, so don't worry.' The unlit church-warden pipe was clenched in his teeth as he examined Quin's albums again. He had the profile of a Dickens character. 'I can give you something for these. Something handsome. Do you have your identification papers?' This was Checkpoint Charlie. Was Schellenberger an agent for the NKVD? Quin took out his documents. The office was hot and he was starting to perspire. Maybe his stamps had microscripted messages on the backs of them, written in invisible ink. It would only take one lick and he would be implicated. 'Do you believe in an afterlife?' Helmut Schellenberger asked.

'No. An afterlife is what the living hope for, but when you're dead, you're no longer thinking.' Quin was adamant that the pre-occupations of the dead were a waste of time, and of life.

'But the living have to keep thinking and remembering and living.'

'Yes. That is the burden and the pain of living.'

'Professor Quin, you are quite a pessimist.'

'Call me Abe.'

'I have a collector in New York.'

'Yes?'

'His name is Michael Lincoln. Funny that. Your first name and his second. He happens to be a cousin of yours. He says he's reading you. Your books I mean. He's the CEO of an NGO in New Jersey.'

The correct sum was placed into Quin's account in two days. It was a trade-deal. The same the Mongols would have done in Kyivan Rus' in 1237, trading on tributes which converted to land and mainmorts. But what was deposited was a handsome sum nevertheless; and Quin, who could never sell anything to his own advantage, thought of his father, an *epistolarian extraordinaire*, a *pistolero* in correspondence, who would have exacted a much larger amount by going to higher bidders. Nevertheless, it was ironic that even his father's love letters, probably depraved at times, garnered rare stamps from his co-respondents, and now the price of his love and postage returned into his son's odourless account. Deep down, he knew his father was far more of a trader than a bully, but Quin couldn't straddle the difference. In the end, you had to be nine-tenths a bully to buy and sell love as well as goods. *Bonifacio*, for that was his father's real name, which had always been shortened to *Bonny*, was not a do-gooder. Bonifacio said buying and selling was a public service. He was a *compradore*. He spoke several languages. In Jewish history, he would have been a *shtadlan*, a civil and political go-between, who was not without menace to his own people. Quin asked Iryna for her bank deposit details.

When his bestselling book was published, cousins of his were appearing everywhere. *Dear Abe; My dear Abram;* and so on. All of a sudden. *Ancestry.com* was to blame. *DNA no lie*, they were saying. The philatelic societies. The brotherhood of high office. What next? *Frères fiduciaires*? The Protocols of Zion? The World Bank? The Flat Earth Society? His solitude was under attack. He would be linked willy-nilly into a sceptics' network once they started reading him and saw themselves transcribed; metamorphosed; dismembered. They began compiling family trees of their own and inserted them into Facebook and Wikipedia. He insulted them with his lack of factuality. Here's real research! they wrote.

Yes, I wrote to Iryna. I said one was never right to insist on being right in life. I was wrong about suffering. I was wrong to doubt her suffering. I just wasn't quick enough to know fatuousness came early in late middle age. Then it increased exponentially. *Ignis fatuus*. The foolish lightning of an old man's weakness of judgement, then dementia and imbecility. I'm glad you stuck with me, Iryna. Through the vapid fantasies.

You are not foolish and I will not accept charity. You can donate to the orphanage or to the dogs' home. The two are not mutually exclusive. Or you can sponsor a family through the UNHCR. Witold cannot be reached now and I fear he is either missing in action or has been taken prisoner in the Donbas, which means he will either be killed or sent to a Russian camp. They still have Gulags. No doubt you have read Aleksandr Solzhenitsyn and Vasily Grossman. No doubt you have read Józef Czapski. No doubt you know about the fact that in 1940 twenty-two thousand Polish officers were executed by the Russian NKVD and over four thousand bodies with the backs of their skulls shattered, bullet-holed, were discovered in the Katyń forest. Undoubtedly you know of the mass graves found in Bykownia near Kyiv. And the executions at Kharkiv. My place is here. Full of languages, accents and pluralities. Both Witold and I could speak several languages, including Surzhyk, which is a mixture of Russian and Ukrainian, common in the eastern regions. Upon the invasion, we spoke only Ukrainian. Not out of patriotism but out of a hope for a new pluralistic society. Contradictions and paradoxes on all sides. The land is inspirited with our dead, those who came to defend Mother Russia in the past, and now Russia's brutality reverts to all those centuries of her former brutalities and the dead can do nothing about defending Ukraine because they would never have known it would evolve into a sovereign country. I do not run away, and neither does my daughter. Not again. Mariia, my good friend by the way, is coming back from Sydney. A beautiful city, she said, but the people sunbake like sea lions with no memory.

Iryna was swapping wars: from German to Soviet and back again. Now the Germans are supplying arms to Ukraine to fight the Russians. Wars never end. No matter what the pacifists say. But the silt of life is filtered through the dead, and the ashes of the dead are light enough to deposit into a small drone and a small drone can scatter them out into the sea. Sooner or later, all would be forgotten, or maybe a dim memory would remain, not lasting more than one generation. But it is still good to deal in remembrance, to instil it in others when they are young, to look at nature differently, so that they understand there can be such a thing as the last tree, the last animal, and to live the moment as humanely as possible. There is a difference between being guilty and being responsible. One is recursive: I'm not to blame; I wasn't there. Let me out of here. The other is proactive. I am in some way responsible, albeit indirectly, for not acting. I am not afraid of taking some blame.

Dearest Iryna, Everything that Kafka wrote was proleptic of the historical terror to come, the bloodlands of Eastern Europe. He knew about the notes written by prisoners before being shot; the diaries of children who were starving to death; the words passed along the communal latrines and smuggled out through barbed wire by victims of the early death camps. Even private missives ended in the empty disaster of being unread, the great void of non-reception: written kisses are stolen by ghosts. The Imperial Messenger with a letter from a dying emperor to his ideal lover, can never breach the walls of the courtyard of the courtyard of the courtyard of the Forbidden City because of the crowds. Love is always a casualty of postage and alas, of confession, which the lover always desires. We die through the unfulfilled wishes of our words made flesh. At least consider the possibility of taking some time off, to have a holiday in Australia. That is what your friend did and what you and your daughter should also do. To recharge, to lessen anxiety, at least for a moment. It is not a dereliction of duty or an increase in guilt to know there are countries in which all names are unknown to you, all customs foreign, echoing with the speech of others that you may find banal, in order to return like Ulysses, not as a hero but as a spy who knew that all was not horror. A spy through the keyhole who saw hope and possibility. I think you are Jewish enough to see that.

Quin trawled through his memory and remembered Michael Lincoln, who indeed was a distant cousin. In New York many years ago to promote his book *Smoke and Mirrors*, a critique of non-style in literary analysis, Quin had met with Lincoln in the latter's Fifth Avenue offices. Michael Lincoln was then head of the Asian-American Society, a non-profit organisation devoted to developing Asian-American art and literature. He was also a lawyer. His office jutted out *over* Fifth Avenue, so that this prime real estate was much longer than the actual building. Glass-walled on three sides, you could look up and down the Avenue at what the rich were doing below, going about their business shopping at Bulgari, Tiffany's, Armani and Cartier. Lincoln looked like a young version of his own father, short, stocky and immaculately dressed. He gracefully accepted a copy of Quin's book and read the inscription: *To Michael, with warmth and esteem.* His cousin thanked Quin for 'a great contribution to the study of literature'. 'I suppose you knew Alan Bloom?' Quin shook his head. He had once met Harold Bloom, but decided this was a path not worth taking. 'Let me know if I can do anything to help you,' Lincoln said, obviously pressed for time. His assistant had brought in a bundle of files and laid them neatly on his desk. Quin politely made his farewell. This was not his world.

He was glad to be back on Fifth Avenue and walked a long way in the wrong direction, looking for a restaurant. He finally asked a policewoman where the nearest diner was located. She sent him back the way he had come and he discovered an Italian trattoria, where, together with a bottle of chianti, he paid well over anything he would have done in Adelaide.

Now he thought he would write to Michael Lincoln since he had an excuse. He said he knew Helmut Schellenberger, who had bought some stamp albums from him and that he, Abe Quin, was trying to sponsor a Ukrainian family to come to Australia. He understood Lincoln was now the CEO of an NGO and was working closely with UNHCR in the adoption and repatriation of refugees from Ukraine. Schellenberger also mentioned that Lincoln was still an attorney in the Southern District of New York. Which was serious business; aka the 'sovereign' district; aka the Secret Service.

Multiple times a day I feel the burden of the future. The future can go in many different directions and it presents itself to me in multifarious forms. The only way then, to concentrate, is to go one step at a time like a small animal intent on a single movement, perhaps knowing that moment is brief and may be the last moment. Survival, therefore, is not of the fittest but of experiencing the existential moment, a quickness that does not paralyse a being by offering it choices of direction. It does not will a way or a path but takes it without thought. It is for this reason that I have abandoned going to the medical centre. The centre offered multiple paths, batteries of tests, and invasive procedures. Bone, bowel and brain scans. I have had an endoscopy, a gastroscopy and a colonoscopy. The last was the worst, where you have to prepare for at least a day, eating no solids and swallowing laxative mixtures. I went to the toilet ten times a night. Given my recurrent nightmares of dirty public toilets, which are always well-appointed or well pointed out, privies lacking in privacy, I even dreaded private bathrooms in house and country exchanges, where lifting the toilet seat revealed a horror which I was obliged to clean since I would be suspected of having caused it. The colonostic preparation weakened me so much and implanted a doubt that preventative care was worse than any thanatophobia or fatalism. It was better to live in the moment, step by step, to *count* rather than to recount. Government health departments, likewise, keep sending me letters (3), plastic test kits (2), invitations to attend mobile testing buses(1). All of this is to stop me from clogging up the hospitals by having my bowels cleansed. All of this is an economics of shit. It is a problem for those who are alive, that they are able to decrease the burden of the health care services of the future. But it is awful to die in a nursing home, which is the future for at least ninety per cent of the aging population. Nursing homes smell overwhelmingly of shit and echo with the verbiage of dementia, a Morse of logorrhea.

I am always trying to express something small which cannot happen without large tragedy. Small ills we can tolerate and overcome without writing anything grand. But time stills me and perhaps the small future is not worth recording; fatuous perhaps. There is however, an element that remains – the history-spark that is quickly snuffed – the experience of having lived certain lives; the complete waste of it all.

In moments like these, Quin wrote. Writing was a small animal inside of him which took moments step by step, without plotting death, trying to exist without a knowledge of death. While there were raging wars and epidemics, a small animal knew little of them. It is therefore good, he wrote to Iryna, that taking a small step to one of the furthest countries away from her own inscribes a *distance* from others and their familiarity with horror, that even if it is a brief sojourn, life that is taken away from us is untenable without the Ultima Thule of having the experience of strangeness. *One is out of the moment of death; out of its knowledge; understanding a homelessness that is not horrific but is like an abstract game, for example, just as entering my life, but at a distance, would be an exercise.*

On the fourth of June, he stopped wearing a watch. If a dog can die within two minutes, then clock time was useless and redundant and worthless in death. All this timekeeping was a human obsession and did not keep to the rhythms of biology. So it was important to keep the time of the body. To hear the heart and gauge the movements of all the organs and to feel the sonar of the bones sounding back the skeletal signals of breakdown and repair. All in their own time. With attendant noises, the croaking of frogs, barking of dogs, wailing of ducks. Not for nothing does nature mimic the human, which is the most threatening of species, and thereby it sees the human as complicit with its own mortality; as Heraclitus noted, the word for life – *bíos* – is also the word for bow – *biós* – albeit with a different syllabic accentuation; thus killing, the hunt, the weapon, is very much the work of death inside life.

War, I said to Iryna, is constant angst, but don't worry. Eros will not manifest itself when at my place even God has taken a break from it. You won't have to talk. I will hold a big party for all the Ukrainians in the hills. I will have caterers. I will personally oversee all the invitations.

Others, however, in the bowels of the inferno of information, were working hard. Michael Lincoln got back to Quin from New York with an encrypted email that needed a passcode: *Zarębin is a political activist. Anti-Russian, but deeply implicated in Donbas local politics. He's known to have infiltrated Russian sympathisers in Donetsk. He may still be alive but is an expert impersonator. He may have gone underground or undercover. We have no news of a prisoner swap or whether he has been 'filtered' to Russia. Given the sensitive nature of his relationships and compromises, it is probably imperative to get his wife and daughter out of Ukraine. Australia is a good place to begin.*

December 2013, Iryna said, we were sitting in the snow listening to the blues. We wanted the Yanukovych government out. We heard guitarists playing just like Robert Johnson, and Stevie Ray Vaughan, and vocalists imitating Bessie Smith. Ukraine had a great understanding of the blues. The blues was what hit us, in a soon-to-be-occupied land. We locked into singing it on Independence Square in Kyiv, or you may know it as the Maidan Nezalezhnosti. We actually called ourselves *batiars*, which meant bohemians from Lviv, or the old *Lvov*. If we didn't get rid of the government we were going to be slaves, not Slavic, but enclaves of dissidents, collaborators, pseudo-Russkis (*Rus* meaning 'men who row' when they took slaves in Viking times in the ninth century, rowing down our rivers and along the coast of the Sea of Azov, before the Mongols arrived overland), these modern-day pretend-Vikings who would in time be known as the 'little Russians' would be wiped out in forests and camps and Gulags as spies and would be shot by twenty-year-old Russian conscripts with shaven heads looking like Mongols. The blues, which in the Western-educated world would be categorised as 'melancholic' was something other than the comfortable cosy rooms of warm, sad writing. The blues was about despair but was also liberational and pregestational, agitational and confrontational. It meant you could howl without being able to explain, while police dogs took bites out of your haunches and you camped in the snow with no shoes. It meant nothing to explain yourself in an inhuman system. The Russian onslaught, despite the warnings of Dostoyevsky and Tolstoy, was that the un-humans will always win the propaganda war through the sacrifice of millions of their own. That is how it works. Then we all become refugees. There will be no time for the blues because as refugees we will get low-paid jobs in another country and will have to dumb down our brains so we can survive in those jobs. Sooner or later we will become zombies simply to exist. We will think with nostalgia about our former nation. But what is 'nation' after all that? 'Nation' is expressed by large tears and huge suffering and if we return we will be sitting in the dust and ash and rubble of our former homes which no longer have a roof and parts of the walls will be ready to break off and bury us there. Nobody has learned anything except the old lesson of despair and false pride. So, I would ask if you would like to have a holiday in Lviv before Ukrainian cities are entirely levelled? If Witold is still alive, Marika and I would both welcome you into our humble apartment. Warmest regards, Iryna.

Iryna was astounding. Exactly the correspondent I needed. For over five years now I have isolated myself. You may not think that is a long time. I was not lonely at all. I had mostly three dogs and in one period, five. The local Council mandated that you could only have three at the most and that you needed a licence to have more if you are a breeder. That meant you had to be registered. I was not interested in breeding, but in rescuing. All those puppies nobody wanted, left to die in cardboard boxes in deep bush and valleys. Even feral hounds and half-dingoes adopted them. In isolation, which some people call antisocial disorder, sociopathy or agoraphobia, you do not harm others. You just avoid them. Because they harm you. But you see how human proliferation and abandonment affect animals and you take them in. Because animals do not harm you if you are not afraid and if you are not aggressive and lie still upon the ground and don't use words, which are always a threat to them. This is the natural principle I understood without articulating it to myself. Cruelty is inbred in humans. All because they think they are at the top of the pecking order because they have language. And psychopathy lies deep in the brain stem. Now and again I have uncontrollable thoughts, which are not impulses or thoughts which lead to actions, but which overload my imagination with terrible incidents, war experiences, and violent results, which are worded and not imaged. I do not know whence they come. You can trace the Middle English *whence* as an indirect question distancing my pathology of intrusive and involuntary word-memory: ancient; ancestral; not nuanced and refined. Self-protection. Too much vocabulary doth violence upon the self.

Where is the silence and what does it serve?

But let's understand each other. Most humans like clockwork. Production. Achievement. Key Performance Indicators. A-type personalities. Anal. No small animals have these aims. They play, eat, sleep, and try to keep out of trouble. Human time was invented by the clock, not by the seasons or the weather. The weather is greater than all of us. The weather works, in its fashion, by serendipity, unpredictability, and delayed or precipitous eruptions. Humans are not in charge of it. Though humans can divert it, disrupt it, and massively ruin its rhythms and upheavals. We are ants building a lifetime of anthills, huge monuments, and then a bobcat knocks everything over and then instead of destroying all of us, we build elsewhere. Those who are left. The survivors without KPIs simply do what we do: build and secure a nest and serve our queen.

Isn't that the true penal colony? Joy through work?

It isn't the same in wartime. There is nothing to build. Nothing to repair. Everything is about destruction. You live on hot water if you can get it, and potato peels. There are degrees of abjection. Peelings, rinds, bark, insects, human flesh.

You cut down trees that were once the most beautiful in the most beautiful parks. You burn heritage furniture like pianos and violins and violoncellos. You bury bodies where once whole families perambulated.

All to heat a potage of borage to treat fatal ailments. Which silage smell have you now forgotten how to distinguish? And whence did it once come and in what circumstance did its perfume leave a wake and a promise of cure?

These are too fine to sensitise.

Dear Iryna, my daughter's daughter is autistic. My daughter grew up with her mother and never knew me as her father. But then, how many children have men fathered without their knowing? It's best to describe the condition as that without any euphemisms. But me, my daughter and I, do our best to understand the genius of her daughter's autism. It is just like any genius, looking at different aspects of life as fascinating and obsessive. It is truly wonderful without sensitisation, which gets in the way of obsession. Like a computer that is fed with information and thrives on its variants and proliferations and algorithms of non-feeling; a great advantage in certain roles. Strange use of the human brain because it is incredibly focused without the restraining handbrake of sensation. So now you know a little bit about me and my family...a missing family, that is, since they now live in Canada and speak French and a singsong kind of English. I have only met them once when they holidayed in Melbourne. Her mother is now dead. She was a classical guitarist with an obsessive bent and the saddest face you could ever encounter. She wore short skirts like a little girl and she showed off her legs. She never smiled, not even when she climaxed, with dark furrowed brows and deep concentration. We were in Madrid. She wrote to me about her pregnancy; she didn't want a termination. I was still a student, living in digs back in Balmain, and had little money. It was another failure of mine not to have been *in situ*. My daughter is called Aisha. She found me through the notorious *Ancestry.com*. Emails from there always meant trouble. It was a kind of trolling until it bit the cat's curiosity. It was strange but not awkward when I met her after twenty years, someone who had the same eyes, who spoke French and for whom I had a mixture of love and desire. I will visit Canada whenever this damned pandemic is over and if my heart still beats.

Dear Abe, I very much fear Witold has been murdered in a Russian prison in Olenivka in Donetsk. I am too full of grief to write more. Here, people queue to give samples of their DNA in order to match them with bits of bodies arriving daily in a refrigerated van.

Quin again did not know how to respond. He decided that for the time being at least, he would not do so because a response would sound hollow and no words would be able to describe adequately any comfort or condolence. Silence and time sometimes can heal, but rarely. Hard times insist on words, but they are wilted weeds and soon become widow's weeds, worn for at least four years. That is the time taken in silence. Half of Marika's lifetime.

I'm not sure how I felt upon receiving this news. I seemed to know Iryna like a friend and was saddened by this brutal event. But the human heart is a flawed organ and deceives itself by ascribing an opportunity to all those hidden selves with different motives, to now convince her to leave Ukraine with her daughter. I could afford to bring them to Adelaide and they could stay at my house and there would be dogs and a school within walking distance and if she wished, Iryna being a refugee, could further her tertiary qualifications at less than half the cost paid by regular international students. I could even start inquiries at my university.

My university...he caught himself claiming this belongingness when the truth was that his time teaching there had been pitted with the minefields of his colleagues' resentments and envies; after all, he was a published bookman who had never earned the academic ivy garnishing his high windows. (In fact they were aluminium-framed, stoppered at six inches to prevent professorial suicides.) And he was multicultural to boot, which universities were embracing at the time, in their statements of inclusion. Insider-runner, silver-spooned, he came with the baggage of others' complaints. He had been named by his mother: *Bok Mun*, the well-read one. *Bookman Quin* would have been a distinguished appellation, but his father said *Abraham* was the more fitting (Abraham was unquestioning), and his mother didn't argue with whatever faith was being put forward. She was sacrificing her son to the West, and that was that.

Quin's first response to all these issues was to open a new bottle of whiskey. He thought of the ubiquitous banality of people's responses to the griefs of others. Had he possessed a different character he would have responded naturally and ingenuously but he was disingenuous and unnatural and highly sensitised to his ignominious upbringing which saw each day as an apocalypse, each morning a ritual of depressive tasks, a past which generalised grief with a silence that was not unfeeling, but was an honesty shared and meant to be shared. But how could anyone have noticed it? Silence was the worst expression of empathy.

I've always believed it is the novel that carries all the indirect notes of empathy. It may even be violence that brings empathy to war and its suffering. It may be anything. Yet, the plasticity of the novel bends to all the obtuse emotions and accommodates them. Then all is confined to the scrapheap of the having been read, having been experienced, having been second-hand and second-read. Major libraries are throwing out paper books.

So Quin thought. But you needed to get beyond the clever and smug superficies of what he had always denied: that he was any kind of specialist in human affairs. Words were the translations of human affairs, and they were often untrustworthy, and by being thus, brought about that dreadful alienation called literature. Real readers love pain and then catharsis, since they cannot stand outside or above, to write pain and catharsis.

So what? So he played school rugby to roughen up his brutality, and by this, without any ideology or ideal, to be engaged in the rude world of war. It didn't take much to squeeze a trigger with precision and deadly effect. But it was a different matter in love and sex.

In grief and in pain, one can never be alone enough. The brief distractions of others and their words, all meant out of kindness, make things incomparably worse than if one were entirely solitary and dealing with life's pain and worse, the memories that are even more painful. One who is feeling the pain can sit and cry until the hours dry up, or they can sit and write and relive the experiences as though telling them to others. But writing in this way is to avoid the most brutal form of distancing and judging, which is needed in order not to tell a story, but to reveal something about the writer, and hopefully to move others through their own benign judgement.

Kafka, apparently, was interested in that overwhelming feeling of not wanting to be seen; all the better to imagine seeing by being unnoticed. In other words, to sense and to smell. Dogs, by the way, don't see very well, but can hear and smell something more than a kilometre away. Kafka is the name of my male dog. He patrols the fences and finds the highest spot on which to sniff the air. In Ukraine he would smell rotting corpses, nitroglycerine and burning chemicals. The sky would be blue and black, the yellow wheatfields ablaze. In order to counter all these sensory losses, I would need different colours and smells. Petals soft to the touch. A bouquet of particoloured roses called 'A Carnival of Love'. These can be ordered through Flowers.ua. One satisfied customer, Sofia, writes: Чудесные розы! Свежие и радостные! Meaning, 'Wonderful roses! Fresh and joyful!'

They can deliver ten bouquets to the orphanage in Lviv.

It takes a while for the exchange rate to come through on Quin's credit card account – 1159 Ukrainian hryvnia per bouquet, or 45 AUD per bunch. The flowers are all addressed to 'Iryna Zarębina'. He was hoping she still worked there. Or that she was a real person.

Nevertheless, the staff and children would appreciate the colours of the roses. And the dogs would have a smell they would not have experienced for a long time.

Like some Ukrainian dogs, my father only knew war, imprisonment, drunken street-fights and unemployment, after having known the opposite. But no hard feelings. It's better to start from the butt-end. What I've inherited from him is a fatal attraction and connection between music and sadness. It is a deficit, a loss, because it always presupposes the 'I' as the receiver of music and sadness, when in fact, that 'I' is the giver of music and sadness and that is where it all goes wrong. There are few to whom I can give this, and as that rarely occurs, I am safe from damaging relationships and I am mostly condemned to solitude. In other words, the caged bird in my head hardly ever sings and never flies.

Existence may be made up of atoms of perception, the ones that had been retained, insignificant enough but perpetually disconcerting, ordinary anomalies, irrational clutter, a small thorny virus pressed between pages, the grey of an office door, the yellow fog of anxiety in a funeral parlour, the smells of embalming, not wishing to be dead, coming back to oneself...are corpses things?

LOOK WHAT I'VE DONE! Paul Boswell is yelling again. LOOK WHAT I'VE DONE!

He yells it with anger, pain, despair. The whole valley can hear him and people have learned not to approach him. It could be a cry for help. But then again, it could be a cry of achievement, unrecognised, pure failure, creation which can only arrive through pain. God may have yelled in the same manner when making a man out of mud.

Paul Boswell owns the property next to mine. He is one of the last gypsy Boswells in Adelaide. His most common response to anybody else's remarks was 'true enough'. It means he was sceptical. Of the remark; of truth itself; of the teller of the tale; who knows? But he does know that what is true and what is false depends very much on the fact that you are not confined to an institution; on whether you are free to judge. Otherwise the fluctuations between truth and lies are blurred like wild weather and illusory mists.

At two a.m. the dogs bark. Regularly at two a.m. someone is walking past the front of my house. It is Bartby, Paul's son who is half mad and who once called from a phone booth, ringing the emergency number, that he had overdosed on methamphetamine and that his address was my address. We shouldn't use the word 'Gypsy' for Paul. Instead, one should say 'Yenish' or 'Sinti' or 'Roma'. So the ambulance came posthaste and the dogs barked without letting up and the paramedics, a man and a woman, wanted to know who lived in my house and what was my surname and I started to mount a subterfuge as though I were in Nazi Germany and gave a false name which I knew would be checked against police files later, and I would have to disappear myself. Not go out for a while. Watching for the transports which came along the level crossing three times a night: ten p.m.; two a.m.; five a.m.

Bartby thought he was Spartacus. He needed a slave revolt. He also knew his father Paul had been incarcerated in the program known as the *Oeuvre d'entraide des enfants de la grand-route,* an organisation of boarding schools for youth in Switzerland, that peaceable land of fairy-tales and breadbaskets, whose aim was to ethnically cleanse bands of wandering ethnic children – ('surely wandering was a form of insanity? Gregarious and *Unheimlich!*') – by injecting them with methamphetamine. *Entreaide* – mutual aid.

Two a.m. A dog is full of synapses, reactions; reflexes. What we should never doubt is that they are more connected to the world than we are. We romance the world as cloud-sailors and are defeated because of that damned text called *language* in our heads, but in reality we love the silence, the angst, and are the first out of town when it comes to any other commitment. Is that not the fate of the messenger of the void? The passenger of narrative? That's when the dogs bark, isn't it?

Paul found out I was a professor and a writer. He asked for evidence. I delivered a book of mine to his house, a very English cottage on the edge of the grove next to my orchard. It was small, tidy and laden with rugs and carpets rolled and unrolled. There was something of an industry going on, and when I knocked he told me the letterbox on the drive was large enough to accommodate all letters and parcels except for lawn mowers, which he doesn't expect through the post. Yes, there was a stone pillar with a large slot above which was labelled *Circulars*, an old-fashioned direction to indicate community open-mindedness. Most others stuck up warnings: *No flyers or pamphlets.* But Paul was interested in community spirit and feeling, though he was the most cantankerous person in the area. Rightly so, if people of the area had known he was deposited in a mental institution at the age of five by his father, who believed his son was so bright as to be accepted free of charge in a fancy boarding school. Now Paul was toothless and angry and sported long white hair to his shoulders beneath his fedora. He stalks along the road wrapped in a red blanket and berates anybody within range. He engages them at first in simple conversation: about the rabbits and the flowers – those yellow roses in someone's yard he would like to pinch; the Council's laziness in not constructing footpaths. Then he will take issue with any opinion, aggressively staking out the opposite pole. If a car passes, he will refuse to move and will threaten the driver by brandishing his walking stick, which is of a thick, gnarly rosewood garnished at the top with a wolf's head cast in pewter. *My family's mad*, he will say. *They're all mad. Where does it come from? Somewhere way back. Lunacy. Inherited.* A good shtick like that balances ordinary life, Quin said.

He used to stop me on my bike, adding an extra half hour of interruption to my solitary day. *When I blink*, he would say, *I can hear the fluttering of feathers inside my head.* I wanted to tell him that it was a kind of Morse code for staying still; staying calm; for staying on watch. Time was ticking. What is still to come requires patience. Watch the fire. Watch the light. The doves. Listen to the flapping of wings. He was always on the move. He had four houses, all of them run-down and needing much repair.

Paul trapped rabbits at night with wire snares which hooked up into their necks and the more they struggled, the tighter the noose got and by morning, they were cold, not so easy to skin but easier to gut, then there will be curried stew for dinner, heartwarming winter fodder. Cold to hot, warm to bed. I thought trapping was a cruel process. Paul called this survival of the impoverished. He did not rely on Centrelink or charity. Charity, he said, was the worst form of any curse. You never recovered from that kind of curse.

Sometimes I'm not sure if I am Paul or I am me. But I am quite sure I'm using him as an imago of what I could have been or could be still. Going downhill, we run out of words, Paul and me. We don't know where the other is at, but there is some kind of reckoning with anger at the ancient past and with the world and with the humility of compromise.

We always move on. Gregariously. Besides there is always a smell of urine that comes with routine, as when he irascibly swings the bunch of rabbit carcasses up his driveway like a wet bouquet, anointing his yellow roses.

I understand his anger with his drug-addled son, his useless daughter who had a nasty dealer for a lover who kept her in cash while she watched television soaps and lounged in a dirty house, moving slowly, vaguely, withdrawing and then reappearing. It was not the way of the Yenish to have stayed in one place for so long. There should have been ponies to feed and water, tents to be pitched, odd jobs to be sought, new places to be savoured or fought over. But as I may have intimated before, it too is like that for me: I am flat, uninspired, I have no lust for life. Even endurance is too tiring, but there is no choice about that.

Just for the record, Paul said, *Norma came home aggressive and bad-tempered because she went to church and I had to supervise an excavation on the property as I knew where the taps, drains, underground wires were. It was not my lack of faith, but I am not the enemy*, Paul said. *That is how things have got to now. The blame is that I refused to be coerced into a public expression of faith as I have a private means of expression. Norma is led by the whims of our daughter. Children, even if they are in their twenties, continue to manipulate adults. This is the huge problem with aging and with immaturity, which occur simultaneously. And I will probably see more of this. Passion, precipitousness, ill-temper and importunity. It is mine to suffer as I prefer peace and order. I really do think this relationship is at an end now. I will call the police myself. Have her committed*, Paul said.

I was thinking Paul preferred trauma to peace and the ill-temper was his alone. You can hear him shouting from streets away. I do not know why an anxious shadow hangs over my life when I hear shouting. The double is the trouble; one is not oneself and not wishing to send a message to Paul about anger takes the double in me to the extremity of anxiety. I cannot even reach the outer courtyards of the city of anxiety. It is something one carries as a burden but also as a boon when the double disappears, for then the self is externalised and I am able to deliver simple messages to others. But then I feel like a fraud. It's like being drunk and is a great relief, but only for the moment when it occurs. Then the double always sneaks back in and convinces me it is better never to reach out to anyone or to even think there is a receiver or anybody else in a conversation. The Other is so impermeable and opaque that I become a camera revolving through the day, removed and dissociated, but leaving a spectre of dignity as the recorder of reality.

Paul says Norma is finally going mad. She storms into his bedroom and berates him about being closed off from her. When they argue she gets so enraged she slams doors so violently the glassware in the shelves fall over and shatter. He wants privacy. He wants to trap his rabbits in peace. He wants to tinker in the shed mending things that Norma has broken. He, though, is not alone in his ill-temper. Norma barges into the shed and demands that he sign papers to annul their fifty-five-year-old marriage. He sees that she has written these so-called legal papers herself in illegible longhand. He ignores her. They do not speak for two weeks.

His son has lost his driver's licence again and this time it is a two-year suspension. He drives his son to the beach at first, where he has rented out a house he inherited from a deceased aunt. They sit on a sand dune and he notices that Bartby is unable to put whole sentences together. The whole idea, he said was to be able to speak to each other, to get their lives in order. Paul likes order. But he does not speak much and when he does he usually shouts pithily with repetition. He needs to marry his words with action. He subscribes to newsletters which instruct handymen on the use and maintenance of tools, how to store them and not misplace them. For example, he learned that you hang them on a back board above the bench and then spray paint over the whole thing and *voilà* each tool has its own outline. He wanted to help his son, who is thirty years old, understand how not to misplace his life. Spray an indelible paint over him. Bartby looks at him blankly, with a smile on his lips. His father loses his temper. Wants to clout his son, but his son is made of muscle and can split huge logs with an axe and employs the same anger as his father's and it is better not to engage with him because Bartby believes in Spartacus. A revolt takes time. Paul always carries a knife which I've seen stuck in a tree at times, when he has had to remember where it is in order to skin the rabbits by the creek. Not a large knife but a skinning knife, sharp as a razor so he only needs two or three strokes to go up the hind legs, forelegs and the belly and then to take off the head. Paul could skin his son but goes silent. He does not like development of arguments or of frustrations. Sometimes out of kindness and pity he tells Norma not to carry a knife backwards, so when she holds it by the blade he says she might fall and stab herself. She yells at him for telling her what to do. Men are always telling you what to do. She will do what she likes and besides handing a knife to someone by proffering the handle is polite and considerate. He feels for the knife in his pocket. It is there like a good companion. Bartby smiles inanely because he knows what to do with a knife or an axe when the slave revolution takes place. He has been reading about it and has been watching movies on the internet and revenge will be all the sweeter in time. Like his father, Bartby does not speak much, but when he does, he invents or mixes up words, as when he said to me, upon disentangling a fruit-tree net, that it would take an eternity to *entwangle* it. A good word for a divorce.

I am moved all the time by music. All kinds of music except toneless music. I traverse Brazilian melancholia to Franck's *Quartet in D Major*. It is a language of my own, when no one is coming into my room, for which I am labelled agoraphobic, though I simply abhor the marketplace, the noise, the faux camaraderie. If only there were an impossible staircase like Escher's, from which I could have thrown myself and then find that I am ascending it again and again, with hope.

Paul shouts and screams and howls in the night while walking in the grove. People call the police. Perhaps he is being murdered? His son Bartby is certainly capable of it. He is Spartacus with an axe. But I suspect it is because Paul likes to shout too much. No one wants to talk to him because he only has his opinion and will not listen to anyone else. He wants you to know that his views are correct and true, as if you were deaf. He acts according to his will, but he cannot will others to agree. He, of course, *expresses himself*.

I can hear Norma in the stillness, murmuring to herself, a bird twittering in the night for fallen chicks and windblown nests, her children drugged and wayward. One's mouth is the mouth of a small stream, emptying into the vast ocean. Language can be the stream of memory or dementia. We live the life of rabbits: from moment to moment, and are happy when we stop fearing memory or dementia.

Paul once read a lot. I admire his past aspiration. He had a large book collection in plastic crates beside his house, leeward, he said, and he rammed into several of them while backing his ute. Now, the books weren't really damaged – remarkable how sturdy they are to all except fire and water – but Paul said they carried a hurt with them and should not be read again. He said most books carry hurts and curses and to go there was to court disaster and depression and reading didn't put food on the table, because books were unlike food, and it was food which alleviated almost every ailment, both mental and physical. Like his pipe, which calms him down. His Amphora tobacco in a perfume jar. Like his miniature paintings of clowns on the backs of cigar boxes. No more words, he said. Just different depictions of clowns; sad, happy, mocking, mocked; funny to children but always murderously misunderstood. I looked at the clowns. Our people, Paul said with a sly smile, would always grant one wish to a friend. He did not add that it may not be what you wished for, like a child of yours you did not know existed, something repressed, a letter that you wrote which though received, will never have a reply.

Books carry hurts. Ancient Greek *phora* – *φορά* – *carrying*. Paul has an immense belief in the real so he understands that the real content of life is the carrying of burdens. Metaphors lighten the load. Like alcohol is to the heart and brain, time to emotion, melancholia to memory, his gift was for metaphoric enlargement, taking pleasure in the transfer of trauma. But that is as far as he trusts words. Numbers are far more profitable. And I am his listener, imagining him already in the grave, burying stories. On these days I can smell the earth receiving me. I do not draw a straight line under my life. It is a squiggly line to the edge of time: electricity through a curly filament; not heat but mortal light. My wish is often for extinction. In this sense I've connected with Paul. He says life is all pain and that's all there is and it only gets worse. More pain. The good thing is that you get to forget. But like insanity, you have to do it alone. Counting helps. Count the days; count the nights; count everything. Weigh it all up and assess the bottom line like an accounting book; a double-entry. Did you get through without a loss? True enough, Paul would say.

My father the accountant, the journalist, the impresario of lives. I should have said to him that bee-keeping was far better than book-keeping. At least it was far wiser, since bees are wise beyond vice.

The thing that keeps me going is Iryna. I share and carry her hurts as well.

The previous norm was solitude. Fear of the marketplace. Which is not fear of the social but of bargaining. The social is not imperative, though people like to make it so, just in case they get terribly lonely. But they simply haven't trained for solitude and that makes them reliant on chatter and company. Chatter and company is always a bargaining. Someone is always trying to get the better of someone else. Hold court; see how entertaining, witty, hale, likeable, attractive, I am. Dogs, for instance, don't actually enjoy the pack since it is fraught with domination, backbiting, submission and rebellion. They pack together out of fear of being hunted down alone. That is their bargain and it is a better one.

You be careful, Paul said to me when he spoke to me about Norma. *You*, he emphasised, poking his index finger at my chest. Did he mean her dementia would cause me personal trouble? Would she complain he's poisoning her? Cooking her rabbit curry with Rat-Kill? Small things happen in small increments. *Look what I've done!* The dogs are barking. I expect sirens at any moment. Shouting neighbours. Flashing blue and red lights. A knock at my door by fluoro-vested authorities. All true enough.

After all the shouting, on the Sunday of the next week, the two of them were walking to the church like scattered stars in a darkening empyrean. For Paul, it was not faith but superstition: he belonged to all denominations and attended different churches on different days. There was thunder and I was heading home. He was striding out in front, having lost his driver's licence, she ten paces behind, muttering loudly that they were going to be robbed by leaving home. Did I look like a robber? Did I steal lives and bury them? Small things happen in small increments until they reach the next crescendo. I slow down on my bicycle and take the first available corner behind them before they see me.

I do not want to become someone like Paul. He reads the cards, he says, but I do not want to know what he sees in my cards. Lots of spades, I would think. I now smile at people on their *passeggiate*. It is perhaps because I have sent some flowers to Ukraine.

Dearest Abe, How delightful your present of flowers! Our orphanage is full of them and the children are delighted! Oh how you make my heart lighter, knowing someone from the other end of the earth cares and concedes that civilisation understands that barbarism is not the norm! I hear music again, since I have been deaf all this time since Witold went east and threw in his lot with the Asov regiment. I have a bouquet in my apartment and the perfume is delirious. A carnival of love! He bought me flowers when he first met me. I can imagine you now, and the pain is reduced by at least one degree, maybe even more, because you are a simulacrum of the past. I have seen your image. You are a kind old man. An old Witold. My ever kindest regards, Iryna. PS: the dogs have become gentler and are forming bonds. Their tails are wagging, finally, and they lick the children's faces.

But flowers wilt, and time, which may heal but also fades, reminds Quin that a man of the moment very quickly becomes a has-been in-between breathless commas of age, the comatose moments of the twilights of gods which used to flicker in and out of a life without remorse. We can die at one a.m. or one p.m. Not a great hour for a lifetime of feeling. A kind old man is an irony. He who doesn't understand his grumpiness. Who wishes to be alone. To be with oblivion. Yet ever doubting what could be, knowing it could grow ever worse for what you wished. And there it was. Youth has suddenly gone to the hell in which it began. Is not birth that moment?

In the Citizen's Military Force at the university – we were called 'The Weekend Warriors' – we bivouacked in long grass and got our faces bitten by hordes of mosquitoes so we looked moon-faced, as I already did, so there was no discrimination, those who could not shoot through no fault of their own, but because their 1970s FN (*Fabrique Nationale*) rifles from Belgium had bent sights and went off target in fully automated mode, got to do latrine duty. I never did latrine duty because I was a sharpshooter who shot one round at a time, or as a *franc-tireur* as the French would say, adjusted to the conditions, not that I was frank, but at least I was sharp. The field latrines were quite awful but doable if you sat over a log and let the trench and stench do its work. Nature was always amenable to my nature. Shoot one at a time; shit one at a time. The platoon took this slogan on. We were effective in the jungle. In boarding school it was second nature to avoid the dirty toilets, which were only cleaned once a week, and seek the ones that were broken, cracked or choked with toilet rolls. The cleanest were the ones without toilet seats. No one used them. But I did. Not to sit on the porcelain rim but to squat over it, developing strong calves and thighs, which I did over my squat toilet in Hong Kong. The problem was that the other boys, who went through the toilet block with canes and switches, whacked those who were shitting. When they discovered there were no legs and no trousers in my cubicle, they climbed upon the adjoining toilet to peer into my privacy. Chinaman! they yelled. He's not used to Western sitting-bowls! Which were of course, filthier than any squat toilet, since in that position you didn't miss the target. And if you did, there was always a bucket of water to sluice the foot-plates. Birch switches were useless in this geometry; like a cavalry sabre in a jungle. So I can imagine what a wartime ablution was like in the field and in the house-to-house fighting in Ukraine. There was no time to do up your trousers if the sirens sounded. And besides, you did not hear a high-mobility artillery missile or a thermobaric bomb if you were unlucky enough to be relieving yourself. Shit yourself later if you were surrounded. Then swallow the bullet you saved for yourself. Drunk enough for heaven, they say. And do it alone.

I don't have much else to say for myself, Quin said to himself. It is much easier to die at seventy-four than at twenty-four despite all the heroics of the latter. Immortality is so much more a lie now, rather than a myth. So too is *pro patria gloria, mori*.

Then again, I used to clean toilets and glean ironies and while Iryna Zarębina will not be that girl in Frank Moorhouse's *Forty-Seventeen*, according to his lyric account of an older man–young girl relationship, I still dream of a Platonic emulsifier, smoothies which old hacks like me still use; a credit card; sartorial splendour; charm and wit; which will always please younger women.

In Olenivka prison they moved the most rebellious and suspicious prisoners to a warehouse block, which was then supplied with new water tanks filled with accelerants and set on fire. The men were burned in their bunks, too disabled to flee, too wounded from their torture to crawl out. Witold was among them, Michael Lincoln wrote to Abe Quin. You are my cousin. I share this with you, knowing you may write about it. So be it. Now, it is unclassified. Civilisation or barbarity: it is not a choice.

Daša Drndić, in her book *Canzone di Guerra*: *In the early nineteen-fifties, around two thousand Ukrainians, former soldiers of the Galician division, an exceptionally fanatical organisation of the Nazi regime, were allowed into Canada.*

The main thing, Quin wanted to say to Iryna, is that the truth should not be abused.

Unlike his cousin, Quin doesn't believe in good guys and bad guys. There are only bad guys. Instead, war is the norm and in a war you have to be bad. After that, everybody harbours a past that is mostly distasteful, like soured wine or the fishy smell of blood, with only a memory made out of words, the most common of which is *incognito*.

Learn the wrinkles, my neighbour Paul said to me when he came to replace the windows in my hut, which I called my 'pad' but was now my 'studio'. When building a paling fence, Paul said to me, rub your tomahawk in the soil or grass to give it a stickiness. Then your hammering and cutting won't slip and miss. Paul played the bugle as a hobby and had elastic bands in his teeth. He was pitch perfect with plangent Gypsy melodies. It was a terrible sight when he ate. You always had to look away. True enough.

I have to learn the wrinkles. So I don't slip and miss. When writing letters, whether they are belles-lettres or not, rub in some dirt and grass so you are in touch with reality. So your words don't slip or mash in your mouth. Cut true. I want to look after you and your daughter, Iryna. Even for a very short time. My dogs are showing a return to their dogness. They bark, chase and hunt again. They do not hang around the house in front of the fire. Instead, the three of them sit in the rain waiting for me to finish writing to you. Then I take the walk back to the main house through huge puddles of water. They wait for me at the top, follow me into the house. Shake all over the walls. I hope you will not mind this when you get here.

When he took lectures on Milton, he remembered that Professor Wilkes said God's providence, divine guidance and control, was actually about provisioning and foresight and previsioning by man. Milton was implying that you had to cure yourself and provide for yourself. But there is much available outside. Learn to be self-sufficient and you will never be wanting. Learn the wrinkles, in other words, do your own ploughing and listen to the seasons and the land. The harvest will come and you will thank God by overlooking science. Learn how not to slip and miss, not to be taken prisoner by grief, to cut through and to cut loose.

There had also been loves he could not requite in his past. He kept going somewhere when she, or another she, would want him to stop, to say *let's go to my house...or to yours?* But he never answered or asked anything like that because to stop still on this question would be cruel, and curious about seeing how far one could go. It was not him. Courtly love. Refined love. Non-aggressive love. Keep moving. That was more like him.

Now he was asking her to his house. Perhaps to read Proust in the afternoons, aloud, over a few glasses of wine. Once, in a reading group, after several meetings, a few members started to have pulmonary or cardiac failures. He stopped smoking cigars. Stopped drinking. Stopped the reading groups.

Aging is a mess. Best to get neat and tidy and do it yourself. With lots of style but with caution.

But think of the near past: mentoring girl students some of whom I would take to long lunches in the East End where there were many gourmet restaurants to choose from and then wax lyrical after a wine or two and in the heat of literary finesse find that the life I needed was just this mixture of solitude and encounter; mind games and projected futures; but not relationships, and certainly not the jeopardising of any person's career. I didn't care about my own, but never got close to being reprimanded; I loved rumour without proof. Literary festivals; love without materiality or even touching; no haptics; chivalrous departures. I retreated from girls who were too insistent. I agonised. I drank. I imagined. And that was the best thing that can happen to a writer.

I used to love the cold and the wet winter weather. Now it makes me anxious as though I were about to die. It's strange what age can do to the mind, let alone the body. The mind withdraws into angst and this condition becomes more and more the norm; uncertainty, pessimism, unease about sitting on the ground for fear of not being able to get up. I don't think I can do a squat toilet anymore. Nor can I travel on an aircraft for more then two or three hours because the anxiety of the toilet trip would turn the journey into a nightmare. In toilet-world at the back of the plane, people are particularly untidy and unhygienic, and with my bladder I have to go often, wash, refresh, re-attire. There is no regular cleaning of the toilets by staff. There is often a pool of pee on the floor. So it is better not to go there, to perform the parade across knees and down the aisle and wait by the occupied box while the plane shudders and one has to retreat to buckle back into the seat according to the pilot's announcement. One has to be compliant as well as uncomfortable. And these days the literary festivals are a form of dread as well: uninterested audiences; ignorant or show-off type questions; mobile phones that people had forgotten to switch off. The only camaraderie was with older writers who wondered why they were doing all these gigs in competition with the twenty-somethings, the theoretical or the glamorous, the former elucidating chiasmus or aporia, the latter, usually blonde, criss-crossing their long spandex legs as if illustrating the frustrations of sexual inversions and the perplexities of idealists.

On the seventeenth of July 2014, Malaysian Airlines flight MH-17 flying over Hrabove in Ukraine, was shot down by a Russian surface-to-air missile. On board was my writer friend and his wife. Nobody survived. I therefore have an investment in the struggle in Ukraine, I wrote to Iryna. In footage of the body-recoveries, I saw an arm and a wristwatch amidst the wreckage. Time stood still at that moment, and the minute before, the steep fall into the Ukrainian farmland.

Iryna replied that she had witnessed body bags arriving in several refrigerated railcars in Kharkiv. She also said she was very depressed and sat motionless for some hours every day in a kind of apoplectic concurrence with traumatic anamnesis. Lapsed time and real time passed without notice. She saw Witold's face; ambition in his eyes; he was technical and logistical. He could speak Ukrainian, Russian, Polish, English and German. He was working under an assumed name in the separatist regions, the *oblasts* sympathetic to Russia. The FSB was able to trace and track him through informants. Iryna thinks he was cornered in the Azovstal steel plant in Mariupol. The wounded and the sick were 'filtrated' into Russian territory. The others, of which Witold was one, were taken prisoner and transferred to a prison in Donetsk. There they were beaten and starved and the survivors moved into a warehouse which was then set alight. An escapee (who had turned informant and was in peril of his life in the prison), phoned his own mother, who then phoned her sister in Kyiv, who phoned...and at the end of the party-line or the grapevine...it was learned finally that Witold had been burned alive.

We always phone our mothers, mostly when we are about to die, Quin was thinking. Although he was not one to communicate with the dead. His mother smelt of oolong tea and fresh flowers until the dogs knocked over her urn and her ashes slowly slid into the dam. The dam was built in 1943, as part of the war effort in the Adelaide Hills. It was on a large pig farm and from here they made Spam for the Pacific theatre. American soldiers loved Spam. It could also lubricate a rifle and waterproof boots. War again. It never left him.

In order to live, we need little life. In order to love, we need much. – Joseph Joubert, 1793 Notebook.

Quin was in a train in Sydney, visiting his publisher and then his lawyer. There was a young woman opposite him, who had the saddest face he had ever seen. It was so mournful that it had a remarkable beauty, as though the pain of what she was feeling turned her into a portrait of a grieving Madonna. Perhaps she and her partner had just broken up. Perhaps someone had died. He emitted a great sympathy without staring or appearing rude or curious. He simply nodded very slightly. The girl looked at him and then at his former wife sitting next to him. The mournful Madonna seemed to relax a little, to feel slightly more secure that someone had silently and safely understood something. She then alighted at the next station.

The significance of mourning is its utter uselessness, until it is relieved for the reassurance of memory.

Quin and his wife had been estranged for some time. There had been an interlude when he found himself wandering the streets of central Sydney, lost in anguish, lost in his bearings, unutterably alone. They had discussed breaking up several times. She had applied for a job in another country. He had applied for a job in another state. Vengeance had become too near for either to dwell in the same house.

Thus Professor Abe Quin accepted an invitation to give a few talks in China.

The National Museum of Modern Chinese Literature in Beijing was an imposing Stalinist building on 45 Wenxueguan Lu, Shao Yao Ju, Chaoyang district (朝阳区 芍药居 文学馆路 45号). It had many lecture halls, a Great Hall and chronological rooms of author artefacts, their publications, their desks and inks, their photos and even their cigarette packets. Most of the honoured were dead. There were only a few under the age of sixty. In Australia, the old made way for the young. It guaranteed a juvenile legacy. In China, the young had to earn their way into being old and honoured. It would be hard to imagine a similar museum in the Western world, the anglophone world, where writers were less honoured than bitched about. There were sites of interest, in Sydney, for example, where Henry Lawson's erstwhile 'cave', in which he spent nights with the DTs, was noted in tourist guides. Now full of cigarette butts and the odd used condom.

A new idea for Quin: in China, acknowledged writers had pensions. Of course some were anointed; others ignored through their politics or their bourgeois decadence. The thing that most impressed Quin about the National Museum of Modern Chinese Literature was the toilets. Here were rows of cubicles kept meticulously clean. Indeed, he noticed an army of cleaners who emerged from their smokos every fifteen minutes. The toilet bowls shone, were much lower than those in Australia, had water more than halfway up, which meant no splash-back and a secure evacuation. He didn't know why Western toilets were designed to be punitive rather than pleasurable: high, wet and easily soiled. Yes, the Chinese knew a thing or two about bodily functions. Indeed, they used to read the Emperor's poo to divine the future of his rule.

Speaking of which, Quin's hotel was the Jade Garden, only a block from the Forbidden City. He decided to visit the Imperial Palace and queued for a ticket then wandered aimlessly in what he thought was the path to the main building. He was completely lost in the vastness of the ponds, lakes, avenues and steps. He didn't know enough Mandarin to ask directions. He could speak in Cantonese, but nobody understood him. It was as if two peoples inhabited one country. Like Canada.

Perhaps the point was that the Emperor's residence could never be reached. There was no centre. A message from him, in the other direction, would never be delivered. The crowds of people made it difficult to orientate without a compass. The signs were almost non-existent. Maybe, Quin concluded, it meant that navigation made you think rather than speak. That being lost brought on an eternal anxiety as well as an unending flânerie, which forced one to observe immediacy, faces, shoes, the narrative stream of movement, all of which created an uneasy feeling of never arriving. Without centrality you could not be attacked. His mother was like that; unknowable and decentred. So Quin sat down on a stone wall by a small lake and watched the golden carp patrolling the reeds beneath the water. He was a fish then, in search of a mother. He would never find her again. No one remembers the pain of the mother upon the birth of oneself. Thereafter, existence was a strange experience of grievous bodily harm.

He was a stranger in China just like everywhere else. Only in China, a lot of people stared at him, and a couple dressed very colourfully once approached him in English, smiling and asking if he were Uighur. He shook his head, but they were unconvinced, and kept smiling as they melted lightly into the crowd. Two young, very beautiful people. Yes, China was an enigma for him, both familiar and massively disquieting in its acceleration into the future. What it would sacrifice for that, as what it did in the past, was frightening.

Quin decided to find the Hyatt, which was reputed to have a great restaurant, great wines, great steaks. He walked along the main boulevard, which was hardly easy as boulevards go, not only because of the crowds, but you had to avoid tree roots, ungrated gutters, smoking joss sticks that a shop owner had laid out on the pavement. Cars careened disconcertingly up onto the kerb. Then suddenly, the Hyatt. He thinks it's an oasis. It would undoubtedly cost a good deal. But he was determined to have a good French wine, oysters from Australia, a steak with bearnaise sauce. He was immediately accosted by a head waitress, who moved incredibly fast from the other side of the dining room. She asked him in good English whether he wanted lunch. Yes. He was taken aback by the swift smile, the stilettos which didn't seem to touch the floor, the unfurling of a huge napkin and then she asked for his credit card. He fumbled a bit with his wallet and placed the card on her silver tray, which seemed to appear from nowhere. Perhaps she had hidden it between her jacket and her white silk blouse, and if he touched the surface it would be warm. She bowed, took it away. He did not see it until he had completed his meal.

All of which made enjoyment, gustation, lingering between courses, impossible. Such a difference from the toilets at the National Museum of Modern Chinese Literature.

I shall send Iryna a photo of my dogs. There are now three of them: Kafka, Murphy and Djuna. Djuna is a little smooth fox terrier whom I rescued from the pound. She is very lively; too lively for me, but her unlimited energy is good for memory and distraction; distraction enables a faulty memory to recover. She's brought me a dead bush rat since, according to her, I was not good enough to hunt them. It is not something of which I approve, but it's a gift nevertheless. As an incompetent human, I am encumbered by words and she knows that jumping up on my lap would be much better than the words I use to console myself. So I shall send Iryna photographs of my dogs performing their various antics. Like Murphy shooting off along the banks of the lake after some noise and suddenly everything erupts in the water: ducks fly, herons screech, cormorants dive, and there are mysterious geysers and ripples for quite a while after. He follows behind me when I investigate, without out-guessing me, without reflection, ready for action. It is anxiety of a differing kind. Positive, not backward...existential happiness a clear and present thrill. There are plenty of emotions out there for which to forage.

Marika, Iryna said to her daughter when she picked her up after school, *a Chinese man is writing to me from Australia – yes that country furthest away from us, thousands of kilometres away – a man who is a writer and who was a professor, has invited us to holiday in Adelaide, which is named after a German queen who also became queen of England in the 1830s. You see, the Germans and the English were always in and out of bed with each other. Should we take up the offer?*

Yes, mumiya. You already sent him flowers.

Carnations. Because his dog died.

How did you know where to send them?

Got in touch with his publisher. Why do you want to go to Australia?

Because I'm scared of here and I'm tired of the school where everybody pretends to be normal but is damaged inside. My friend Galnya screams for no reason and last Friday she went up to the roof of the school and wanted to jump off but the teachers talked her into coming down. It was like a real drama performance. Her father was also killed in the east so maybe that was the cause, but I don't believe so. She is just acting spoilt to get attention. We all want attention from the teachers but we don't all act out selfishly.

The first snowfall of the season. It was another coming winter, Iryna wrote, since the Russian invasion. Many of Ukraine's cultural luminaries have been killed at the front. During the last winter in Kharkiv, it snowed for almost five months. There was a lot of blood in the snow, alongside musical scores. At first, the blood was bright red, then pink and then yellow like the scores, Iryna informed Quin. It was then that I learned anatomy through war. I also learned how to read music.

It was another strange vision for him since he had always associated snow with a kind of Yuletide joy, roasting chestnuts, skiing trips and his first serious relationship with a woman.

Lutum fecit ex sputo dominus et linivit oculos meos (The Lord made clay with spit and anointed my eyes...). Quin remembered his Latin from the plainsongs he had to sing during mass in boarding school.

So I didn't know, of course, that the ski trip was already organised by my half-sister and her friend Sonya and that something was going to happen which they knew well in advance, because my father had written that something *had* to happen to me and would my half-sister get some help to create this scenario where, when this thing was over, they could all write about it? They would send aerograms whizzing across oceans, paper planes in their light-blue thinness, almost translucent so anyone could, without tearing them open, read the ball-point indentations backwards or in a mirror, and decipher the whole ski trip during which something would happen at Thredbo or Smiggins or Perisher and during which time I would learn to snow-plough or climb slopes forming herringbone patterns in the powder or descend, executing stem-Christies, parallels or simply schuss into a tree and get myself well and truly killed – but it wasn't going to happen that way because my father wrote that this had to be *well-planned* and it wasn't going to be about skiing since I was a slow learner and that the trip would be a significant experience for me and because slow learners don't really understand what experiences they are having at the time anyway. My father seemed to think: it would be a waste of time teaching him how to ski, better to get him into the mountains and slowly – he tried to italicise with lots of underlining – you would educate him, which was what he wrote to my half-sister who now shared all the aerogrammes with her friend, *slowly* he *will* awaken to the fact that he *is* a man since it has taken him *all* this time at university reading books and losing his eyesight which we all *know* is caused by the *imagination* – you see, he is *haunted* by his imagination – and will you *please* get this friend of yours, Sanja, or whatever, sounds Russian – you know, I knew some terrific Russian girls in Harbin who could skate the pants off any man, but my grandmother told me they were just escaping the great Manchurian plague which came with the railway... anyway, get this Sanja to collaborate with you to cure his blindness, but the best thing is to check it out first, as to what kind of blindness it is, whether it is ignorance or introversion and not inversion, and don't do the experiment on your own because you know how *that* will turn out, get a friend, preferably a friend who is not too close, but *someone* – as you say, Sanja would be a good bet – who is older than he is, who can handle the game and take some fun from it, like lead him to one of your favourite haunts blindfolded or something and *reveal reality to him*... and mind you, doing him this favour would last him a lifetime, so that's all from me for now and I remain your loving papa etc... And thus it came to pass that the three of us drove to the snow and at Perisher I had a small bunk in the chalet and the women had the big bedroom and there was a lounge with a fire beside the French windows outside of which the snow was piling up and I felt very cosy and excited that tomorrow morning we could all ski out the front door to the bottom of the ski lift and then I would learn from Sonya how to disembark the chairlift properly and then ski off to the left over some easy slopes which would soon begin to get steeper, mined with moguls, and where snow-ploughing wasn't going to work that well, so firstly Sonya would teach me to do a 'Christie', which is some kind of beginner's trick: forming a wedge by rotating one ski outwards from the stemmed ski and by shifting your weight to the right, let's say, opposite to the downward direction, then making a V in reverse and then drawing in both skis to the parallel position perpendicular to the slope, you slowed before plunging again. Easy. I must say Sonya was a good teacher, patient and caring, and while we were doing it there was a brief moment when she bent right down in front of me and held the tips of my skis and we skied down, she going backwards gently and I feeling very thrilled in this position and then she let me go and I fell a few times but by the end of the day I was turning Christies, which is a name derived from Christiana in Norway (not Denmark) where it was first developed and now, back in the warmth and comfort of the chalet I went into the large bathroom by the big bedroom, luxuriating in the hot steam. I then went next door to sit in the sauna and suddenly Sonya came in totally naked and sat next to me so casually that I thought this was what one did in saunas and tried not to notice her nakedness though I had the beginnings of an erection beneath my towel, not missing the point that she was very blonde and her nipples were dark and this sent me into a curious swirl when just as suddenly in entered my half-sister also entirely naked who sat on the other side of me – my half-sister who was very dark and her nipples light. As the steam rose around us the two women began a conversation about skiing that morning, and as Sonya was showing how important the downhill ski edge was in turns, she placed her hand on my towel, and my half-sister was leaning on my shoulder to absorb Sonya's expertise and before too long, covered in perspiration and steam, I was sandwiched between them, my obvious desire proving something to my father, at the same time releasing my half-sister from subscribing to *Man* magazine and *Penthouse* for the express purpose of leaving them under my pillow because *obviously* I wasn't too bookish *now*, and was instead covered in embarrassment, though Sonya was kind enough to wipe me down and as a much more mature woman, comforted and cuddled me while my half-sister smiled painfully and left the sauna to go to her bedroom, somewhat disappointed, I think, that the experiment was so quick and easy, and on the way home none of us spoke very much, so I presumed it had all gone wrong because they couldn't establish an understanding between them – not even about skiing! – and I grew silent as a sphinx until we ran out of petrol and the trip began to unravel as a disaster since there were no service stations open and I, having now become a man, finally got out at one and knocked at the house behind the shop and an Alsatian dog was suddenly lunging at me from behind the heavy glass door before a grumpy old woman with lilting German like she came from Bavaria brought out a can and filled it for us and at that very moment I felt that Sonya liked me and would have wanted to continue our relationship while my half-sister sat sourly in the back seat betrayed by this new liaison, since in the dark Sonya was driving with one hand and placing her left hand in my lap except for when she had to change gears, the two of us playing a game of naming one's favourite novels and I could imagine my half-sister writing to my father saying the experiment had failed, that her half-brother was definitely an invert, too obsessed by books, and though he may look normal, the books are definitely holding him back from normal life, that when my father eventually arrived in Australia he ought to force me to play golf or go to the races and they would all arrange girls for me to take out on these occasions, sporty girls who would teach me how to breathe underwater and do handstands on the lawn but of course this never happened because in less than a week after his arrival, my father asked Sonya, whom he still called Sanja, to accompany him to his new club where he would give her five hundred dollars to play the pokies, since he thought five hundred Australian was worth the same in Hong Kong dollars and so my mother and I stayed home sitting up late, watching television – I, who was suffering an exquisite jealousy though no longer blind, could at least now parallel ski in tidy tight turns in my imagination, sending up puffs of powder behind me so that I gradually disappeared from view.

Robert Walser understood snow best, when at the age of seventy-eight he walked out into it near Herisau, intent on taking his daily walk from the asylum, and lay down in the snow forever, Quin wrote to Iryna.

Here is a photo of Djuna the smooth fox terrier, and me. The other dogs cannot be rounded up as they are males and tend to be solitary.

Djuna is a realist with her wedge head, and a poet amongst dogs. She has her rhythms, habits, doing her rounds. She checks the fences for rabbit diggings, finds the scents of koalas who are also checking their territory above ground, puzzles over the ducks on the dam who are too fast and after all, can take to the air. Djuna likes a beer and was once caught drinking Guinness out of my stein. Guinness: established in 1759; the year Wolfe beat the French in Quebec, decimated the Indians and died in the process, and in the process, revenge will bite back eternally. No more. No more. I cannot cope with the inundations of history. I have to look after my dogs much better. You would probably agree, Iryna.

This was supposed to be my year. The year of the Tiger. In fact, it is the year of the Water Tiger. That is probably why things have gone awry, since I am born in the year of the Fire Tiger. So this year has been diametrically opposite to my Chinese sign. Fire Tiger years come only once in sixty years. This was never going to be my year. I should keep a low profile. The only good thing going for me is relationships. Great if you're young. No country for old men. Adventurous but realistic, Fire Tigers can also be easily deceived since they trust others too readily. Perhaps because I've missed my moment in life I do not like to talk much. So friendships are difficult for me as there are no models to follow. I do not know what comprises a friendship, since the very word describes a kind of acting, as if one cannot be entirely oneself. Without this stage-play, there can be no friendship. There is only a confessional relationship or a power relationship.

Dearest Abe, The last photo I have of Witold was the one I took on my phone the day he left for the east. I discovered it buried there in an unnamed file. He was waving with his back turned to me as he got on the bus, so I didn't know if he was waving to me or to his comrades who were already on the bus. He was so thin, and death was dancing in his eyes. As soon as I saw the photo, I started to cry like mad. I was still crying when I fell asleep. The night before, he was saying that all the sadness that goes into a separation will ultimately emerge as a sickness.

Quin has been busy doing his research. He discovered that the Ukrainian government was closing down orphanages to save money until the war began. So war did have unexpected benefits. He searched through all the Children's Homes in Lviv for the name Iryna Zarębina. After a few days he found that in the Municipal Institution of the Lviv City Council, 21 Tadzhytska Street, Lviv, 79038, there was someone with the same name. Painstakingly, employing the Cyrillic alphabet, he found an image. He was pleasantly surprised. His heart skipped a few beats. Was this really her? She was not blonde but was a brunette. She looked like the Polish actress Karolina Wydra, who had a role in the medical drama *House*, though of course Quin had never watched American shows, least of all crime series or vampire movies. But there was a resemblance to the forty-one year old actress, given the angle of the photo-shot, the slight defect in one eye, and the seriousness of her expression. But you could never tell, since the willingness to believe in his own fantasy only led to an unfinished reality, an unsatisfying suspension. He would never dare to ask her for a selfie. Iryna would probably say it was inappropriate, and their correspondence would be at an end. It was simple to be deceived, but difficult to hide his awareness of being deceived.

My former dog Molly was so trusting and was even happy to visit the vet and she slept in the car when I went shopping and when she needed me I was missing. I lacked the surplus energy at the end, which is something the aged cannot summon up because they are too tired to be bountiful and every hesitation is a failure of trust and the world becomes more tragic, and life and death become less available for love and grief, and then suddenly, you go missing when you're needed, trying to retro-erase sadness for an impossible, happy, future in whatever minuscule time is left.

Dearest Abe, The autumn counteroffensive has liberated my home city of Kharkiv. I am joyful, but not overjoyed. As you know. The irritation is that I am getting distanced. A kind of dissociation. I don't know what I'm feeling, that I'm self-censoring because I just want to escape my life. Warmest, Iryna.

The thing, I always say to myself, is that I'm in this isolated bubble, that in my mid-seventies, I'm tired and cannot do too much. I'm tired of production, of striving for *the big work*, the big show. I too want to escape my life. Like Jean-Luc Godard, who opted for euthanasia in Switzerland. I think instead, I would opt for carpentry in my workshop. If I could drug up the pain. But of course, those who are dying would say this is an ideal and not real. These are different kinds of bubbles.

But now, life. LIFE. Because Iryna indicated she would like to visit me. It is not something bestowed on Professor Quin; aged seventy-three; divorced three times; no children from known natural causes; carer of three dogs, possibly of more; esteemed author of thirteen books; lover of the victimised; sympatico; non-argumentative but playfully championing the less-accepted case for sainthood; ill-condemned romantic; able to jump off a cliff if challenged to a duel.

Kharkiv has been liberated!

Dear Iryna, I would like to deposit some small amount into your account to facilitate your visit to Australia. Please let me know your details.

To Ricky Dupont,
DFAT, Australian Foreign Affairs and Trade,
Querido Primo,
Nice to hear from you. I want to sponsor a Ukrainian family, mother
and child, the mother widowed and the child disturbed. Is there any
way to fast-track a visa so they will not linger longer in a purgatory in
Lviv? I would be most grateful and remain your *primo* with the usual
saudade for our families and lost places. Yours, Abe Quin.

Quin sent this as a handwritten letter in a stamped envelope. He knew
many hands would open it before it reached the addressee. That way
it was an open secret.

So the Ukrainian counteroffensive retook her home city of Kharkiv.
The locals were rushing out to present bread to the soldiers. Flags
were flown. Other flags torn down. The President himself drove to
congratulate the troops and to pose for selfies. It was triumphant. But
there was a lot to do and a long way to go. The President had a car
accident on the way home to Kyiv but was unhurt. Unlike Italo Svevo,
who was killed by his chauffeur in an encounter with a large tree.
Italo Svevo; Schmitz was his real name. A Jewish-German Italian who
had young James Joyce as his English tutor. Addicted to cigarettes
which didn't kill him. Inspired by repetition which didn't kill him.
Enamoured of failure, which didn't kill him. Got famous, and rushed
around in a limousine, which killed him.

His pseudonym translates as 'Italian Swabian'. He was painfully
working on his self-identity and never quite got comfortable with
how it slipped through his fingers. Which is what happens to people
who agonise. Over everything. Some people, Quin was thinking, just
agonise; with different parts to play and with different voices. It's a

big part of Jewish life. And identity is the greatest agony. If you don't pretend. Pretence is the easiest of gimmicks; since it is a web of lies. Quin can do pretence. *How're you mate? Thanks buddy. All good. No problem.* Assimilation. But he can also do the police in different voices: the working title for T.S. Eliot's *The Wasteland.* Good cop; bad cop; authority and prophet; believe me, this non-compliance in poetry can land you in a garbage-skip picking out dinner; the end of the world as we know it. Ultimately, a web of voices can lead to a hollow man. Then you had to sit down and write, if there is anything left. On the agony couch or in your green leather armchair doing overtime in the bank or publishing house just to avoid the mad wife at home itching for an argument because you didn't want lentils again for dinner.

So the Queen has died. Knowing that pomp and ceremony would come after coma, it would have seemed valueless without being present to dispense some grace, a gloved and royal wave or two for all the effort. I doubt if it made much of a splash in Ukraine. We will all die and some of us will keep fighting for our anonymity. It's best to keep below the radar...like Adorno, with small aesthetics and exaggerated polemics which revealed beguiling truths.

But you can't talk about any of this. It's like brain fog for others. In one of my previous marriages she would always say: 'a penny for your thoughts', and I would say it's worth more than a fortune, my thoughts, and I would be irritated that thoughts should be bought, toted up, as though at the end of the day (that's another phrase I hate, since there's no end, for in battle if you fall asleep or try to doze you will be bayonetted in your sleeping bag at two in the morning), some kind of bookkeeping of thoughts could be weighed, as though production was the most important achievement of a writer and that words could be bargained for weight and achievement balanced against failure, since for me, all was failure and failure was my glory and any Protestant ethic of work equals edification was anathema to me since work only equalled *macht frei* over the gates of Auschwitz and failure was my right and my duty and it's okay to keep failing, since the goal of a book was never achieving it, because in doing that achieving you were betraying the best part of yourself, that is, the inexpressible agony of not being able to even start.

Dearest Iryna, I wrote, I wonder if I could employ you as my amanuensis since I can no longer remember my own dictations and write words I find alien to what I was really thinking. That way you would be in employment and I would be relieved of a deteriorating condition and Marika would be in a good school...a Steiner school just close by. In secondary school, it is called Waldorf education, also known as Steiner education, and is based on the educational philosophy of Rudolf Steiner, the founder of anthroposophy. Its theme is holistic, intended to develop the pupils' intellectual, artistic and practical skills, with a focus on imagination and creativity. Yes, he attacked anti-Semitism in Hitler's Germany and advocated biodynamic agriculture, which appeared apolitical, but he also cannot be forgiven for promoting a total assimilation of the Jews in his anti-Zionism. In this way he was walking a tightrope, but was not imprisoned by the Nazis, avoiding the wire-snare set for him.

Franz Kafka: 'The true path is along a rope, not a rope suspended way up in the air, but rather only just over the ground. It seems more like a tripwire than a tightrope.' (*The Zürau Aphorisms*)

Everything does come back to me in memory if I detect the fragrance of a woman's perfume or of old wine. I told Iryna this and she responded that she had a weakness for Ralph Lauren's Polo Black, which was an aftershave I suspected Witold may have used, but I did not ask about that and she did not elaborate on it. *Nevertheless*, after some months, with the victories in the east and south of Ukraine, this seemed to me to be the beginning of an intimacy and a trust – the alienation and reciprocity of correspondence *notwithstanding* – these Middle English etymons, occasional collisional words – *notwithstanding* – intrigue me, like the fragrance of Polo Black – like an unforeseen car accident driving home after a match – *nevertheless* – the leather and tweeds and the aftershave before the evening fire – sentiments after the fact – did not Putin also aspire to such fragrant empathy, champagne and *class-coldness*, notwithstanding?

But I haven't stopped smoking class-conscious cigars. It comes upon me when I need reflection and *The Magic Mountain* brain fog in which I can summon up all of Mann's nostalgia. I have however, stopped too much physical outdoor work. I cannot lift heavy logs or chop redgum in one stroke of the axe. I now take two or more strokes and sharpen the axe more times than I swing it. I am a procrastinator, when once I was an achiever with a long list which was fulfilled by the end of the day. Instead of mending leaks in the roof I put up an umbrella (after buckets were no longer feasible, since having to empty them made a menace of my lower back), and then the ultimate solution was to resort to alcohol, because alcohol made everything disappear until the next day, when slow plodding took hold and streams overflowed their banks and one thing or another overwhelmed the day.

I didn't realise I was saying all this to Iryna in my writing and that I was burdening her with my old man trivia and that I should at least realise she was in a much more perilous state than my real estate.

But courageously, she understood and wrote back, first about her father, who died of colon cancer, and then about her grandmother, who having endured the Holodomor, the terror-starvation in Ukraine caused by Stalin, died by alcohol poisoning forty years later, probably as a result of constantly reliving a period of cannibalism. Iryna said her grandmother told her how village after village was ransacked by the local authorities, ordering the Kulaks, the wealthier peasants, to do the dirty work like cleaning up the dead bodies. The bodies came apart when tugged at. So they burned all of them, some still sitting up at their empty tables. She said her grandmother told her how a terrible silence came over the entire region. All the cats and dogs and worms and grass had been eaten. The most fertile region in eastern Europe had been turned into vast deserts of snow and unburied corpses. No one had the energy to talk. The sign of starvation was always a thick silence, which fell like night after the last whimpering of the children, since they could not send their children to the cities to beg for food. Then the terrible thaw came and bits of bodies appeared like signposts to hell, the thick, unmistakable and distinctive smell which never left your nostrils for the rest of your life.

Iryna, God bless her heart, counselled him to slow down, to take things at his own pace and to take pleasure in animals. At the end of the day, nothing was worth killing oneself for. This was chastening. Quin took this on board. She was caring for an old man many thousands of miles away, she who had no father of her own; and now, no husband. He needed to step up, stand up and be counted.

My mother was a hunger artist; not because she wanted to be noticed as such, but because she wanted to understand how drastic her own experience of famine was in comparison to what she was observing in these comfort days: gourmet nouvelle cuisine; diet fads; her husband's motto of living to eat. She wanted to do away with aspiration through starvation. Only then did the brain succumb to the meaty scramble of the heart for attention. Then dementia solved that for her. She simply forgot about eating.

When he was a young man, Quin used to experience certain moments when an attractive young woman (ideally blonde), took an interest in this shy and non-macho man who invested a great deal of attention on women. He glanced at them fleetingly and listened in silence, nodding periodically and making low sounds of agreement. He would always be reading a thick book…William Empson's *The Structure Of Complex Words* for example…and they seemed to find this warming and honest, though Quin would be the first to disagree. There are no more of these moments now, but he has a dream now and again, of winning the most desirable girl in the room, he, despised by all the other jealous males, and she would say I love you, in his dreams, and he would say I love you too, and for the rest of the dream he was looking for his hotel and a private ensuite planning to meet her again *through preparation*, since rehearsal was everything in courtship.

Iryna wrote that Mariia was not coming back to Ukraine from Sydney until January next year, that she had found a fellow Ukrainian, another vet, a younger woman who had clicked (*vlashtuvalysya dobre*) with her. Mariia has extended an invitation to Iryna to stay at their Clovelly flat if she were coming to Australia. *What do you think Abe? Should I accept?*

Quin replied that it would be a great stopover on the way to Adelaide. And would it be okay for him to send some funds to her for their journey?

But for a long time, a matter of two weeks or so, there was no reply from Iryna. Then she emailed to say Witold may have been alive and may have been exchanged in a prisoner swap along with other Azovstal fighters. In her next email she said she was so overwhelmed with joy when he rang her to say he was in Ukraine. She could not believe it. She didn't recognise his voice, so much had he suffered. He was on his way to Lviv. There were emojis with hearts and flowers.

So there is a happy ending of sorts. Quin felt bittersweet, an emotion that he understood was chronic in his life. He got up on the roof of the main house, slid and almost fell. He found nail holes and squirted silicone into them. He was shaky coming down on the ladder.

I am alone again. Without emails from Iryna I cannot live from day to day because I have lost the aim of life, let alone the aim of writing. Why write when there is only a prolongation of reflection? Why write when wisdom is exhausted, and the body is exhausted and Pasternak's dictum that every novel is a woman is now outdated in its very premise, since no novel by a very old man can sustain the fantasy of being driven by a love affair. Foolish Falstaff! That is how I see myself now, succouring the young Prince Hal, only half suspecting his deceit and betrayal in taking me for a fool. But I am prophylactic to my own productions since pessimism had already prepared me for failure, from the time I was born. Yes, the womb was where it nested and bred. And failure is really the staunchest friend. Who would look askance at me? Who would find this withered skin a kin to that young fellow of twenty who once danced the jitterbug swirling girls so their skirts became revolving fans of colour and scents? How quickly a relationship disappears in how short a time! How tempered a look falls into disrepair or plumpness, enlarged livers and sagging jowls; how simple the transition between charm and jaded calm, when the weather changes and the rain rolls in and all there is lies in the cemetery beyond the hedgerow where the silence is only broken by birdsong at dawn and dusk.

He was not going to write the novel of the great affair generated by the great Russian novels. He would have to wait to come into his aging. His mother waited; and waited. She always had a clock, a large alarm clock beside her nursing-home bed. When she woke in the mornings, she wound it up. When she slept after midnight, she wound it before bed. Then she forgot to wind it, once, twice, then always. She slept more and more. Time went still. She waited: for the BBC news bulletin; there was a lot on Dag Hammarskjöld, the UN Secretary-General. She waited for the Rediffusion news; for Hong Kong Radio news. She waited for him to come home. Not her husband, who was long gone. She waited for Reggie, the ginger-haired RAF pilot stationed near Kai Tak Airport in Kowloon City, who paid her several visits, all very proper, for afternoon tea, as her son played with the model Spitfire Reggie had brought him for a present, buzzing the fridge like an ice-wall, whitegoods always cool to the touch in their arctic resistances, while inside, in the freezer compartment, there were the survivors of a forced landing, pilots placed there previously, frozen solid in his imaginative wars. And then quite abruptly, in the same reality, that Hong Kong humidity of sweaty British servicemen, their armpit odours tingeing the afternoon with the violence of missing fathers, taught him jealousy.

It is important to be serene in everything you do. From getting out of bed until retiring into it at night. I am more alone than ever and therefore have to take every step with some consideration. No one will notice if I disappear. So it is with some bemusement that I regard the rabbit in the grass who is only fulfilling his hunger, but cannot afford to relax as he does it, ears and eyes ready for endless flight and it is his survival not to be noticed, sometimes freezing, not in meditation but by conserving movement in not attracting attention. For this very reason, I decide not to travel again. Travel is a means of attracting attention. It puts paranoia under a lot of strain, especially when going through immigration. There is always guilt, but guilt is the least difficult layer of anxiety. The most serious is *wanting* to be suspicious. In other words, the death-wish of looking so dubiously like a terrorist that officers who believe they are trained in such detection always succeed in grabbing a nervous person, rather than a real terrorist or smuggler or spy. But another thing about travel is that I notice all the other passengers are incredibly selfish and bloody-minded. They overflow their seats, take up extra room, cough and splutter into other people's airspace, emit their body odours in extremis, bump and push their luggage into confined areas and do not worry about body language, noisy conversations, politeness when alighting or boarding. Once when Quin was helping a young mother with her baby and luggage, an Irish priest told him to get on with it and to move on down the aisle, since the priest had no time for women and babies. Another time a fat salesman told him to 'hang on, Charlie' when struggling with a suitcase from an overhead locker. Then there were the nursery rhymes mothers sang to their children; on and on; over and over again, for a whole two hours. People stared a lot at Quin since there was nothing much else to do, particularly if he walked up and down the aisle. Sometimes there wasn't even alcohol. For Quin, alcohol relaxed the rabbit's eyes and ears and the endless flight seemed quicker. In any case, alcohol made up for thirty years of bickering: the gender battles were hard; the practical versus the emotional; the war was never over.

Once in Paris I went into a bric-à-brac shop, a *brocante*, and found a menorah and crystal glasses and purchased them because I had a feeling they were stolen by the Nazis or by Céline the writer, or whomever, and boxed them up and sent them home like dead bodies, and later in my library, I drank out of the glasses simply to understand their afterlives which were entering my body, all the pentimenti that had been done to them, and I knew then that I wasn't forgetting that the world was neither poetry and truth, nor dream and reality, but nasty actions of history painted over suffering, as Joyce said, *palimpsestuously*. And so travel was equated with layers of suffering for me and I have never lost the taste of travel as grimness, historical displays of the worst of human nature.

There are, of course, relationship matters. Whenever dealing with relationships, there will always be arguments. The longer the relationship the more numerous the arguments. Human nature is about dispute. Dispute arises because of self-interest, laziness, the *domestic* history of painting over past experience. Relationships are never easy, though they may seem to be in the first years. Then if insensitivity accrues, they harden and encrust life with an irreversible progression. And all life is a sort of progression and then a regression, when it is too late. So people in a relationship never look to caring about how forward or backward they go. If they manage the present in unspoken terms, they are lucky. If the unspoken frees itself from repression, they are lucky. If other joys like sexual health and understanding occur, then they are lucky. But the worst is resentment. *Ressentiment*, as the French say, is a cancer that is under the skin. That way, not only divorce, but hatred, hides like a survivalist cockroach between the floorboards. That can never be eradicated, like a bad temper that is an uncontrolled itch, an eruption, an infinite volcano of rage and burn.

It is best, when thinking over his past three marriages, never to say too much. A quiet relationship is probably the wisest. Maybe even an epistolary one. Dogs, for instance, don't say too much. Except in extreme mourning or joy, they howl or yelp; their expression is then much more valued. He likes quiet women and men. He understands their understanding of quietude. Their acceptance of manner and speech. Their mystery. Talk for them is the quickest way towards a separation of souls.

But now I miss the talk between men and women, having isolated myself for quite some time, since death had entered the scene and since I have been enjoying my *finca* in the cemetery, which allows me to listen to the voices of the dead and the three-note fluting of orange-beaked blackbirds and having cut myself off even further, let alone from the difficult encounters with Paul, I have had no *dialectic*, until my correspondence with Iryna, thus externalising my inner self into the discipline of observation. The correspondence with Iryna was like having a real relationship, where awareness, dispute, agreement and sensitivity all went hand in hand, and I even imagined walking her around the valley, pointing out all the peculiar (to her) Australian fauna and flora bred of my long observation, and we would both be curious and enlightened because there would be silences in this walking together, which spoke of a certain consciousness, both singular and communal, before breaking out into questions and answers, exchanges which would bring my self-questioning to an end. During the time of correspondences I did not once think of my father's revolver or the need to consider it in its drawer, and proved to myself then, that I was not writing a slow suicide but encouraging an inflammation of joy from a distance. Such is the growth of brief hallucinations, which may not be seriously harmful to existence, but should probably be left to dissolve by themselves in a contraindication against excessive self-medication. Exaltation is almost always brief.

What I mean by this is that today I discovered a white ball of foam at the bottom of my large ash tree. At first I thought it was some leaching from the graveyard, but upon closer inspection saw that it may have been slime flux, which is a bacterial infection growing inside a wounded tree. Inside my wounded tree, in which fermentation is occurring, carbon dioxide is released and alcohol can form.

On the other hand, rain can dissolve chemicals from the tree bark and foam forms at the base of the tree, the surface tension creating white bubbles as I also notice in creeks. So there is tree foam and rock foam.

I prefer to think of the latter, which is more positive than the former, and rather than fermentation from within, I am simply gathering the surface tension of the world, a nervous stemflow which harmlessly deposits soap suds at the base of relationships.

Perhaps Quin saw himself as a purgative for wounds, but more likely, as he had once graffitied on a toilet wall, he was smugly enacting what he decried: employing ethics as a detergent to excuse himself from any further communication with Iryna.

Instead, Quin finds himself reading about the history of Lviv, once known as Lemberg under the Austro-Hungarian Empire, then it became part of Poland and was briefly called Lviv during the Ukrainian Republic in 1919, but again, it was returned to Poland and named Lwów, then in 1941 it became Lvov in the USSR of Ukraine and finally Lviv as we now know it, Iryna being incorporated into the city's emigrant and transient existence. Ukraine is still winning the war against Russia, but for how long? What twists will eventuate? Quin waits. The young are flooding the book markets with weightless reading. There are very few catafalques; sarcophagi; wooden overcoats where there is no war; it's all overdone and easy for them in the West. This is because publication doesn't have real consequences. In war-torn countries it can mean life or death, which removes the indulgent candy of self-destruction. There is smell. You literally write your own warrant about experience. Who is up to the task when you know you are playing for keeps?

I'm not happy about going to the doctor. I feel sick before I go. I am reminded that *pharmakos* means both *poison* and *cure*. Once there, I try to avoid blood tests, faecal occult blood tests (with all its vampire secrecies – Cristóbal Colón was fascinated by those in the New World in 1492 when he landed in the Bahamas), encouragements to undergo 'procedures' – and by the time I leave I've decided to do none of these invasive things for my own good, but am fixed on feeling better as soon as I'm freed of them and take myself to a healthier world riding my bicycle through the hills and gradually, even the warm exhaust emitted by the closeness of cars feels refreshing and less menacing, since each overtaking car is an achievement of having survived death, followed by a lessening of fear and finally an erasure of it and a joy of ghosting amongst traffic without angst. The soul loves superhuman freedom embalmed in the warmth of extinction.

He once felt a strange freedom in San Francisco. He was in a cheap hotel which didn't have food, though you could order from the pizzeria next door, which closed early and opened late. As he arrived at night, he had to go look for a restaurant. Outside one an African-American man was arguing with a taxidriver and it was turning violent. But Quin felt strangely unperturbed and calm and perhaps he had had too much to drink on the plane, but he took the black man's side and said taxidrivers always gouged their fares and they needed some standardisation of their meters, and at this, the driver backed down and the African-American man struck up a friendship with Quin and they had a meal together and spoke about jazz, and as it turned out, the man was a musician, a pianist, and he knew some of the best in the business, saying Quin should do the nightspots with him sometime, and of course Quin was very flattered and of course he paid the bill at the end of the night.

In the morning, he still couldn't find a good place for breakfast, but walked into Market Street, which housed all the druggies and the drunks still sleeping off the night before in the gutters. Again, that same calmness in him; no angst; no special alertness. He was in a Dantesque underworld and nobody hassled him and he imagined he must have walked like he too was drunk or drugged, weaving and ducking like he was in an imaginary boxing match. He quite enjoyed it but then came across a very large African-American man lying on the pavement and it appeared he had just fallen over and was holding out a hand to Quin for help, or was he? But at that moment Quin became lucid and knew there was a good chance of being robbed as he was much smaller than the man on the ground, so he stepped to one side and walked on. And then he felt a terrible shame. It kicked in like it always did, for much of his life; the shame of over-wariness; of suspicion and self-preservation. He interpreted it as a very Chinese thing, this reading of danger, this *inscrutability of foresight*. Nevertheless it was a shame; a human stain of alienation.

And besides, it was all about accounting for deficits; counting and accounting; credits and debits; all Confucianism and Mencianism and the public service of duty to the people; long before Communism, which is so Chinese and not Chinese, as you needed the communal will to service the people and then the people became viral offenders to the commonweal and then anarchy came and aneurysms of greed and corruption and finally, neo-liberalism and the people starved and died in cold-water flats and alleyways and you wondered what your aims in youth were, those silly ideals which are now reduced to simply surviving the next bully in the age of oligarchs.

This is all down to the regression of age. Shame recalls childhood in all kinds of circular motions. I once naively asked an Auschwitz survivor what it was like being there. He looked at me with some bemusement. It was very ordinary and routine, he said. People behave the same way in or out of the camps. I did not believe him and thought he was taking the micky. But I didn't know what he did there or how he survived, maybe as a *sonder commando*, those who collected the bodies, and having weighed all that up, decided horror was pretty ordinary once you're deprived of freedom and food and dignity. In boarding school there was nothing of the first and the last. Food, though, caused fights, and the thump of fists landing on someone's head was an initiation. Brutality is ordinary. Death is ordinary. It is as ordinary as a small child being caned for a slight misdemeanour. It is as ordinary as an abusive, dysfunctional family; as ordinary as being homeless or walking alone to the airport after a divorce. It is a matter of scale, the horror, then the greater horror. Once you're inured to it, through drink or otherwise, it regresses. That is, if you didn't know what was ahead of you. The unexpected shrinks mental reality. Looking back, experiences fit into all their different sizes. Bach knew about this accounting. In the end, his rhythms all added up like a double-entry.

What Quin missed most was what Dante called *intelletto*, the immediate rapport and understanding expressed by a woman with the gift of speech; in other words, sensitive and loving *understanding*, which took the place of mute male understanding, and which *understood* by expressing. He imagined Iryna possessing this gift; he fantasised about their walks in the valley; he forgot his age. And then he understood his pathos. Emotive words were not what he needed. Cognition wasn't it either. Bitter experience, perhaps. But then, he was tired. Wouldn't it do to remark the foam at the base of the ash tree, the rakali swimming up to the bank looking first like an otter and then a rat, the mallard grooming its feathers within a hand's breadth on the grass?

No it wouldn't do. Because of the writing which needs its drills and practices and tries its notes upon the time left to me. And then Iryna wrote. *He has changed beyond recognition, Abe. He is no longer the man I knew. He was changing even before he left Kharkiv. But now he is morose and angry and lashed out at Marika. It is something I cannot tolerate. Marika and I are living in the 'internat' until he calms down.*

It is a burden that can be shared, Quin wrote back. And it will continue for a long time; perhaps even after I'm gone. Because a connection should not be broken, as I've broken them many, many times in the past. It's now beyond phone-lines and cloud signals. In these circumstances it's beyond the ludic, which at times I've found to be of help to me.

No longer. After catching Covid on a flight to Sydney for a conference, he suffered a brain fog, which came in like dementia, a void without a middle C for guidance to the centre of the musical universe. He lost his perfect pitch and he lost his usual skill in playing with words and coupling etymologies to invent new wakes for old Finnegan. He was plagued by opaque dreams and night sweats when he found himself floating over Niagara in a barrel. He aged in six months. His eyes grew bags above his cheeks and his hair turned completely white.

His eyesight was getting worse. Bats had a lot to answer for, but as for eating them...yes, some delicacies are deadly, like torafugu, Japan's favourite poisonous tiger puffer fish, which is more lethal than cyanide. You dice with death, but it is said to bring good fortune...if you survive the painful fugue that comes after, which is what post-Covid feels like to him, exhaustion like a bad hangover; forgetfulness; he wrote as much to Iryna; it was like PTSD, and so Witold needed to be treated; who knows what he went through? But it was the wrong thing to say to her, or perhaps Quin had lost some of his delicacy since his illness, because she skewered him with her intellect and poured out her passionate scorn for Witold and all men, those who go to war to be with men in order to die as brothers; it was foolish to think he would ever be the same man she knew and he was already thinking about going back, to the south this time, as soon as he had recovered physically, she wrote, her words erupting in a more violent manner than Quin had ever encountered in letters, which he had always considered a gentle art and not a ruthless attack, her reiteration that Quin had been too eloquent about war, and now, what was worse, he was defending the self-destructive violence of her husband! It was too self-centred, she wrote, sending Quin into taking umbrage, taking to his bed under the barrage of her anger, so that he had this strong urge to open an umbrella above his bed for security and comfort since this epistolary relationship was now wearing thin.

What he was missing was *fun*. It's a funny word. From the middle English *fonne*, that is, to cheat, make fun of, jest, fondle, folly. Iryna was not, at the moment fond of fun; obviously. War is also fun; a game; a dice with death; a *fugu* or fortune; a soldier of fortune. The games people play. Quin wasn't going to present this interpretation to Iryna. But under his umbrella, above his bed, he was floating downriver in a barrel without laughs.

In the morning he went back to trying to play Schubert while his dogs howled. At the same time he was thinking that canines don't survive as long as bovines. The average life of a cow is twenty years. A dog would be lucky to go at fourteen. EGBDF in the treble clef, *every good boy deserves fruit* was weak though melodious, and short-lived. Goodness quickly turned to the rottenness of fallen fruit. ACEG, *all cows eat grass* was far more stolid; the bass carrying its weight in space. And so, he gradually weaned himself from the loss of Iryna's emails. He was Charles, not Emma Bovary. He was not clever in affairs but he was plodding towards Bethlehem. There was a possibility of redemption for the rough beast. He wrote to say he was sorry for his gaucherie. He should have minded his own business.

Which he can do in letters and emails; disappear, reappear, remain hidden, pop up when needed, great for second-guessing, reading between the lines. It is a relationship of sorts, but not a real relationship since there is no presence, no body, no body language to note, no voice to gauge emotion, no charm of accented English. There are only dry words remaining. The Dry Salvages, *les trois sauvages*, a bunch of rocks off the coast in Eliot's Quartets. And words can act like savages, excoriating and then resigned. But much is missing in this shell of typography, ebbing and flowing with the tide and movement of sand: for one thing, the absence of sexual invigoration and submission, the yin and yang of coupling, the frowning brow upon orgasm and then the huge release of happiness inside one another's bodies, unloading rocks off the coast, exhausted, blessed by divination and satori. And then from such lofty heights, play begins again.

That was years ago. How quickly age, illness, death can enter!

She wrote back, mollified. *My daughter and I will come to you*, she said. *I'm much in need of a holiday.*

On the beach, the bottoms of his trousers rolled, he felt the surge and suck of the water, his feet capsizing beneath wet sand. He was already planning to bring Iryna and Marika here, to the Fleurieu Peninsula, where the wild beaches stretched between rocks and bays. They would never have seen such a coastline and the Southern Ocean in all its moods. Everything needed to be planned. He bought a camping swag and rolled it out inside his hut and he liked the comfort of it, the built-in mattress, the sleeping bag inside, lying amongst the books and firewood, and his dogs came in to lie down as well; a clean, well-lighted place with a small chest of hidden whiskey. He called a cleaning company and they washed and tidied the main house and he thought he would not use the main house too much, so it would be welcoming for his new guests. He was excited; he had a project; he was busy.

So I'm thinking: it can come very close this thing called death and it can be very trivial as well, since I can step down steep paths onto the beach here at the Fleurieu wild beaches, and what a name, that Frenchy who explored this coast and there are certainly wildflowers, both blue and white up on the cliff paths and how they can also herald a funereal colour in the wild wind and I go back into the warmth of my Rover and turn on the engine and think to myself I could fall and die right there in front of the car and not many people would come this way and maybe I would be found a couple of days later, maybe a week later when the salty winds would have washed over me in some kind of preservative. But right now I'm not ready to die because I have a purpose and this purpose fills me with life and quite suddenly I'm thinking of practical matters, how I must buy a second-hand car for

Iryna so she could explore all of this South Australian coast without me tagging along, a coastline which is surely one of the least touristic but most interesting in the whole of Australia? But she would have to drive on the left side of the road in a right-hand drive car, not on the right side of the road in a left-hand drive car, which is the case in most of the world except for the few Commonwealth, former British colonies, like Australia, which are exceptions to the rule.

I'm worried about the way I feel in the mornings. Ill until eleven, recovering by noon, drunk but still lucid by six. I will have to correct all this. Then there is the constant angst, or dread as Kierkegaard described it, the 'dizzying freedom' of nothingness. But is my anxiety a prelude to sin, or is it my salvation? All this, I have to weigh up. Embracing it, I must not judge myself. Because I have to leave this open book, this book open, for Iryna's sake.

In battle, you have to watch your brother die; in battle you cannot help your brother as he is dying; there are arms and legs everywhere; in battle you have to move fast because they are shooting at you from the woods; in battle you smell the shit and the blood and sometimes you can't feel anything until the blood fills your ears and your eyes and then you are grabbing at the wet earth with your right hand, rubbing your head into the soil, having realised you are hit and your left arm is gone.

Funny how paper letters are always associated with wars or disasters. There are no happy letters except bland ones...the phatic ones, to stay in touch (or not). The last tragic letter Quin got from a relative was that one of his cousins who had joined the Marine Corps in the US had his leg blown off in a training accident. But somehow Quin is starting to like emails rather than paper letters, since he can express things more rapidly and not go over each line, agonisingly poring over his syntax or burying hidden meanings and poetic messages. He can write without remorse and with very little correction, which is not a good thing, but hey, emails are a form of repartée, a brief dialectic not to be mulled over, nor kept or drawn out later for literary love-making. There's no shaving mirror in emails and little reflection or imagination, but plenty of bitter experience. Since he grew old very suddenly, he's stopped caring about his belles-lettres, his toilette, his dress and his appearance. He was once dapper and elegant, they said. All that effort and no romance ensued. Now he's not even nimble-minded and is simply dogged, plugging up the hill on his bicycle, never giving in, never getting off to walk.

Even ordinary life, mild life, gentle life, lucky life, was a battle. But maybe this will all change when Iryna and Marika arrive. He will have a family of sorts. The house will become noisy with laughter and music.

Hardly had his joy begun when it was short-lived. The Russians were firing cruise missiles at Kyiv again, hitting civilian areas, and Iryna wrote that Lviv was without power, so she didn't know if her emails were getting through at all because she couldn't charge her phone. The orphanage was blacked out as well and walking the dogs in the small garden behind the building was a hazard when air raid sirens were a constant, their wails frightening the children huddled together in the basement. The smell is terrible. There is a lot of whimpering and wailing, and the teachers and volunteers are holding onto the youngest children, trying to comfort them when they themselves also require some soothing, not knowing exactly what to do in this waiting period when there is nothing much one can do, let alone move around in the filth and darkness.

Schoolchildren should not be brought to heated classrooms; they should be made to attend abattoirs; it is only from abattoirs that I expect understanding of the world and of the world's bloody life.
Thomas Bernhard, *Frost*

Well, Thomas does tend to exaggerate. That verb *exaggerate* means to heap or pile up or accumulate. He doesn't hoard or store, he's not a minimalist, but he emphasises and magnifies and repeats and goes beyond the limits of reality in his own universe, but he also intensifies and aggravates to stimulate the *névrosité* of smugness, which is always beneath the bourgeois skin, when people refuse to see the absurdities of human behaviour. He's been a good friend for many years and accompanies me on our walks through the woodlands. Indeed, there is a pocket book of his called *Walking*, which I always take with me.

To cure sundry ailments, go to the abattoir and drink a cup of warm blood. Quin's father swore by that remedy and forced his son to take several spoonfuls of horse blood each day. There are very many viruses in animal blood. It's probably why Quin's haemochromatosis was causing him fatigue, joint pain, and a lowered libido.

The Ukrainian winter will be grim, he wrote to Iryna. *Please come soon.*

All of this over-activity was wearing him down. Finally he did the blood test and it came back with urgency: the liver of course; that renewable organ was tired. He couldn't admit too much to the doctor though the results were there in plain sight. He couldn't admit there was no life without the whiskey and the routine dullness was killing him faster, at the end of which was the revolver, five bullets in the chamber in case he missed, took out a jaw, a cheekbone. He would have to attempt rude health by not speaking or imbibing or imagining. Empty out all the wiring in the head, stop wandering in the caustic lunacy of words. He would have to be dumb to the door-knocks of adventures and misadventures. At least he had stopped smoking after the fire. Now, to give up mirrors was the next step: no reflection or signalling; just sit and watch the rain; close the door against ambition.

Yesterday he erased his diary entries; a whole twenty years' worth. No point to them. One thing good about computers was that he didn't know the first thing about recovering files lost in the ether. The thing was to resist the temptation to salvage all the savagery from the sea of lost time. Yes, he was tired and was winding down, himself and the clock. Dementia may not be such a bad thing to get if it relieves him of all the nightmares, those dreams of bad toilets, wartime eviscerations of buildings and bodies. Fatigue came upon him more and more often. His balance was unpredictable. The bicycle was a liability, but a tool for health, the doctor said. She knew paraplegia and quadriplegia lay in the worst recesses of bike accidents – she had seen enough of them – but she said nothing to him. You can scare some but some are beyond scaring. In the end it's all about economics. Death costs money.

'Describe; prescribe,' he said to the doctor. You people are too scared to prescribe another addiction less harmful than the previous. Give me paraldehyde; naltrexone, it's the mildest. Don't self-medicate, the doctor told him. But Quin would write to a friend in Canberra who was a pharmacist and who was dying of stomach complications. *Gavin, can you send me enough boxes of the mildest anti-alcoholic drugs?* It was warm in the clinic and he was composing letters to the ferment of smells. Chemistry must be an interesting science of trial and error. Vasily Grossman was a chemist before he became one of the greatest of all war writers. He wrote micro scripts on tiny bits of paper. The rest he committed to memory. In this way he avoided the Stalinist trials by not committing to writing 'errors' that would have sent him to the Gulag. An old man next to Quin in the waiting room said he would hate to be a doctor and have to deal with the dying constantly. Yes, *in cineram redigi*, that's life, Quin said. 'What?' 'Reduced to ashes.' 'Very pessimistic,' the old man said. 'No time for hope in an age of apocalypse,' Quin replied. The waiting room fell silent. That was the result of climbing above one's station when the train of chit-chat had already departed.

Trials and errors. Hospital toilets were okay but best not to linger there even amongst cleanliness and order. Any complication was a threat. Do not press the red button, mistaking it for the flush. You may find yourself wheeled out into a cancer ward of no return. At the university Quin once wandered into the women's toilet and a pretty professional staff member came out of a cubicle. She didn't scream, but said softly, 'Professor Quin,' in a rather husky voice and he came to his senses. He should have undergone training in orienteering.

He didn't know why toilets obsessed and terrified him. (Perhaps the tell-tale wet patch in front of his trousers told him that toilets were always too late and unpromising.) Perhaps because in Hong Kong he lived in Flower Market Street (now named Second Street, New York style), which had nothing of flower smells or flower stalls in it, but was full of chicken slaughter and wet lanes, and from the kitchen window you could see a football oval on the opposite side. He went back there in his sixties and found his flat was a now a public toilet, still opposite the football oval; the too-late toilet; on second thoughts. Outside, you had to put up your umbrella as the residents above tended to empty their cat-litter onto the street.

Back from the doctors, he sat at home in front of the fire and meditated upon living among drunken greats like Lowry, Thomas and O'Neill. It would not be enlightening and there would be a steep learning curve on how to die slowly, with dignity and cleanliness. Never think about writing without a pen or pencil in hand. But something was missing. Giving a shit was really important. It's not the same as taking the piss. Not just relief but a sense of wellbeing without mockery or deceit – honest excretion and full-strength urination made you fit for the next drink after the first, that lull and buzz before blankness blanketed thinking. That was the time for conferencing without aggression. Conciliation and arbitration took place best after a relaxing shit and then a bottle of good whiskey. That was also the time for ideas, a time to write. A good toilet like a momentary window, was also a still, a health-giving respite, rest and mental revivification.

The trouble with balancing his addiction to alcohol through good toiletry, Quin decided, was that you needed a project, an aim, a *plan* which took the place of despair at four in the afternoon when the slaughter of sensibility was at its worst. Yes, sitting in front of his fire, not a fire philosopher but a fire architect-designer, he would map out the most desirable toilets, preferably in an exclusive club, most likely in Japan, where they are obsessed by toilets, a country club perhaps, not pictured on the internet, toilets for a secret society of super-wealthy golfers, etc., then work from this design as a template for lesser clubs and hotels around the world, all the way to airport toilets and lounges. Ordinary people deserved the best. A good toilet was a great leveller and a teacher of good grooming. The Romans knew this. They sat together on outdoor toilets and had interesting conversations and instead of reading the news, they *brought* the news, all sorts of gossip, and beneath the shitters ran a fresh stream and around and above them, parks and gardens, birds and bees, all the renewables of life. In Paris in 1843 a patent was taken out on a toilet fed by the heat of a pigeon loft whose currents of air were funnelled through aromatic plants, emerging into a lavender-scented private *cabinet* on the roof. So Quin, the fire-philosopher and toilet-architect, started by sketching floor-to-ceiling cubicle doors; air supply and quiet extractors; choice of music; Japanese-designed bowls with built-in bidets and temperature-controlled sprays, flushing with a foot pedal; lavish sinks with automated taps at the right volume and heat; motion-activated handwash; heated handtowels; anti-mist mirrors; a scale model electric train which circled the anteroom on whose flatbed carriages stood all kinds of aftershaves, lavenders, disposable combs and razors; and most importantly of all, a small army of quick and silent cleaners every half-hour. Happy times in the midst of miseries. Sanity through sanitation. Perhaps the Chinese President Xi Jinping got it right when he called for a 'toilet revolution' in 2015. Like Mao, who said a revolution was not a dinner party, Xi took the politics out of public sanitation and made it a point to personally inspect country toilets to see if the squat-pit was still in use.

Had there been happy times? In his life? He supposed there were, but they were not in his memory. There was excitement of course, but that was not the same as happiness. Happiness may have been an emptying; of mind, of words. A white-breasted shag on a branch waiting for fish. No, he couldn't remember anything pronounced or prolonged. The fish swam in, the shag dived, life went on and on. And death too. He had seen much of it and how quickly it can happen, not necessarily the clinical lingering in monitored wards, but the motor accident, the mortar shell left exposed that blew the guts out of an older cadet on bivouac as he bowled it against a tree like a cricket ball; the pallor of his face, the fading eyes. Today, one of my dogs killed a rabbit and tore it from limb to limb. The carcass was very red on the green grass. It reminded me of the distance I had come, from living an animal life in which the seed of adventure was indifference, to the mannered and meditative inaction of age. Could any of this represent happiness?

There are bits and pieces of rabbit here and there. I shall not bury them because they will be exhumed by all manner of creatures in the nights and early dawns. Instead, nature will bleach the bones that remain and after a month or two, it will be like an anthropological excavation and there will be a certain happiness in that discovery; of a time of violence and its remembrance, and marking time, as in marking places, a continuance, like writing, that filters out disgust with an understanding of the betrayal of words; and surely that understanding is a kind of etymological joy of discovery? Of being released from a prison? Of having already betrayed? A dog, who without words, is truer to its nature.

It is thus, that without alcohol, I cannot be true. The blandness would be ludicrous, and therefore the human element, sociability included, would be false and worthless. My nature is of intoxication by both words and the chemicals of ethanol. It is as ancient as Zeus and beyond. So I would like to presume that religion is as potent, if not worse, since it doesn't second-guess its own drug and certainly never questions its dependency. Religion is sex without guilt; missionary-prone, procreative and therefore frighteningly potent, leading to infinite potentates and continuous pseudo-happiness beyond individual extinction. Theogarchy is the power of the future. The god of one-in-me, not three persons schizophrenically and communally spreading out power. There is no categorical imperative. Religion is beautifully built like an automatic rifle and just as universally deadly.

Iryna wrote that she doesn't want anything from me except a place to stay for a few weeks with her daughter while her own country is threatened by a nuclear event. It is legitimate, she said, that revitalisation and recuperation in preparation for the fight ahead be strategic. She can afford the trip on her own. I therefore understood that my role as mine host would definitely be distanced and professional and was quite happy with this circumstance. I was reminded of my father, who had a number of English 'secretaries' in his line of work, a Mrs Morris or a Mrs Robertson, or a Mrs Harbulow. They were always referred to as 'Mrs'. They were very proper and drove him everywhere, in Morris Minors and Vauxhall Victors. As a child, I wouldn't have noticed anything improper except for the women's very closed and clipped vowels. In fact, if I had the phrase to employ then, I would have said 'uptight', dressed in their sensible shoes and straight-seamed stockings. My father was never uptight. He was elegant, charming, a little too garrulous. But something was very wrong – there were illicit fragrances – and my mother grew more depressed as my father took longer and longer trips away. But when he came home he was always mine host and entertained lavishly, catching up with friends, realising perhaps that any moment of silence and solitude and conversation with my mother would end in fights and dark moods and silences that lasted weeks so he and Johnnie Walker would have to go away again.

So much for familial forensics. A drunken genome gone AWOL.

Paul Boswell came to visit. He said he was visiting the dogs and not me. He looked much older than when I saw him last. He had no teeth left. He said Norma had died in her nursing home. Would I have some sugar for his tea? I'm sorry, I said, referring to Norma, and he took that to mean I couldn't spare him any sugar. But we sorted that out. He said he didn't like the phrase 'passed away'. Passed where? Passed what? Paul said the word 'dead' was a better way to describe Norma. Much more final. And why are you sorry? he asked. I shrugged. It's what you say. True enough. Paul said I should make a will instead of being sorry. Wills were really important otherwise the government takes it all away, he said. It's the same as passing away everything you've worked for. He showed me some of his miniatures painted in oil. 'Look what I've done,' he said without shouting. Munch replicas; Norma in a headscarf silently screaming. There were the clowns of course, of which I dutifully bought six at a small price. I had told Paul Boswell too much about my life and now I had to buy it back.

The next day he left me a package in my letterbox. My letterbox is not labelled *Circulars* or *No Junk Mail*. It is ridiculously small. The parcel was wrapped meticulously in newspaper, folded with manifold corners and triangles like an origami puzzle. It was squeezed into the metal box so I had some difficulty extracting it. It was a miniature done in oils on a cigar-box lid. The figure was identifiably me: on a visitation to the librarian's widow. Standing by her gate in a birdcage hat and holding my pipe, recognisably there in the distance, the figure was growing smaller and smaller as I tried to scrutinise the painting up close. My eyes were deteriorating. It was me all right, unmistakably *visiting the dead librarian's wife to offer my condolences*...a tiny figure full of hope as though fishing by a stream, whiling away a summer, fading into nuances and tints and it seemed very peaceful there, without crowds of people, waiting by a closed door, the Imperial Messenger believing he had reached his destination, which was, as usual, only a deviation, because messages dealing with the human heart never truly arrive.

Quin decided to make a will. He sought out one of his former students, who had taken a degree in law after doing a course in Creative Writing, during which Quin instructed her on how to translate the pauses in a poem. Otherwise, he said to Tamara, who was part African-American and whom he called Tamari, you're playing jazz strictly to time and there is no such thing except amongst white folks, he chuckled, playing the cool coloured man, but unable to change his inscrutable Confucian expression, which could be read as that of either a saint or a sinner. How he loved teaching! It was like being on stage, yet masked, and it was intimately erotic, paronomasian and vaguely antinomian. *The law is nothing but the theatre of the law,* he said to Tamara. *Too much sweetness can form caryatids in your teeth. Farting is such cheap callow…* etc. He rang her to make an appointment for drawing up a legacy.

Hospital. The word scares him knowing there will be the end, some coma-driven sleep without respite, save for a brief wink at an illusion – heaven or hell? – and then the usual clatter of last things, the cheery nurses or those who bully, the transfer of shit to sheet. To think that once he squeaked in new Nikes across tiled floors to witness his father dying on the day he had a golf game with his friends; but there it was, the presumption of health beside death and the weight that was carried in time to the pall-bearers' rhythmic shuffle. His father looked very small in his coffin: in his over-large suit and polka-dot cravat. No, no hospital for me, Quin thought; he'd much prefer the paralysing stroke, the long sleep and infinitude if not found amongst the marshes where no rabbits roam, they who in their sixth senses knew of a massacre in the past, then at least as instantaneously as possible, on his bicycle. No, no hospital would hold him if only his failing heart failed finally, in defiance of Beckett's dictum to fail better, which rewarded young ambitious men. No, he said to Paul, who understood him without too many words, can you build me a bathroom, a wooden hut next to the stone one, a pine-log structure in praise of shadows with a deep Japanese tub, vertical, to belie the sleep of the dead, narrow, water to the chin, where he can sit undisturbed? And then a simple composting toilet, clean and ferny, constructed out of old sauna-soaked Scandinavian cedar? Can you, Paul, use your knowledge and skills and I will provide the materials?

My mother is in Kyiv and cruise missiles are raining down, at least a dozen a day. Blooms of orange and white. There are friends of hers who have been injured, one killed in the apartment block just up the street. So Iryna wrote.

Quin wrote back immediately. Then bring her with you to Adelaide. I'm constructing outbuildings so you will have a large main house for your family's use. Please keep your phone charged if you can. I'm now quite versed in text messages, though you couldn't say I was all thumbs, exploiting both indices of inaccuracy. But I'm unused to flowery Ukrainian, which I'm learning to use. I'm glad that flowers in all senses, are employed, even if they be flowers of evil or flowers of love, funereal or matrimonial, their perfume is conditional, reliant upon transience.

The terrain here is stopping my heart, hoary cobwebs embrace my face and the ground slips away beneath my feet. Paul's van creaks in by the cemetery gate and we unload heavy sleepers and then ancient wood for the bath, steeped in sedation and compiled like a Beethoven score, with dove-tailed crotchets and semi-breviary prayers and curses. Nails. Paul hates them. Get it all to fit first time, he said, the master of grooves and bird's-mouth notches, footings and long-points, pitch and purlins. The old Chinese, he said, despised iron nails. Paul sees me in that light, he, an amateur Sinologist and I a pseudo-fabricator, both sinecured structuralists, now intent on building a bathhouse together. A flock of duck wings overhead was beating the air with layered music. Paul looks up. We are strangers here on the ground, his look to me says.

In Lviv Iryna lives in a four-storey house on a wide tree-lined avenue. Quin tried to imagine the heavy wooden doors which opened onto a landing with ornate tiles and then one would walk up two storeys and in the stairwell you would see the ceiling painted with yellow flowers and a blue, cloud-studded sky and pass to the next landing, the floor patterned with blue and white tiles and opposite an ornate balustrade would be her door and you would be reminded you are in an old city with a layered history, bearing all the scars of past occupations and the current veneer of peeling paint and chipped façades. He moves in and out of her house in his dreams, awaking in a metachronistic miasma, uncertain of whether he had written these scenes or dreamt them or felt her kiss upon his cheek.

It would be very different to a stone cottage in the Adelaide Hills whose terraced gardens and lawns were bisected by a creek of icy water and across the road, down the hill a little, would be the old cemetery dating from the early nineteenth century. Not a long history if you were white, yet everywhere, on account of the flowing water, there were the roaming ghosts of the Indigenous past. Quin wasn't sure how Iryna and her family would find this place – either intriguing or boring perhaps, after Lviv. It was a good place to forget other places.

Paul, what happened between you and the librarian's wife?

She had three small kids. Her husband was about to be sacked for arguing with the Council over the burning of books.

Book-burning?

Yes, the Council ordered several thousand books to be culled and he refused. He had to organise them to be given away to second-hand shops or to Oxfam. They gave him three days. He couldn't manage it.

What happened?

He had a car accident driving home one night, his van loaded with books. Took a corner too fast. Rolled down into a ravine. They didn't find his body until dawn.

I'm not sure about Paul's stories. He has been on something much of his life. I suspect alcohol, but now he seems sane and chastened. He is prescribing me a cure for addiction. It goes in several stages. He's made a a study of it since he acquired a laptop.

Meanwhile, he is constructing my bath, which is called a *hinoki*. It is put together with western red cedar which is air-dried, fine-sanded and dressed. Paul said he learned the trade as a seaman when he jumped ship in Japan. I'm not sure about this either. Though he knows a lot about Japanese wood, especially about *kiso hinoki* and *aomari hibari* wood, he says he can get the same product in western red cedar. It's too expensive to ship from Japan, he says. By the way, Paul says as he lifts the cedar planks from his ute, the librarian's widow saved me from my mental atrophy. We were friends and not lovers. She said I should go back to building healthy structures and not the hand-carved coffins which had become my morbid trade. Paul bursts out laughing without showing any teeth.

Today I read an article about the dogs of Ukraine. About abandoned dogs, who were being rescued and fed by a guy called Nate Mook – I once took my dogs for a holiday in Mollymook NSW – Nate Mook set up feeding stations with PVC pipes and dried food outside libraries, hospitals and churches and the dogs politely lined up to eat, instead of haunting the crematoria. Even when abandoned, Ukrainian dogs are very obedient and polite, Mr Mook said. They keep their distance and take their turn.

Paul has two old dogs, a large Old English sheepdog who was dying, and a small Pomeranian who was lame. He brought them over to meet my pack and they all got along without much jollity. Paul told me how rescue dogs needed homes and animal shelters needed money. Why do you do it? Paul asked me. Do what? Write books. I was at a loss as to an answer. Then he answered for me. Nature doesn't need words or ideas, he said. It can do without human thought and it is human thought which has destroyed much of nature. Humans want to acquire things. Property, for instance, I said, to push him on why he had four properties. They are simply dwelling places, he said, because it is in my nature to move nomadically from place to place. But they are not possessions, since anyone can dwell in any of them. A couple have roofs that leak. But anyone in the tribe can use them. When they come from England they are very happy to camp in a couple of them by the sea. His houses are neither for rent nor for sale.

Anthony Burgess, né Wilson, said good writers write for their own entertainment, not for sales. Writers never make good salespersons. Quin noticed that Boswell-Wilson was one of the most exclusive real-estate agencies in North Carolina. Janette Turner Hospital gave him that piece of information.

The bath is deep, five feet deep, so you can sit on the ledge or stand, semi-floating, fresh hot water being pumped from a gas system with a permanent pilot light. Quin imagined Iryna ladling the warmth onto his head and shoulders; the steaming glow of wet wood; candles in the soft night...the dogs are barking again.

I pay Paul for the cedar and the labour.

In turn, he pays me by teaching me some Romani. Your name, he said, is pronounced *Chin* isn't it? I agreed. It isn't *Quin*, is it? No. *Chin* in my language, he continued, which is a secret language, means 'cut' or 'carve'. I'll let you have this one out of the box of secrets. By extension, it means 'to engrave' or 'to write'. So we both carve in different ways. Paul bursts out laughing without teeth.

My dog Murphy barks up at the hill, hoping that Molly will come running and bark with him. But no one comes. Molly is dead. Djuna runs to him and is curious about why he is barking at nothing in particular. Murphy takes no notice of her and keeps barking up. He barks for Molly. She is his conscience...the way he ignored her before... except when they hunted in tandem, veering right and left through long grass after a scent. She is now ghosting him with the same colouring as a magpie, in black and white. Kafka ignores everything and guards the gate, waiting for the postman.

Paul has bought the cement footings, round biscuits weighing fifteen kilos each, and I have dug the holes, each half a metre deep and we place them in the holes and make sure they are even in uneven ground and some have to be deeper dug and others raised a little. Nine footings in all. And then Paul disappears and there is no way to reach him because he doesn't own a mobile phone and his house next door is empty, so he must have gone to the seaside, though the storms are brewing and the wind is strong and sooner or later the rain will come scatter-gunning on the roofs and my dogs will come in and lie by the fire. I will not do much on these days. But I will have to complete the building before Iryna arrives. She is arriving in January, when it will be warm, not as hot as in the city, where I used to soak through two shirts a day toiling at the university, where all was anxiety, angst every minute of the day because it was required that I speak and speaking was a horror for me, since everything and anything said should have been thought through three or four times and corrections made in the head, adjustments of grammar, syntax and pronouns, and quotations looked up, and the greatest anxiety was that speaking required replies and questions and nothing could prepare one for speaking without writing it first, the outline of a whole life and an edited narrative with a meaning that is finally given which cannot be achieved in the rapidity of talk and the exchanges of ideas, which are usually neither generously nor warmly *given*, nor are ideas generally an inhabitation of an other but are more often a *display* of knowledge, and even more often, a display plagiarised from others.

The person who lives in precarity, I wrote to Iryna during this time that no outdoor work could be done, *gives herself to the imagination of an other, who receives her as a vision of suffering and sorrow, yet her risk in precarity engenders a kind of enjoyment and freedom for her which the other can neither fully understand nor appreciate...or perhaps only in the context of a dubious irony*. In this way, questioning and replying in long durations of delayed time may have had the effect of altering each other's thinking in an ethical direction, I suggested to Iryna, careful not to put into too many words the precious nuances of my thought.

It was here, sitting in front of the fire with my dogs, that Iryna's reply opened up a new existence for me. *It is*, she wrote, *the unavoidability of people who see eye to eye and think together the same thoughts and imagine the same visions. It is a reciprocal investment.*

It was at that moment that Quin, who for most of his life had to tolerate the adversarial thrusts of others, to debate and defend and make watertight arguments, to negate the vulnerabilities of being a novelist for duels which scarred the soul for life, it was at that moment that a new warmth came from a different fire and the shape of time started to look very different, a new time and not the end times of the catastrophe philosophers.

In Anatole France's short story 'The Procurator of Judea', L. Aelius Lamia, a young man, licentiate and licentious, was exiled by Tiberius Caesar for consorting with consular wives. After many decades wandering through Syria, Palestine and Armenia, he retired to the Baths at Baiae on the gulf of Naples. There he meets an old and gouty Pontius Pilate, who cannot remember who Jesus was, either through dementia or through a willed forgetting. Lamia pleads the Jewish case against Pilate's anti-Semitism but does not succeed. Instead, Aelius Lamia dreams of his own past affairs with Jewish women who had left him for Jesus. But Pontius the Pompous knew more than he would let on. In a moment of pain in his left toe, he said he was the one with INRI on his tombstone: In Need of Rest and Inspiration. Maybe I'm making that up again. Playing fast and loose with irony and satire.

Quin did not know why this story came to him while he was waiting for the rain to cease. Some of the cement footings had sunken below the required depth. The timber that had been delivered had to be shrouded in tarpaulin. He maundered about, ascribing all this to self-exile, punishment for bad judgement, the vicissitudes of gregariousness culminating in expiation. Why should nomadism be a sin? There were ten ducklings on the pond and overnight, none were left. Even the best intentions for a brood, a stable home, were doomed by savagery. These fragmented thoughts had disturbed him for some time now.

History is either a forgetting or a self-serving narration, I'm assured of that. Herodotus mocked it in his first five chapters on the Greeks. At the university they do not know that forty years ago I once inhabited rooms which gave onto the lawns of learning. I believed I was one brick in this institutional history. No longer. Now those who sit or lie in the sunshine below do not discuss ideas but partying and sex; the ones who don't discuss but are swatting in the library are uninterested in ideas or language; entrepreneurial administrations change from day to day only to employ history in grand narratives for logos and ads. The whole country sways from drought to fires to floods and pandemics and having exhausted those disasters, sinks into recessions. The latest desperation is possibly the only remembering. Yes, Iryna would find it very strange here.

Quin levels up the footings and digs a shallow trench around the bathhouse site. As the weather leavens he uncovers the timber and begins to build the wall frames. He is fond of galvanised nails and power nail-guns. He is a fan of metal braces and tensioners. After some mistakes and corrections, he has constructed a frame. Moderation is what this building exercise does for the human spirit. He resists a whiskey at the end of the day to go with his honeyed beccaficos. Later in the evening and switching into the past tense, he admitted that forgetting bygones, erasing eras, periods, nostalgia, was a discipline he needed to follow. Isn't this the only way to avoid the paralysis of old age? To aim for the unification of subject and object, so that the present is both joyful and sorrowful?

It was hard to hold that state for long. Relationships don't last. He had found it in alcohol, now he has to find it without intoxication. He has given up drinking alcohol entirely. He collects old wine crates from his sheds and uses them for kindling. He sits and watches the pine slats burn, some of them engraved with the names of vineyards; 14% alc.; *Première Cuvée*; an elaborate signature next to *Calvados*. The present is both joyful and sorrowful. He wonders how long he will last. The relationship with himself cannot last. The rains do not stop.

Kyiv and Lviv have been attacked by Russian cruise missiles. I do not hear from Iryna as there are blackouts and water shortages. I send a blackly humorous email saying that if she does not come soon I will return to alcohol. This may not be funny to her at all. But then two days later, she replied feistily: *I will meet you soon, when you're not on alcoholidays.*

Actuality is what is most important for me now. Will it ever happen? Will world events eclipse or produce an outcome? Iryna and her family could possibly change my life in one way or another, but a piece of good writing, I said to Paul Boswell when he next delivered me some timber, is not quite the same thing as starting up a chainsaw. Both may be firing, but only one, the chainsaw, puts you at risk when the tree you're cutting twists as it drops. Risk is what writing lacks; it is an armchair ride on metaphors, no match for a close shave with half a ton of timber. I am nimbler now, without Sir Arthur Guinness, but we'll all kill ourselves in different ways.

Iryna, seeming to have read Quin's mind, wrote a short email to him. *People around me have grown old overnight,* she commented, *they do not tell jokes anymore. Freud may have been wrong in saying the unconscious is revealed in jokes. Or I may be wrong in saying the unconscious is too precious and tedious to reveal at this moment, if it still exists. If I could say one thing, it is that chance has taken over from fear. Chance is more real. And by the way my mother is now living with Marika and me in Lviv since she had to abandon her apartment in Kyiv, which is without water and power. It is freezing there at night.*

Paul Boswell has turned up finally. He is grumbling about the fact that I put together the walls of the bathhouse before assembling the floor. Once the subfloor is in place, the measurements change, he shouted. Nevertheless, adjustments can be made. He chocks up the corners with short lengths of hardwood, indents grooves into the tops, constantly measuring each stump with a spirit level. When I insist on paying him he spits on the ground. Barter is more important than money in our culture, he said. Undoubtedly money was important in Australia, but he preferred to take cuttings of my yellow roses, the mint from the back garden and the lemons and apples from my trees. It would mean he would have free access at all times, since I'd seen him cruising the orchard at night like a ghost. He gleans fruit but not books. Something happened to him regarding books. It was after he started to call on the dead librarian's wife. Gleaning was fine by me, if only he would not shout so much and grumble about the way I use a drop-saw or a hammer. Learn the wrinkles, he said, or you'll cut off a hand or break a finger; you may even die without practical knowledge. Paul's instructions were always full of fatalism. My father used to say that thinking of death all the time was sinful. We were born for survival. The sun will rise tomorrow and he'll win the jackpot lottery and he will buy everyone something and give a handsome sum to the ticket seller and he will drive a nice car, all of this dreaming in his prewar flat on Saturday afternoons, paying his two kids twenty cents to rub his feet, watching and betting on geckoes stuttering up the flaking walls.

Here the weather is fining up. Soon it will be warm, perhaps too warm, and Quin would have to sweat it out in the city waiting to see his doctor. He found the pains in his stomach too much to bear in the mornings. He shuffled to the bathroom, groaned on the toilet, thought he could see blood in his stool. His nightmares of crowded cities descending from plush to nondescript to deplorable, without cool and clean restrooms, increased. Summers depressed him, those long bright days the English loved so much, going out to the beaches and burning red like lobsters. Those warm nights that were only good for dripping love-making denied him now, and not even lurid memories lifted his depression. He hated beaches, hated the display of flesh, the crowds wading in knee-deep water oblivious of the shark cruising just beyond the first line of breakers. He hated the cheap food stalls, the sandy-floored restaurants with inedible food, the steaming traffic of bad-mannered children. Above all, the hammering blue of the sky, which slyly sent cancer to heads and backs of people in denial of their squamous moles, their bumps and lesions. Where were the fine baths of Baiae? But like so many civilised places, Baiae had turned into an archaeological park, its thermal springs underwater, its buildings half-buried in petrified lava. Yes, the future, Quin was convinced, lay in sybaritic senescence or in painful surgical digs. Look at all these fine young bodies! He saw them with arthritic limbs, heavy ankles, dolloping rolls of fat in floral dresses, stroke-induced ricti, a paraphernalia of canes and walkers. But maybe it wasn't as bad as being in Ukraine.

Dear Primo, Quin wrote, it was exceedingly kind of you to arrange the visas for my Ukrainians so quickly. Quin thought about his cousin Ricky Dupont, who grew up in the same street in Hong Kong, always the more studious of the two of them, smarter in diplomacy, the favourite of his teachers. He used to keep to himself when Quin took on dares from other boys, slashing a bus seat, throwing a golf ball through the school window, pirouetting on the high dam wall of a New Territories reservoir. No, Ricky came from a good family and was sent to Australia before Quin finished primary school. The nuns at his school didn't think Quin would make it very far in the world. His father couldn't afford the International School fees, or he would have learnt French and German like Ricky and be sent to a prestigious boarding college overseas. Dear Primo, I have a further favour to ask. Iryna wants to bring her mother here, at least temporarily, now that Kyiv is being bombed. He remembered that Ricky always used to look slightly down his nose when he spoke to Quin, peering over his fine gold-rimmed glasses. It was precocious for a ten-year-old to judge class so clearly and decisively. Quin had not heard from his cousin for over forty years, and then suddenly, a letter congratulating him on an autobiography that Quin took pains to label a novel. Ricky had finally discovered through Ancestry.com that they were related. But the letter was probably ironic, since a character in the book called Ponting was cast as *déclassé*, a refugee child to whom Quin's mother donated his old shoes. Or maybe, Quin suspected, Dupont was saying he knew that I knew that he knew, Quin concluded, always suspicious of his own writerly motives.

Women, Paul Boswell said to him when they were carting the lumber that had been delivered – the driver didn't know he had to go in through the cemetery gates – so they had to lift each piece over the fence, women – you can't live with them but you can't live without them. It's best if you become more nomadic and only come home periodically, with or without notification. I go off to paint...what do you do? Quin shook his head. I don't intend to do that when Iryna's here. That would be a mistake, Paul said. You can't be a full-time tour guide. It's the first thing that would send you bonkers – making up things to see and do. You know as well as I do that the Hills are not for women. Nothing interesting has happened here since 1836, when the Lutherans brought their German names and devout consciences to till the soil for vineyards. Women need the city, restaurants, parties, gossip, talk and more talk. You isolate them here and you end up alone. This country life is no good for talking, only good for carving up time...you know, like your name...all done in silence. He smiled toothlessly. And you, with little in the bank, are in the encyclopaedias. Cultural capital, Professor, won't get you far in the world of divorce. They'll check your tote bag and see if it rattles. They'll list every misdemeanour and hold it above your head. King of one weekend review and then forgotten. Yes, you would have nailed it briefly: INRI – In the Next (200-word) Review Insert. Quin had forgotten Paul Boswell was once an avid reader. What really happened with the dead librarian's wife? He thought this a good moment to ask.

Impetuous, Paul said. Too eager for the big city. She wanted the distraction of noise. Musicians who didn't read books. Long-haired *dinlows* who rode Harley-Davidsons and who should have known better than the throbbing beneath their balls.

Quin knew. Marriages were soured by stillness. Look at the Garden of Eden, the red apple, just there waiting to be noisily eaten. Better still, have a big apple-pie cook-up; invite the whole neighbourhood and then, God only knows, bitch about them later. At least that was a kind of solidarity. The fact though, in his experience, was that marriages lasted only as long as the last book; prizes, cocktails; the short fuse of fame and fizzes.

In the Lvivian blackouts, text messages made sense. Their brevity suited Quin, who at university was a radio operator in the Citizen Military Forces until he slept in long grass on operations and was so severely bitten by jumping ants that he had to be taken by ambulance to hospital with anaphylaxis. He was feeling confused, on the point of collapse and a strong sense of impending doom came over him. It was the beginning of his neurosis. He was a failure, a quitter. He couldn't hack it. He was anxious, obsessive; he needed an adoring lover who would take over his life, grant him achievement; an ideal lover who was never forthcoming. One girlfriend broke off with him because she said she was looking for a man who would never come before she did. Quin didn't have the discipline of the ancient Chinese. Nor could he practise at it, since romantic love always came first and it was beautiful and it took the longest time before it was extinguished in that little deadly shudder which turned the world back into the grim ordinary of daily existence, of choking buses and buzzing lawnmowers, of wailing children and suburban Saturdays.

Iryna, what is your mother's name?

Her name is Aneta Graff. Why?

DFAT, the Department of Foreign Affairs and Trade, needs to know for her visa.

Trade? My mother has retired. She has nothing to trade. And she has been foreign all her life, moving from Poland to Estonia to Moldova to Kyiv in Ukraine. So what's new?

Nothing. I want very much that you all have a smooth passage to here.

There are many other refugees, asylum seekers, who do not have a smooth passage to Australia. I do not want to hurdle over them, but I will come under my own steam as a tourist. How could you even suggest any kind of inside-running?

It is not inside-running. I do what I can. I wish I can save all the dogs of Ukraine as well.

That is good of you, but you know that almost a hundred thousand of our people have been killed or wounded since the war, dogs or no dogs. A dog is no more human than a human is a dog. If you can think that, then you are halfway to understanding war. I could hear her tone of rebuke. It was the crackle of frost before some sweetness returned.

Yes, I know. Is it you are coming or not? Please no silent treatment if technologically possible.

This stichomythia was full of holes, misspellings and techno-suggestions, auto-corrections and misunderstandings. Indeed, the shorthand had dispensed with codes and hidden meanings.

He wrote as though he were foreign himself. It helped to speak like the Other. Get the message across. He had read Levinas: 'The face of the other'. He was trying to negotiate a gentle face-to-face with Iryna and not use English as an imperious tool. Persuade the moment to come to some premature crisis. Did he dare to Zoom when power in Lviv was restored? Did he dare to show a bewhiskered cheek beneath his thick glasses while eating an avocado to declare his nonchalance? No, this was not a courtship or a trawling for a relationship. J. Alfred Prufrock knew that. She needed to know that. There was nothing in it for her.

He recognised he had moments of madness, not exactly psychotic episodes, but when he left his first wife he was neurotically recognising everyone in the streets of the Sydney CBD as kin; her cousins, aunts, sisters and brothers. It was as though he had never left. Her family was everywhere. They were coming for him. He tried to say hello and they walked away, looking askance as though he were another crazy, though he was better dressed than most of those. Then again, he understood all those foreign crazies because they knew that in isolation they would never survive and it was only hallucinatory families that saved them. They called out, in the Sydney streets, for all the dead, the ones who didn't make it across the Tropic of Capricorn or the gates of heaven. Yes, you had to be stubborn; you had to be a goat, sure-footed and climb to great heights. But you couldn't make it without family to whom you could write with an urgency. They would hear the call. Now of course, he was unsteady on his feet, the world was slipping away from him; there was no family and the valley below was covered in mist into whose translucent cushions he wished to dive, short-circuit his own frail dreaming with oblivion.

But he had always felt like that and the thought had kept him alive. It was funny how habituation became survival. Argument after argument did not solve the problem of coexistence. Ordinary life tested one's capacity for larger ideas and Quin felt he was choking every time he entered social life with its banal excitements and less than satisfactory takeaways. But he never complained. You are a glide, Paul Boswell once said appraisingly of him – smooth and silent and never argumentative. In the past, ultimatums to move house were like an invitation to his hanging. Now, after a decade or so of celibacy, he knew that familiarity was the killer – those habits of the Other; menstrual negligence; leftover fish; mice under the fridge; the way money ran through his fingers in attempting to straighten out life – he called this his *Ukrainian gambit* as he had sacrificed prime real estate for cemeterial gravitas, obsessive tidiness and deadly silence, at least, during the day, though at midnight in the summer, town youths used to come to dance and drink through their macabre rituals, smashing bottles until Quin laid rabbit traps around his gîte that might have taken off a toe or two. After over a decade of celibacy – Germaine Greer was right in many things – Quin understood he had had a lucky escape from dying of heartbreak. Solitary as a stone, cloistered, he read Gerard Manley Hopkins and bought Japanese paper upon which to write his life with neither compromise nor the seething blackmail of relations, the soundless paper absorbing his ink with a warm and seeping permanence.

On a more optimistic side there were always flowers, some fresh, which spoke eloquently about memory, as the graveyard ended its intake in 1945. Perhaps it ran out of room, but I suspect it was because of all the Lutheran-German names there, which embarrassed the town councillors of the time, some of whom wanted to relocate the Krauts, but due to strong opposition from Teutonic vignerons, only succeeded in renaming the town of Grünwald *Verdun* and German shepherds *Alsatians*. Not a great victory, but proleptic just the same.

His pond had grown into a lake. The rains did not ease for long. The water was shimmering in the strange light as though thousands of tiny fish were breaching the surface in joy while the wind set up a howl of disaster. Quin thought of Blaise Pascal, of his wager that if you believed in God there were infinite gains, but if God did not exist, there were only minor finite losses. But, Quin thought, what were these? Were they whiskey-afternoons or Stendhalian-nights, the library and music, the Sassafrasian biking ecstasies, the imaginative Shangri-Las of other-lives and after-lives? And what if you *pretended* to believe? Who would know? What consequences would there be? What about the pleasure of contradiction? Would that be a sin? Isn't gaming dubious, but is it a sin? He thought of all those sleazy men at the roulette table in Macau's Venetian casino, gangster types with scarred faces freshly flown in from mainland China, high-rollers who had kept women in cheongsams standing beside them for luck. Maybe that was pure authenticity if your fingers were at risk of being amputated in the morning with bolt-cutters for unpaid debts.

One thing Quin has worked out is that there are definitely gender separations in dogs. His alpha dog Kafka, possibly a misnomer, sees all affection as coming from females. But at the same time females are to be fought off in case weak male submission became the norm, with unsuitable partners like Djuna the terrier or Félice the fiancée, baring dog-like teeth. Amazons would extinguish Quin and the dinosaurs forever. He however, can give affection to his dogs but not of the cuddly kind. Kafka the dog distinguishes this as a kind of pack brotherhood with hierarchies, and probably in a *literary* but totally instinctive reaction, takes naturally to the brutal world of hunting and protection, confusion and trauma, animated by adventure without restraint – self-destruction as a *modus operandi*. It is the same in war. It is the same in Ukraine. Kafka the dog understands Quin, and vice-versa. They go out into the rain and cold, looking for incidents of fallen trees or wandering hostilities, trials by disorientation, and then before settling down, there is the firelight of the inside-outside; restless; on the *qui-vive*; angry as well as contented.

Iryna texted as Quin and his dogs were out walking. Her midnight was his morning. She was ill with Covid. Marika had brought it home from school. Everything came from school: viruses, news of deaths, frontline footages, available foodstuffs. Quin told her she needed to look after her health. In order to enter Australia, don't cough or sneeze, make your cheeks pale so you don't appear feverish, don't ever put food into your luggage. Next to mosquitoes, humans were hunted down by sprays and sniffer dogs; gloved fingers went through your underwear; don't bring any wood or plant products. Speak the King's English if questioned. *Yes, the wong twip was wather teddible.*

In the spring, Quin succeeded in finishing his wabi-sabi toilet hut set amidst moss and ferns, camellias and plane trees. He installed an eco-composting toilet with a remote flush generator stationed fifteen metres from the toilet. The bathhouse would take a lot longer. Inside, next to the fine-grained wood of the toilet walls, he could sit and watch the soft rain, his feet on the warm tatami matting; all was cleanliness and elegance, quietude and balm. The small hut was asymmetrical and angled so that a waist-level window facing away from the weather could be opened to the half-light filtered through ferns and he could see the dark pond beyond, its halite surface suddenly disturbed by gliding and skating ducks, and he could count the widening ripples on his morning visits. He meditated on the filth and stench at Versailles in the time of Louis XIV. Such grandeur could not solve the problem of sewage. There were cesspits, but the servants found it too tedious to carry the brimming chamber-pots all the way (sometimes a walk the length of a kilometre if you had to service the King's apartment, which was furthest from the cesspit stench if the wind was blowing the wrong way), and servants being servants, those entrusted with the lowest order of ordure-disposal, would take a shortcut from the King's *cabinet des affaires* down one flight of stairs and would simply throw the shit out the window and into the courtyard below. To promenade in the quadrangles would require parasols or *paracloaca*. Louis planted orange trees in the vain hope of clearing the air. These *orangeries* were sometimes fertilised, by a circular logic, from what was in the nearest cesspit.

Two white-faced herons are building a precarious nest way out on a limb. It's their third nest. It's a messy perch of twigs which falls into the water at the first serious gust of wind. Meanwhile below, a little shag is happily and busily diving, without a care, without having any partner, without any weight in the world, diving and eating minnows, happily alone. Sitting on the toilet, I learn the importance of perseverance before precarity; of self-dependency without the burden of consciousness. I was against failure now in this *amour épistolaire*. I also concluded that Iryna may have been very much like Ginnie: stubborn as a Pole. Or maybe all this was just world-weariness, because age doesn't just creep up, it sprints. One day you're starting a great project, the next, you're flattened by gravity. Sisyphus had it better than he thought, rocking and rolling uphill and then down again. But if you wanted to build anything, then you'd better be thinking in frames and boxes. Frames when clad, kept out the weather; boxes, when filled, provided the strength. Wood, like the human spirit, was the most forgiving and unforgiving. The tree of man was also a crucifix if you failed. That was the wager. Will and skill determined the futures of people.

But all of these lessons did no good at all. Quin was going back and forth between the voices in his head, those third-person dialogues and reprimands, and his wordless instinctive self, which could be depicted as a mass of knotted anxieties, such as sitting in front of his phone or blank computer when a courier company failed to deliver his goods which he had ordered online. He couldn't imagine such incompetence. His father always said to him that one small mistake would be the end of your business. The customer was always right, etc. The word 'business' was paramount in his household. As a child, his mother said doing his business was essential at least once a day. So competence rested on bodily evacuation and brain mobilisation. Where was his parcel? Irresponsible couriers could have left it in some bushes for midnight ramblers to steal. Even tracking was impossible if there were no laws to indemnify the receiver and prosecute the middleman. Big companies were paying out for non-deliveries. Refunds referred the guilt back to the buyer. The customer was always right, but such an ethics needed proving. Someone was cheating. Someone was sleeping in the expensive linen sheets he ordered for the advent of his guests from Ukraine. By early evening he was worn out. Quin relented against this optimistic/pessimistic expectationary pressure and pulled out a bottle of whiskey. His fury was then dulled and he quietly admitted it was just money. That's what an intellectual always said as an excuse, his father would have said before hitting the roof. What, you think money grows on trees? Just go climb one to see, and hopefully you'll fall and maybe pain and fear will fix your head. You're nothing without money; just go ask the Communists queuing for blocks in their threadbare greatcoats for half a lump of butter! Then you'll know the State has stolen your time and you're suddenly an old man in a cold-water flat, a thin reed still glorifying Stalin with your last bitter breath before oblivion. His father waxed lyrical in his hatred of professors, claiming they had talent but no imagination; otherwise they would have squandered their money along with their learning. That was true authenticity. Gamblers, risk-takers. None though, were professors. His father called the humble schoolteacher who lived downstairs 'Mr Professor'. I saw him buying Superman comics at the corner-stall, Abe's father said with malicious glee to his son. That's a start, at least.

Dearest Abe, today many missiles flew over and some landed on the electricity plant. We are very close to Poland. One or two exploded there.

I was brought back to this war. I'm now personally involved. I send money to the orphanage and to Mr Mook's animal welfare. He who is feeding the strays. He replies with candour and elegance: *I am only a shepherd. I look after one flock but am saddened by news of others who have shrapnel wounds, who have been run over, who are traumatised and who are wary of humans.*

Was Quin's philanthropy founded on whiskey? Did it matter? He didn't have the answer, although he took comfort in the fact that in the mornings he did not feel he had wasted anything, except himself. He was a poor judge of human motives, but like a dripping tap that keeps you from sleep, it is better to change the washers rather than over-tightening them and better to slip into a deep, warm, wooden bath at the end of the day than to hurry through a lobotomising shower against the clinical tiles. Maintenance; orderliness; attention to ritual detail; they all stilled the mind's agitation.

There was no need to hurry now that he was fixed on the last action of his life. Introducing a Jewish-Ukrainian family to Australia was what his father would have done. Baruch Spinoza would have done the same thing in the same circumstances. Yes, his father was called Bonifacio and if you go to the Amsterdam Jewish Museum which has been renovated, refurbished, you will find the column on which the names of benefactors have been carved and the name Castro in a line of Castros who were chemists, merchants, makers of glass spectacles. Baruch/Bento Spinoza was a rationalist in a time of intolerance and he too, ground lenses in order to see better the fanciful idiocies of faith. Bonifacio Castro had no time for metaphysics. Why can't you study to be a physicist, he said to his son; send rockets to the moon? So Quin decided to be Quin from his mother's side. The Ch'in Dynasty was the first imperial Chinese dynasty. That was good enough for him, but they said that the first emperor burnt books. Practical but unreasoning, mired in superstition, Quin's mother did not read. Was this a dynastic legacy? Was Quin's burning library an unconscious regression towards incarnating his avatar? His mother glued herself to Chinese-language radio and lived her life not in the news but in the gossip of communal tales. It was richly textured, had some sense of bodily wisdom, like putting soap up your bum to induce a motion, but where she excelled was in bitter medicines which she bought from her dealer in the Walled City in Kowloon: dried snake, centipedes, scorpions and tiger spleen. It cured cancer. A boy wasn't allowed day-old eggs or sitting on stone. You would be infertile if you did. But hundred-year-old eggs were fine. She used to like watching the typhoons and thunderstorms come in with that slanting 'rice rain' familiar to the Chinese, observing with delight and trepidation until it was time, in the late afternoon of depression and dim fluorescent lighting, for bitter herbs and teas.

Now he was catching up to her age when she died. You always caught up, like the young catching up to you: twenty-five-year-olds were still possible when he was fifty. Half his age. Then it became 40/65; 50/75; the gap was narrowing but though the math was in his favour, the body wasn't. And besides, women weren't on the hunt at fifty. They settled into their children's lives, twin sets and pearls. They went bushwalking with other women and bitched about grumpy old men.

The succulents were growing around the Japanese toilet. Soon they would engulf the bathhouse if he didn't get moving on building the retaining wall behind, so there would be a terrace and good drainage. He ordered railway sleepers. Then he made lists for the main house; hardware, kitchenware, dinnerware; bath towels. The main house was cavernous and lonely but could be filled with laughter and light. What about a menorah? No, she may not be religious and would have missed Hanukkah anyway. He couldn't concentrate; his fragments of instructions to department stores, delivery companies, couriers and post offices engulfed him. And what about Marika? What were the interests of fatherless fifteen-year-old girls who were war-traumatised? What about books like *Girl At War*, or *Why Is Dad So Mad?*

Iryna wrote from Lviv. The trams are not running. Russian cruise missiles have hit many of the electrical substations. The schools have shut and Marika frets inside our cold apartment, where we have purchased a fuel stove. The wood we have doesn't burn well. It fizzles and exudes sap. Do you remember reading *The Story Of A Life*, by Konstantin Paustovsky, when he describes our beautiful boulevards lined with trees? That was at the beginning of the First World War. Lviv is still a university town. It was, and is, a lively hub of cafés and bars. But the boulevards have been denuded of their trees. It is now minus one most afternoons and will get colder soon.

Iryna gave me much hope. She wrote last night to me: *When I come, you will have no reason to have to write. You will enter the 'haven of secure taciturnity', as Denys le Chartreux wrote at the end of the middle ages. He laid down his pen and wrote no more, for he had met a woman; the Virgin Mary perhaps.* Iryna sounds like quite a woman.

He began reading Oswald Spengler's *The Decline of the West*, volumes one and two. It was written after the First World War and it was something of an eye-opener because the rot was inside, and for Quin, there was no equality in humankind to be rescued. Beginning with the *Untergang*, the downfall of Aryan, Apollonian, Faustian intellectuals and the rise of the zoological primitives, Spengler intimated that no new culture could find its own expression. The new cannot be born. We all slouched towards Bethlehem as beasts of ignorance. Quin did not believe this. He didn't believe that civilisation was at its end. He did not believe in blood and roots, soil and shoots. He believed neither in violent revolution nor social evolution. Nor in uprisings or prophets. Nor did he believe what philosophers proclaimed about systems and means. He was a pessimist, but only in a personal sense. For him, the world had no innate structure even though the mind demanded it. Melancholy was the only position to take against chaos, an anatomy of self-management and not of society. It was not because he felt unequal to the task of theorising about the *hoi polloi*. He was not one of Voltaire's bastards, appealing to the lowest common denominator, but like Candide, he cultivated a safe haven from corrupted reason and power in his fallen garden. Yet there he found bees, and in their honeycombs he saw algorithms, the kind of digital stickiness in which workers die and the élites live off the attrition of renewable instinct, a régime ended only by displacement, smoke and incineration. Nature mirrored humans but it also weaponised them, gave them the idea of dispensing with the human. Indeed, nature was nothing but a hard god.

The war, Iryna wrote, *was always against myself. Once you wage war against someone else, the self disappears. So does anxiety about petty things. In fact, that can be a relief.*

In fact, Quin had fallen in love with Iryna. He was a bookish old man who was not romantically foolish but was now in the grips of a real woman. If it were only these slight phrases that created and ended his life, then he could live perpetually without testament! *I* and *he*, insistently small. Unwitnessed. And *nature* continuing side by side with *civilisation*. How sweet and brutal! It was something Ginnie would have said. Iryna was now Ginnie's reincarnation and had dovetailed into his aesthetics, a fixture in existence. He tapped together the window frames of his bathhouse with pleasurable anticipation; twenty-four small panes of old glass set inside it, distorting and filtering the western light.

He was on a reading tour of Chengdu after the great earthquake. His Australian travelling companion was Kate Jennings, the fiery feminist cum Trotskyist cum poet cum memoirist cum essayist, who told her leftist male buddies they stank from their jockstraps to their hairy armpits. And she was right, and Quin, who was a little behind all the anti-war rhetoric Kate both spouted and attacked, must have seemed a strange, rare bird when she remarked how old-fashioned his attire was in comparison to the Merrill-Lynch company she kept, midst the gay and stock-holding crowd, and yes, his computer bag was out of date, imagine, a Lamborghini brand of super-slow PCs useless except for the tin badge on the front. And here he was with the formidable Kate, who was exhibiting signs of not only a great decline but of New York denial, knowing she had smoked too much and drunk too much and it was now all catching up with her, but I didn't know this, thought Quin, Confucian to the end, and he asked her not to shout at the children who were jumping up and down on the rope bridge overhanging a deep gorge between icy river flows and yes, she was right, we would all die if it broke, but he was too embarrassed to be Chinese in the midst of Tibetans and he looked up at the half demolished pagodas and the buildings buried together with their tenants, crushed by tons of cheap Stalin cement, so they levelled the sites into football fields after the quake because ghosts were beneath and nobody would want to build or live above them. So he read with Kate and she said how could any of us love the Chinese because life was too brief and brutal in China and you threw in your lot with their useless gambling and fortune-telling. But then we visited the Du Fu memorial. In 759 Du Fu moved to Chengdu, built a thatched hut near the Flower Rinsing Creek and lived there for four years. It was the peak of Du's creativity, during which he wrote two hundred and forty poems.

Kate then went to the toilet. She returned with a copy of Du Fu's collected works and gave it to me. That was the last time I saw her.

Two white-faced herons have tried to nest four times since my morning ablutions. They do not build nice and neat and tight nests with spider webs and dog hair but toss messy twigs and small branches together into a windblown cockleshell of fearful fragility. They do not succeed in producing eggs or in hatching fledglings. They build thatched huts in high winds and create image-poems. Perhaps that is their purpose.

But it makes me a stranger in my hide and comfort, sheltered from all risk, a fugitive from being.

Kafka bit Paul's wife Norma on the hand. She was trying to pat him but should not have raised her hand above him. He snapped, probably because there was lightning about and thunder that no human could yet hear. It wasn't a savage bite but it drew blood. Paul grumbled about taking her to the doctor. She can't remember when she had had tetanus shots, he said. He was taking her to the nursing home at the end of the week anyway. Quin said he would drive her to the doctor and pay for everything. So he drove the old woman in the Rover and she was very frightened at first, fiddling with her seatbelt which Paul said would keep her from jumping out. She said very little but asked where he was taking her five or six times. Why to the doctor? Again? There was that nice woman doctor who gave her pills. Yes, he was taking her there. Norma's white hair was hanging over one eye. She asked Quin where he was from. He said he was from next door. Yes, a neighbouring country, she said, confused that this stranger from a foreign country was taking her to the doctor. Once there though, all he had to do was to wait. They would see to it. But he didn't realise they wanted to question him. A young male GP came with a clipboard. When was she bitten; what kind of dog? Has it had its shots? Was it desexed? All incidents like that had to be reported. Sometimes people sued for high stakes. Quin was resentful at such interrogation. Oh yes, he was in no doubt he was a suspicious foreigner with a vicious dog. Maybe the cops will come around and shoot Kafka. He didn't like it one bit and all he was doing was the right thing. Norma came out by and by with her hand bandaged. Quin settled the Medicare gap and drove her home. It was easier this time as Norma seemed sedated. Maybe the doctors knew about her dementia and mania. Maybe she told them

Quin stole her things when she wasn't home. Paul said he had gold sovereigns hidden somewhere. She suspected they were beneath the concrete in the tool shed. You'd have to jackhammer it up to find it, she said. Quin took her home, and no, he didn't want a cup of tea. He made a mental note of what to do in case Kafka threatened the Ukrainians. A dog psychiatrist; hundreds of dollars; medication for the rest of the dog's natural life.

It was probably the fate of all who only wanted peace and quiet and were gaslighted by someone else's tantrums and disturbances, their vengeance and anger; their false narratives and willing audiences. If it weren't for this audience of doctors, policewomen, health workers, psychiatrists, therapists, partial do-gooders of all kinds, these theatrics would cease and fail and only worst-case scenarios would receive real justice, while misdemeanours would not end up in court. If the world of the intellect once dealt in metaphors which linguistically mitigated trivial umbrage, the world of science now dealt solely in medication. Not only was psychological manipulation profitable, but it was the sympathetic treatment by health workers that led to a lifelong dependence. *Pecuniaria remedium.* Payment exacted for supposed damage *ad infinitum.* The crazies win. The doctors win. Everybody wins but the peace-seeker. Yes, Quin thought, maybe wars were healthier in that regard. Fear and stoicism eliminated all the lice of peacetime anxieties and disputes which itched at the membrane of the psyche. It was probably why he felt he was 'connecting' with Iryna.

Dear Mrs Aneta Graff, please excuse my rough Cyrillic since I am a letter-writer and not a scholar. As you may know, I am sponsoring you, your daughter and granddaughter in January on a trip to Australia. How long you intend to stay is up to you. You are welcome for as long as you want. I'm aware of how tough things are in Kyiv and wish to alleviate some of the hardships you are undergoing and the sacrifices you will be making in order to leave your home. For this reason, I wonder if you would allow me to help defray some of your costs, as your daughter very honourably and steadfastly has refused any suggestions of this kind. I am not a wealthy man, but I can do what I can do. It would give me great pleasure to come to your assistance, since I feel I know your daughter through our correspondence, or as Baudelaire may have said *nos correspondances*, referring of course not to our prosaic passing through forests of symbols which utter confused words, but to the transports of our imagination; the perfumes, sounds and colours, the connections of our souls. I hope you do not think this an impertinence on my part, but I have long thought these connections essential in any crises, such as in the atrocities of war, and I would hope that through a foreign intervention and interlude, you would be able to conquer all the fears generated this last year and restore a care of the self in distressing times. I remain your ever trusting friend, Abraham Quin.

He remembers now, those earlier years when he burned his life and relationships one after the other, only thinking of going forward because forward was all there was and things always worked out in the end since risk never quite failed you in youth. What was failure was in not moving; regretting, sleeping in his car wondering whether to go back or forwards and deciding at dawn in the fug of exhaustion, that another way would be to go to a good hotel, drink the minibar dry, sleep with the 'Do Not Disturb' sign out, watch a porn movie and refresh oneself by ringing old female acquaintances...then, feeling ripe with sex, he would have an audience he could seduce without reservation. Old girlfriends seemed to sense it immediately. They knew his moves; they had the afternoon free. Looking back, he now knew how to read all his confusions; not the predictable traits of character but all the irrationalities that shone light on ancestries and legacies: his father.

Get a good job, remember your *tzedakah* and move out and move on, but never be dependent on the blackmail women may deploy – that was Bonifacio's motto. His father only applied the last two pieces of his own advice.

Like a leper, abandonment was my salvation. The cloister was a purer life and it was no coincidence it drew those in the Middle Ages who dwelt there not in scholarship or in peaceful reflection but in violent upheavals of the soul accompanied by visions of the dead. Those who view me with distrust are correct in that I already see them in their graves and have marked their lives in my archive of memory. Of course, all of this is just a management of reality; logbooks of consciousness. Death holds no fear; I live very near to it. Perhaps I'm already sitting upon an old grave in my Japanese toilet. This cultivation of the always-already took place early in boarding school, which was the edifice of abandonment, and I sought out what the boys called 'the Green Dykes', hidden behind the handball courts and shrouded by heavy willows and vines. No one went there since rumours of snakes abounded. The Dykes always smelt swampy, like the narrow canals in the red-light district in Amsterdam, but being unlit, they emitted a tremendous calm in the late afternoons when I pretended to play football and peeled off to sit there in the shadows employing my catalogue of dread, which evolved at a later stage into this logbook of the dead. Now, the eco-toilet brought him deeper thoughts. The great evil, he said aloud to the nesting herons, was everybody's own conception of God. If people would stop conceiving, God wouldn't be born and there'd be no excuse to have any universal need for fake belief. Quin was sounding like his father: maybe it was Jewish scepticism. Or sounding like his mother: maybe it was Chinese Confucianism, murdering God out of filial duty because she'd seen enough: extinction of families, villages, children. She had never heard of the word *genocide*. In that sense, history to her was unmapped and unpredictable. She had her little bag of gold always with her. The world could change forever tomorrow. Whatever the case, Quin thought, we were made of compost; he'd witnessed disinterments in the graveyard; only the stone remained above; below, the clay earth didn't look rich enough to nourish the dandelions losing their hair in the wind.

My bathhouse is coming along, now that the weather is warming. I have built the walls and roof from woodland-grey Colorbond steel and cut a slot in the high floor for the deep bath. The pavilion is open on one side and looks down across the valley. I will clad the inside walls with golden cypress slabs. They will weep sap for a while and for a time glistening, translucent droplets will flicker in candlelight and I will dream of a Christmas taken not alone, but with others, the faint tinkle of carols receding across the hilltops, imbibing champagne and perfumes. But Quin was mistaken. If the Ukrainians came it would be in January at the earliest. Was he dreaming of next Christmas? And they were Jewish, presumably. What was he thinking? How do you do Hanukkah? He would have to learn how to make potato pancakes and doughnuts. Where would he get recipes for these? Maybe in a Sammy Spider cookbook...

He was dry for a week. Irritable from the moment he woke to the moment he slept; it was quite untenable to think health was his priority. Again, those other voices that spoke to him didn't have the reliability of language, just the unreliability of reason. Maybe he should shift to French, or better still, start learning Polish, Ukrainian, Russian. Then the centre of the world would find its weighting. He wrote to Iryna that he couldn't wait to bring the centre of the world to the Adelaide Hills. He asked about her mother, about Witold, about Marika. Just a line or a word, he said. He understood the charging of phones, piggybacked cords snaked in a line in underground shelters. Plastic jerrycans by the public faucets. There were no class distinctions in this new world. He was trying hard to understand it. Then he broke his word to her and cracked open a bottle of Irish whiskey. He had always spelled it with an 'e'. It was the key to feelings. Something about it made him human. You locked it away or you opened it up. And Quin was always careful with the grammar of drinking: his father had a rhyme when rocking his four-year-old son on his knee in those rare times of joy, when business had come good on a horse's mane: *beer, beer, whisky always risky; whisky, beer, beer, never fear.* Ride a cock horse to Banbury Cross. His father spelled things differently. Scotch was what he drank. He was a volunteer with the Royal Scots in Hong Kong when the Japanese invaded. He was never the same again, Quin's mother said, since he went mad when I turned on the fluorescent lamp. It was the only light we had after the war. A white tube we thought was an advance in our prewar, cold-water flat. I couldn't figure it out for a while, his mother said. Then his friend told her that POWs in the Nagasaki mines worked under white, fluorescent mercury lights. Quin's mother had had to deal with this madness and civilisation; what was a Jew doing fighting with the Scots against the Japanese? Quin knew: Bonifacio was a good shot. He prided himself on it: two eyes open; breathe out; squeeze. It must have been the same in his love-making.

There is blood in my stool. My shadow cabinet made this hard to detect, but once I shone light on the matter I was quite alarmed even though I was in denial. For a long time I used to go to bed early in the main house, because I looked forward healthily to a sunny morning, my dogs, the beauty of nature and life. Then it all collapsed upon this new discovery.

The more you live, the less useful it seems to have lived.
E.M. Cioran

Eternity was running out for Quin. Abdominal swelling; change in bowel habits; cramping. He went to see his doctor. She immediately requested a colonoscopy. Yes, they were going to shove a hosepipe up his backside like the Nazis did in the camps and flush him out. Surgically speaking, a colonoscope is used to peer inside for swollen tissue, mutations, polyps. Colonic polyps can display dysplasia. Little mushrooms in your guts caused by stress, Quin concluded. The lab needed samples. These colonising polyps were rioting; Medusas, octopi, mucous tentacles of pessimism; all had been multiplying in his nightmares, and now they were down further, inside him. It was deep geography. It was war. After enslaving the natives, Cristóbal Colón had come home to roost, asshole that he was.

Would Quin survive all this? He didn't want to know. It was better to live in ignorance and to die by auto-euthanasia. He made arrangements to finalise his will. He made plans to travel to the Netherlands if and when it became necessary, under his own steam, without encumbrances like a wheelchair or colostomy bags. He wanted to ingest the journey. He tidied his house. He was feeling good; in fact, better than ever. He rode his bicycle for fifty-eight kilometres and came home to enjoy a new selection of fine wines that had just been delivered to the doorstep. He wrote a note to his neighbour Paul Boswell and invited him over.

Dear Professor Quin, It is not necessary to write to me in Cyrillic since I understand English. After all, I am still an English teacher, though I have retired. I give private lessons to pupils who come to my apartment. Iryna has spoken to me of you and of your generous intention to host us in the Adelaide Hills, which I imagine features a rolling countryside, vineyards, orchards and many good restaurants. It would indeed be a wonderful holiday and a break from the hardships we are enduring in Ukraine. Lately, our power shortages have been difficult, but no matter what, we will get through this winter. The main thing is that our troops are able to fight. As you may know, my son-in-law Witold, is at the frontline, somewhere down south. The south of Ukraine, as you would know, was a kind of Athens, a breadbasket, a cradle of culture. It is now mostly in ruins. While my daughter and Witold have been separated in more ways than one, he does request me to send the best body armour, and as someone whom Iryna says is well versed in military equipment and is invested in this war, I ask your opinion. Yours very sincerely, Aneta Graff.

There it was. Reality. I was not aware of what was being traded in my letters to Iryna. Certainly not body armour; perhaps I was really hoping for bodily *amour*, or at most, companionship, or at the very least, *secrecy*. Nevertheless, Quin thought, ever since he began writing, the inside and the outside was always porous. Besides, sooner or later he would be writing to Dr Death in Amsterdam regarding auto-euthanasia, and the good doctor would reply that the exemplary human being must fashion his life and death without any transcendent agency. Quin decided that body armour was the least transcendent *objet* in the pantheon of immortality.

Dear Mrs Graff. You have my full support. Please allow me to deposit a small amount into your bank, if that system is operational and secure. While Kevlar armour is lighter, I recommend something that resists 7.62 projectiles (a broken rib could be sustained beneath Kevlar), so the best would be somewhere between ceramic and steel: the Level IV ultra-high molecular weight polyethylene plastic, which is both light and has the

added benefit of flotation, is a good one. I have purchased three online
from the US and am having them sent to you. I wish Witold all the best.
Abe Quin.

Quin was busy writing to his Chinese translator, who regularly
commuted between Sydney and Wuhan working as a professor in
China and visiting her daughter, who was in boarding school in
Australia. Eileen Zhang told him that her mother was cured of lung
cancer through taking Chinese medicine. Yes, she would drive her
mother to an obscure village where the pharmacist ground up snakes,
scorpions, centipedes and other poisonous insects with almond seeds
and so on. She could bring some with her on her next trip and send it to
him from Sydney through the post. Quin warned her about the Beagle
sniffer dogs at the airport and the racial profiling, but Eileen was used
to all that and said she didn't worry since ground up medicine was
not a foodstuff or a poison. Her mother's tumour shrunk in less than
a year. She will also bring some T33, a traditional Chinese medicine
consisting of five traditional Chinese herbs including Gansui (Kansui
Radix), Zhigancao (Glycyrrhizae Radix et Rhizoma Praeparata
cum Melle), Baishao (Paeoniae Radix Alba), Jiangbanxia (Pinelliae
Rhizoma Praeparatum Cum Zingibere et Alumine), and Dahuang
(Rhei Radix et Rhizoma).

Quin was impressed. He would put his faith in all that. The mental
side, he was thinking, was just as important as the physical remedy.
Positivity; optimism; Iryna. He studied her photo more assiduously.
He enlarged it, rotated it. He had become a master of the lens like
Spinoza. He was digitally creating a Mona Lisa whose eyes followed
you around the Louvre. She had a condition she was born with: she
had Coloboma, one pupil like a teardrop instead of being round in
her iris of pure blue. It gives her a disturbingly alien expression but

you can see from the photo she has learned how to squint, she may be winking, which altogether makes her flirtatiously concentrating on *you*, the viewer, who may be appearing too intrusive – Velázquez would know exactly what I mean – that she has already got the wood on you; she's got your number; Iryna the iris, Iryna the sunburst, the light in the dark Ukrainian sky. She is spring and peace, the blue over the wheat fields, the teardrop of grief.

Are letters just about passion or profit? Quin thought long and hard about this. To him, it was moral camouflage, not motives that inspired them. Enacting one role to elicit another response. And so on. Gradually the other writer is revealed as either ingenuous or as a player, and if the latter is the case, then let the game begin. Past exchanges rarely lasted more than three or four interchanges. No one had real time; nor the inclination. Yet the most enjoyable part of his life was starting a letter: lighting the fire in his *bothán*, another name for his hut, his back-shop, this time an Irish one, to imbibe the adobe flavour and the Gaelic mood and to give substance to his whiskey; to start a fire across the oceans, weave a spell over the ordinary; to recapture a time that doesn't flow away...this was neither passion nor profit, but a tiny stream of hope, perhaps life, perhaps a way of living. Quin the scrivener who chose life. Easy to say that now when he suspected he was dying. Despite the azure skies the days were still cold. They had something of a *dénouement* about them; unknotting; unravelling; unhooking the chain of being. After a great beginning, he returned to the knot in his bowels at the end of each day. It was hardly moral camouflage now, but reality, and soon to be an unreality.

Aneta Graff wrote to thank him for the deposit. She said Witold was now sourcing new Ukrainian army uniforms for pregnant women.

Reality again. Had Witold found someone new? Maybe human conflict had reached a new level? Pregnant women can fight to defend their turf, and they had more to defend didn't they?

I ride my bicycle with less caution than normal. I move a lot faster than ever, through warm and cold draughts of air, various perfumes of different flowers, septic fallouts and woodsmoke. Sometimes he imagined potpourri vases in Versailles, their scents changing with the seasons, arrangements of herbs and cesspools.

As promised, Quin's translator Eileen Zhang sent him a box of Chinese medicine and herbs. The latter he made as a bitter tea, the former came as pills and tablets of various sizes. He purchased a seven-day pillbox of rainbow colours and dutifully began a routine, a regimen which preceded the start of letters and sometimes replaced the play of epistles, none of which he sent to anyone. Iryna was his only correspondent. The three of them are arriving in Adelaide in the first week of February, she wrote. They will train to Krakow because airspace in Ukraine is closed, and fly Emirates to Adelaide. It will take in total about thirty-one hours. It was an expedition for them.

I wrote to Iryna: Australia was still an expedition, if no longer undertaken on camels. In Australia there is a tendency to erase things and to start again on a new exploration. We use the words *Settlement*, meaning white settlement, as though history began then, in 1789. We use the word *pioneers*, as if this country had never been known before. We use phrases like *opening up*, when we forget this country was open and understood fifty thousand years ago. But this tendency is still there, even in myself, when I plan your visit and pretend that I know what had been known for countless centuries. But I am just trying to start again, in every dying fall, a spark of life in someone who came to this country to start again and who desires to forget all the horrors from whence he came. But the horrors follow any way they can. They creep up in the dead of night, the drone of my mosquitoes and the drone of those sent to you by Russia, and I think of your deadly fear and my trivial anxiety and you strengthen me and give me a resolve to finally meet the one who surpasses me and in whom I place my trust.

Iryna wrote back to Quin with one line: *You must follow your desire.*

It was judicious and wise and it again put him out of his fantasy and into a reality he needed to manage.

Paul Boswell came to lunch. Quin cooked curried rabbit, knowing it was Paul's favourite. But he bought the rabbit from his local butcher instead of catching it in a trap. Ordered it specially hung and followed the recipe:

- 1 rabbit cut into pieces
- dust with 2 tablespoons flour
- baste with 3 tablespoons vegetable oil
- add 1 cinnamon stick
- spread 1 teaspoon cumin seeds
- 4 green cardamom pods
- 2 onions – diced
- 2 tomatoes – diced
- 1 green chilli – use pestle and mortar
- 250ml dry white wine
- 1 bay leaf crushed
- 1 tablespoon masala
- 1 tablespoon cumin
- 1 teaspoon chilli powder

After preparing it, Quin didn't feel he could eat it himself. He didn't feel right. He thought of Lionel's bra-less mother cooking the rabbit he shot. He thought of Lionel, blown into pieces in Vietnam. Paul Boswell didn't speak much but ate quite a lot. There was a knot in Quin's stomach from the Chinese medicine he was taking. Josef Czapski recorded the times in Russian prisons during the Second World War where the only scraps of news were from newspapers pulled out of the latrines, cleaned of all the shit and then read to all the inmates. Quin felt that was what he was doing: cleaning the excrement from what remained of his life to recover news of a new world. To start again. He briefly entertained the idea of speaking about it when Paul Boswell said the rabbit was very good. Quin, he said, should consider being a chef in another life, laughing without any teeth showing, his fedora pushed back on his head like a cowboy in an unpredictable poker game. You have a woman visiting I am sure. Paul always had an instinct for such things because he was an excellent observer, and he noticed the glassware and the silverware and the foreign ceramic dishes. Norma once told me they used to call him Crystal Boswell. He could read the future, and sometimes he stole it, she said. Had Quin mentioned a Ukrainian woman? He couldn't remember. He said he had sponsored a family. Paul grinned through his beard but said nothing. The world was complicated enough. He had seen the Steppes, had eaten snow when he was thirsty. Ukrainian women wore thick boots and kerchiefs on their heads; they were tough broads, Paul finally said, nodding. He fingered the tablecloth, indicating it was probably out of place for me to go to such effort. Then he went outside and lit his pipe, sitting in the white wooden Adirondack chair to talk to the dogs.

The dogs have been hunting rabbits. They work as a team, silently and slowly and then quick as a flash, they pounce, most often without success. That is the way of life and death. The will to live is microscopically brief, a nanosecond of pleasure before a random death that has no goal, simply the end of need, misery and pain. And then there are wonderful moments: swarms of wrens first, flitting and darting, curious and nervous. Then flocks of parrots, jabbering and quick. Underneath this air-protection, rabbits finally venture, safe that the air force is all-seeing.

So we are preparing for the trip, Iryna wrote. She always began with 'So', as if a conversation should begin *in media res*, particularly if there was something she needed to get off her chest. She said Witold had stopped communicating with her, but she happened to read a short piece of his he published recently in a Kyiv journal which always reserved a section for military stories and it was pretty good writing, about love and war, something like war and peace as well, though he is no Tolstoy, and he managed to pen the story in this crazy conflict when nothing happens and then all hell breaks loose. Well, well done on such an achievement even though I do not like his ideas at all (after the uprisings I found his ideas quite conservative; in fact Byzantine). As I told him earlier, true intellectual revolution has not happened in him yet and he still had a long way to go and should read a lot more. I read the whole story and in the end found it too blasé, informed with that typical Slavic mentality that nothing good and prosperous lasts forever. As though we would never have lasted as a couple! But let me tell you, I'm just trying to say that he is not an intellectual or an artist in the classic sense and above all, not a straightforward person. He is a person in love with suffering.

I'm tired now. Drones are coming. They are so low I can hear their lawnmower motors and then the explosions which provide a series of brief lights and then firelights to read by, and then an indescribable smell of apocalypse when you know someone has died or their home destroyed. *We cry at night and are brave in the mornings.*

How would he recognise them when they arrived? Oh, you'll know us, Iryna wrote. I will have on a peasant blouse with a kerchief over my dark eyebrows and golden braids. Mother will be in a heavy and long overcoat dragging a leather suitcase and Marika will be skipping ahead in a smock and apron. He got the joke. He would be wearing a white Panama, though it was made in Ecuador. He loved wearing different hats. Sometimes he looked like Saul Bellow, at others, Robert de Niro. So he imagined.

Cultural atmospheres and music understood him, just as he understood war. He didn't understand himself. He could travel moodily from Spanish-Moorish Andalusian melancholia to Brazilian choro to the blues and jazz, then to Australian folk of the early seventies when he went to the Balmain Town Hall to listen to Doug Ashdown telling us winter in America was cold; the worst and best of his times: those broken and drugged people struggling out of a repression of Australian boredom and conformity and the stinking woollen suits of Australian summers and then suddenly, Vietnam and all of us swaying to a critical yearning which has now become nothing but nostalgia; dead mates and the tunes of the times that went with them – 'Gimme Shelter'; 'All Along The Watchtower'; 'Fortunate Son' – which we can no longer convey except for a feeling which broke all of us into those different worlds to which our antennae were tuned. It was agony to drift in and out.

But enough of this melancholy. Take it on the chin or in the butt. Freud had it on the chin. He spat a lot, especially from his staircase in Hampstead Heath. Down the stairwell and sometimes onto the maid. At least I have a toilet of shadows and then a deep Japanese bath. Oh, the repressions of anality! That Type A personality was a curse on those of us who were dutiful and then turned sideways into literature! But it paid to be nimble. Quin had always been light on his feet. He was a good dancer unless he was drunk, which turned elegance into shame. Women peeled off then. So he practised beginnings; if he had enough of them, he would be able to transition between partners smoothly. Then he remembered the number of times he was almost killed by vehicles. Yes, each time was vivid. Once outside the Eiffel Tower, where he had had lunch, the tourist bus swerving just in time to miss his erratic stepping while he was looking the other way. Another time in Dublin late at night, where the Irish laundry van wasn't going to stop for anyone, perhaps running guns at high speed, through the narrow streets, who cares about a drunk walker? They were a dime a dozen after midnight in Dublin. And then in Melbourne he ran in front of a tram trying to catch a bus on the other side of the wide street, the driver ringing his bell, which seemed such a festive thing to do on the point of killing a pedestrian. What about the time in Hong Kong, where most of the unexpected deaths are the result of vehicular accidents, second only to suicide from defenestration, when a double-decker came at him in his blind spot and just missed his shopping bag ballooning behind him, he could still feel the tumid exhaust of humid death, the cemetery soil in Hong Kong overpopulated with layers of sea-view legacies, billions to be fought over, foreclosing a life in the place he was born; inflating a shopping afternoon, a sudden demise; that guy we saw dancing at the Mandarin the night before with a blonde American chick who sold us those fake Aboriginal paintings.

Paul Boswell said we should walk our walk in the summer evenings up to the magic mountain and startle the locals out of their provinciality. We could pick a topic, agree to discuss it on the road and talk our way to the summit. We would argue, of course, but not quarrel. It was a narrow path. We could talk about the Ukraine, or about Wittgenstein, or about Van Gogh. Paul didn't know much about Wittgenstein, except that the philosopher lived in a hut in Norway above a fjord. Paul was mostly interested in the hut: its structure; how it kept out the draughts and the cold. We agreed on bicycles. The electric bike was coming into vogue. It would be important that we both bought one, analysed it and then considered the future. It seemed to be a worthwhile and an unending topic. It was a nomadic machine and held a very high Chinese socialist and utilitarian position. It was everyman's notion of transport.

At night the koalas were rutting, sounding like didgeridoos. Possums hissed and somewhere, something was being killed, squealing like a baby. Australian wildlife was not benign. He'd have to inform the Ukrainians that while there are no wolves or bears, little furry spiders were the most lethal. Kafkaesque silence was an efficient killing method. My dogs stay inside now. They know not to interfere in inter-species wars. They snore at the end of my bed and wake me periodically for trivial reasons, which is what humans do when it is not urgent. Hysteria is not a female condition of the wandering womb. It is a nomadic alert to a menace from other humans. Just in case. A conditioning to herd-protection. Dogs know there is no supernatural, only super-instinct, which is totally natural to them; lingering there just beyond the human. In Vietnam, this would have been helpful and possibly life-saving. Maybe the dogs know something was wrong, or that something was about to change. They've taken up howling when I start the Rover. Djuna begins, then Murphy and then finally Kafka; they choir harmoniously along the fence, their song lines echoing down into the valley. The next day, two old ladies stop me on my bicycle and ask if I have heard wolves. Yes, I say. I read that a few have escaped from the zoo. The women looked demented. I'm sure one of them had a meat cleaver in her bag.

The last time Quin went to the university he had to cross North Terrace and a woman in a coupé slewed around the corner, just missing him. Death was popping up exponentially. Walking was becoming a hazard.

Paul Boswell bought two peacocks and a peahen. When threatened, the big male fans its huge tail to the sound of an opening umbrella, a tail of yellow eyes in a field of blue and green, and then it turns its back, folds back the long feathers and sweeps the lawn while it grazes. Paul said that when he was a merchant seaman he once stayed in Ceylon and they ran wild there, and they were good at killing snakes. He painted a peacock in full fantail gripping a cobra with its beak and talons. There was a caption below: *Never swagger in moderation*. I think this was also tattooed on his forearm. Merchant seamen liked that sort of thing. True enough.

It's really strange to be alive, still. It is as though there were a double, a consciousness, which doesn't want you around. You would be better without it, but without it you would not know you were alive. So it is a tortuous monitor, a heavy backpack, which makes you least able to run, to flee and to survive. You have to carry this as a refugee status. It's all you have. It is important to realise you can be anything and nothing at the same time.

At his age, Quin knew that nothing was going to be normal anymore. To get up from the toilet was an effort. To squat while pumping his bike tyres was agony. To control his balance when walking the forest paths, concentrating only on one or two metres ahead, was a mindful endeavour. To read was a Herculean task of concentration. Nothing much held his attention. He spent long hours in the dead of night repeating conversations he'd heard and chastised himself for his lack of wit. *L'esprit de l'escalier* haunted him on the perpetual stairwell of delay and intent. The world he'd known was rending, tearing itself to pieces, between the sexes, between gender and agenda, races and cultures, rich and poor, the theological and the depraved.

Bento Spinoza, speaking in Portuguese to his nurse upon his deathbed in 1677, may have whispered that self-preservation gone wild was his vision of the terrible future; survival working itself towards death. It would culminate in an experiment in 1937: *Work makes you free through crematorium number three.* This would tend to contradict his great posthumously published work *Ethics,* wherein he stated that self-preservation was the substance of life as such, inclusive of others, a social ethics. But society, the State, the commonweal, does not care about the individual. Spinoza's last vision may have come at the behest of his own physical self-destruction, dying of the silica he inhaled as a lens-grinder for much of his life, his phthisis foreshortening his foresight.

And thus Quin satirically fashioned for himself a hypothesis about his favourite philosopher, who may have wagered his benign optical ethics for the brutal spectacle of mass terror. Suddenly Quin felt he *was* Spinoza. At least that was what he saw in his shaving mirror. Matter, not form. The melancholic long face; the black eyebrows; the pencil moustache. Oh, how the world would squash your ethics with its systems and forms and its formation of forms! The weight of death piling upon death! All those broken stones of shattered worlds!

Quin now understood the history of shit. *Les ruines* was the polite French term after the sanitation of the French language in the seventeenth century. Shit was a symptom of lowly creation's failure to survive as gods, a failure which includes a pathetic catalogue of celebrities, party-officials and demagogues at the top of the heap of dung, thriving on undying death. Shit has no hierarchy, just as there is no immortality of the soul or of the body through the crushing of others. Stalin's mummified body would soon become a power-lunch for grave worms inside the Kremlin wall. All are equalised. Quin loved composting his thoughts in this way. Everything could be found in the periodic table, whose valences synthesised the whole of nature, its creation and its decay. Matter was what mattered. That was what made metaphor. Concrete to concrete, through a beatification of language. Through that you found a method, not a form, and it hardened in time. Time too, was what he needed and what he groomed at leisure: he ironed his clothes; sprinkled lavender on the bedsheets and pillowcases in the main house; brewed coffee for a special flavour upon entry; iced the bottles of *Crème de Limoges*; programmed César Franck on the iPad Bluetooth Hyperboom speakers. The *phora* of his house. He felt ennobled by these activities, as if she had already gratefully shaken hands with him, a gentle but firm grasp like good handwriting, filled with character, memory and culture.

He had to be very careful now, when driving into the big city. He took one last look at the hills. The fire next time, he was thinking. He had not taken a drink that day, respectful of his guests. His thirst was agonising and prolonged as he ate his bento-boxed Sushi from the local Japanese takeaway before driving out to the chorus of dog-howls. He had memorised the flight number. The time of landing. It would be the arrival hall on the ground floor where he would receive them. The Rover brought him to the short-term car park safely in its reliably diesel fashion. They would be coming in at seven. Give them time through immigration, time for the beagle dogs to sniff. Time for the luggage collection. It would all take time in this new country. If you walk backwards slowly you would not get lost and you would know whence you came. Here he was again, mocking prophets and propheteers. There was nothing 'new' about a new country. You had to know its colonial past; and it was always going to be exile first, existence second and the eternal return third. Affirmation was a re-endurance of everything in the past. He walked backwards to the annoyance of travellers. They, the arrivals, would funnel through exits which disembogued into the mainstream of receptionists, a flow of love, absenteeism, here and there, funerary regrets. All to the trundle of heavy bags and trolleys. A parade of different faces. Languages into which you swam, in and out.

He was sweating in his dot-painted shirt which Helen had sent him from Hong Kong some time ago. Indeed, he was feeling phonily Indigenous. At least he was in solidarity with their menfolk who died early from all kinds of things. He should have gone long ago. The muffled sound of his heart was in his ear and there was a ticking in his throat. In the short-term car park he had been a matador with the squeaking cars, haphazard, stepping lightly, only he was not waltzing with any skill but spinning, swaying and lurching quite erratically. He had Indigenous presents for the Ukrainians: two Pitjantjatjara scarves and an engraved emu egg. Perhaps they were piacular offerings to atone for past unreliability. He was particularly bad at meeting airport arrivals as they were often ex-partners or an uninspiring group of conference delegates. He practised avoidance and absent-mindedness. Talk amongst yourselves please. But now he had opened himself up to the world in expiation for his lifelong taciturnity, reclusivity, inability to express feelings out of fear of sentimentality, out of cultural embarrassment. Did he have expressible feelings or were they all thought and assessed firstly and not given their moment? He was vulnerable to the imminent judgement of others. Feelings had to be reserved and assessed. Still. Whether this would help explain his fate or not he was unsure. Do scholars take the time to study the corruption of lives these days, or even of language? The way words, when delayed, were richer, more nuanced? A defect of character judged to be selfish, but ultimately a higher devotion? Their dying fall, their dénouement, the untying, the unravelling of the catastrophe were preserves of the old. For the young there was no time. TikTok. Face-to-face. Zoom. SMS instead of SOS. He was on the *Titanic*. He may have quoted himself incorrectly about finding a new direction: that he was not himself, but said he was himself. This Ukrainian affair may very well have been a complete lie or a lifelong tie. The world as spectacle. A storytelling meant as a trap for just someone as gullible as Quin, who was easy prey to fictioneering and the mountaineering desire to scale cultural peaks. And failing of course, falling into the crevasse left there by ambition. On the other hand, he was brought humbly and numbly to his own assessment. He was fooled by the world as spectacle. Theory deviated from the truth. The TV was not the actual war. It had no smell of decaying flesh. Walking backwards seemed to help; he was regaining time that belonged to him alone, not letting real time catch up. He wanted to remain in a limbo of letters, which was freed from linear time. The cold-rice and vegetable-water man who sang and begged to Quin's mother for his supper in a cardboard shoebox knew only survival. There were no politics or ideologies. Anamnesis was a tricky thing. He had forgotten those past relationships he had condemned to despondency; to their reclamations and recriminations; to the infinity of his ruthless *faits accomplis*. And now it was possible he was *responsible for the damages* which were claims he had to address now. Does the heart ever learn? It was an unthinking muscle. He remembered to take the lift down to the arrivals lounge; overseas flights came in this way, next to the Travelex and the wheelchairs. And there were the pay machines waiting idly for those in the know. He had heavy coins in his pockets ready for their slotted eyelids.

He sat on a bench and counted out his pills, steps, seats, the people waiting, young and old. If he lay down they would soon move him on; get an ambulance. Better not. He scanned the screen again; arrivals and departures; flights landed; those delayed. Counting measured out the minutes. It taught you to draw out death, to draw breath, to live in the end times when survival no longer really mattered. His heart was beating in anticipation, the great wager soon to be upon him, a roulette wheel spinning in his brain as merry-go-rounds of luggage, claimed and unclaimed, circled round and round, the rhythmic click of plastic wheels sounding like stacked casino chips. He turned his head to search the familiar or the unfamiliar. He wore his Panama, it was high summer, for recognition, a fatuous old man looking out of place in all this high energy, people waving, embracing, chatting on their cell phones. *Hello, Mama, I'll be home soon. See you on the other side.* Quin had a bunch of roses from his own garden. A season of growing now, he was thinking, rather than a season of excavating. Iryna's flight had not yet landed. He went up to the bar.

He was a recidivist today. Thinking with alcohol. Just a small one, but good, I do dare to say. Pin the moments. The bones of the work are done now. Repent later, but don't let the moralists enter. They do nothing for the creative explosion, which will be modified and re-edified. A new beginning.

He walked out the back entrance past the luggage carousels for some exercise, holding the roses close to his chest. He was having trouble breathing. He was reading all the signs on the huge hangars: *Rex*; *Corporate Aircraft; Qantas Freight; Pilatus Australia.* The noise of engines was deafening. At least it drowned out the pulse in his ears. And now he was thinking: *Quod scripsi, scripsi.* There it is and there would be no more, for he had indelibly made his move.

Acknowledgements

Several disparate passages included in this work have been previously published. Grateful acknowledgement is made to *Mascara Literary Review*, *Liminal Magazine* and HEAT Series 3 Number 1.

Medieval references were inspired by Johan Huizinga's *The Waning of the Middle Ages*.

About the Author

Born in Hong Kong of Portuguese, Chinese and English parentage, Brian Castro's first novel *Birds Of Passage* (1983) was joint winner of *The Australian*/Vogel Literary Award. *Double-Wolf* (1991) won *The Age* Fiction Prize and the Vance Palmer Prize at the Victorian Premier's Literary Awards. *After China* (1992) again won the Victorian Premier's Literary Award, and *Stepper* (1997) was awarded the National Book Council Prize for Fiction. *Shanghai Dancing* (2003) won the Victorian Premier's Literary Award, the New South Wales Premier's Literary Award and was named New South Wales Book of the Year. *The Garden Book* won the 2006 Queensland Premier's Literary Award. He was the winner of the Patrick White Award for Literature in 2014, and of the Prime Minister's Literary Award for Poetry in 2018.